Lead Me On

A Last Chance Beach Romance

M.J. Schiller

I0664738

CHAPTER ONE

Caleb

People had certain expectations of a guy with a Mohawk. Mohawk Guy was crazy and unpredictable. Outgoing. He was dirt-poor and had been raised on the streets. He was a heavy drinker and into drugs. He was scary. One shouldn't hang around Mohawk Guy or they might end up in prison. This last one made me laugh. Yeah, I'd been in prison, all right. But it was for a crime I didn't commit, in order to protect someone who, I discovered later, was not deserving of my protection. Yes, I had a Mohawk, and I fit none of these descriptions. I mean, it wasn't like I hadn't drank or gotten high, but it certainly wasn't my thing.

But it was okay. I was good with people pegging me as that guy, because then they left me alone. I had a reputation I didn't deserve, and I couldn't have been happier about it. It meant I didn't have to talk to people much. And talking to people was work for me. I don't know what it was; I simply wasn't born with that whole forming a coherent sentence thing. It doesn't mean I'm not smart. I wasn't top of my class or anything, but that was part of the smoke screen. Top of the class meant awards and recognition and, like, talking to people. So, even though I could have aced every single one of those stupid tests my high school teachers handed out, I made sure I didn't. People think it's hard for a guy with a Mohawk to go unnoticed. The opposite is true. It meant I could fade into the background. They already knew who I was. Or they thought they did.

"We're going to take a quick break here, folks. So refresh your drinks and get ready for set number two, because we'll be rockin' it in just a few minutes." Phoenix—who played rhythm guitar for our band, Insatiable Fire, and was our lead vocalist and the face of the band—stashed his guitar in its stand and came to me.

"Man. You've got a live one tonight," he said in a low voice, his grin making the spotlights seem dim.

I stared at him, trying to make sense of his words. "What do you mean?"

Dakota, Phoenix's brother and our bassist, joined us, and Levi, our drummer, disappeared somewhere with Remi Boyd. We were on Last Chance

1

Beach—the home of all the band members, except for me—participating in a fundraiser carrying the name of Remi's late husband. I'd never met the man, but by all accounts, he was a great guy, and now that I'd met Remi, I understood why my crew wanted to help her. It was a shame she was already claimed. Not that Levi had said it verbally, but it didn't take an M.I.T. grad to see he had the hots for her. Not that I needed a girl. It had been my experience that girls meant trouble and heartbreak, and I wasn't down for that.

"Oh, come on," Phoenix continued. "Like you didn't notice *her*..." he gestured over his shoulder, "eyeing you."

I scanned the audience, noting nothing remarkable. "*What* are you talking about?"

"The brunette?" Dakota put in, using the same quiet but suggestive tone. "Ooh, la, la!"

"I know, right?" Phoenix returned. "He's so not worthy of her."

I was becoming annoyed. "What are you freaking talking about? No one is eyeing me." The heat suddenly making me squirm was not from the lights or the exertion of playing lead guitar.

"Dude?" Dak balked. "I know you're oblivious half the time, but you're not *that* oblivious."

My gaze raked the room, trying to locate the girl in question so I could dispel them of this asinine idea that someone was into me. "Who? I'm telling you, no one's staring at me."

Dak opened his stance a little bit. "The three girls who have been dancing in front of you all night."

Sure, I'd noticed the trio of hotties. They were hard to miss.

Phoenix took a quick peek. "Isn't that...?"

"It sure is," Dakota answered, suddenly serious. It piqued my curiosity, but not enough for me to want to continue this uncomfortable conversation.

I busied myself with putting my guitar away. "You guys are crazy. If there are any girls checking someone out on stage it's because they have a thing for musicians, that's all."

"Huh. How come she's looking at you in particular, then?"

Me?

The Blackstone brothers, Phoenix and Dakota, the guys currently torturing me, were the ones all the girls were after. Sure, I'd ended up with a girl or two. But only after they'd been rejected by the brothers and Levi. I was a last resort.

Don't listen to them. They're full of shit.

But I couldn't seem to help myself. My eyes slid in the direction of the three girls, who did appear to be watching us.

"Which one?" I mumbled, not able to keep the question in.

Dakota frowned. "Really?"

"The brunette in the purple top," Phoenix answered quickly.

I checked. She was cute. Straight, sable-colored hair falling like a silky curtain, dark, intelligent eyes, full lips... "No way. She's way out of my league."

"I know!" Phoenix exclaimed.

"*So* far out of your league it's like you're not even playing the same game," Dak said without hesitation.

I grimaced. "Gee, thanks."

"Now, if she'd been going after me," he continued, "that would make more sense."

Phoenix laughed. "Whoa, bro. Be careful of the fan blades with that overinflated ego of yours." He put his hand on Dak's shoulder, and they turned to head for the bar. They'd only gotten a few steps, though, when Phoenix swung around. "Go talk to her. Her name's Sophie."

I glanced at her again. She made eye contact briefly then looked away. Her friend was watching me eagerly. She laughed, said something to Sophie and nudged her, and I could read Sophie's lips as she told her friend to stop whatever it was she was doing.

"What? Like just go up and talk to her?"

"Exactly," Phoenix replied.

Exactly.

They made it sound so easy. Just go up and talk to her. I sighed. But a little voice inside me spoke. It must have been the tequila shots we did before we started.

If they can do it, you can do it.

Yeah, right, I argued with myself.

Come on. Try. You'll never get better if you don't at least try.

I couldn't argue with that, but was it worth the potential humiliation? I lifted my gaze subtly. The girls had their backs to me now and were making a path through the crowd to the bar. I'm a guy, so of course I checked out her ass.

Definitely worth it.

I jumped off the stage and wove amongst the throng myself.

"Hey." Someone grabbed my arm. "Great job, dude." I could tell by the way he was having trouble focusing on me that the guy was trashed, along with his equally wasted date, who was clinging to his side for support as her heels seemed to be so unsteady she might as well have been standing on ice.

"Thanks, man."

I'd barely turned to the guy, but even in that brief amount of time, I'd lost track of the trio, and they'd disappeared into the crush of partiers filling The Rum Runner. I tried to see around people, checking every flash of purple that caught my eye for Sophie, but I couldn't find her.

Probably a sign. Saved myself some embarrassment.

I was surprised by the little wave of disappointment that hit me. I should be feeling relief. I could tell Phoenix honestly that I'd given it a try, but she got swallowed up by the crowd and I lost her.

Would have been nice to meet her, though.

I'd watched them earlier. The blonde who'd nudged Sophie was a wildfire. I mean, she looked like fun, but also trouble. She'd randomly dirty danced with three separate guys and got their engines revving. Her other friend, also a brunette, was pretty all right, but seemed uptight. Or maybe it was merely the fact she had her hair in an unyielding bun. It wasn't really fair to judge someone I'd never even talked to, but that was just the impression I got. Sophie seemed to be the quietest of the bunch. Even though she had a cute way of moving herself, she seemed less comfortable on the dance floor than her friends. When they first came to the front, her friends each had one of her hands, and they were dragging her reluctantly forward, although she was smiling the whole time. The juxtapositions of their personalities had me curious.

But it seemed my curiosity would remain unsettled as I'd made it to the bar without a further glimpse of her.

"Tequila," I told the bartender.

"Lime and salt?" she asked after pouring the shot.

"No thanks."

I drained it and set the glass on the bar. Swinging around to head to the john, I found her standing right in before me.

"Hi." Her gaze didn't connect with mine fully, and she slid a glance to the left, where her friends were trying to be inconspicuous and failing miserably.

She was knock-down, drag-out gorgeous. Long lashes fanned against creamy skin. She wasn't wearing much makeup, and what she had on was subtle. Her lips were done though and looked tempting as hell.

Oh, wait. She talked to me. I should say something in return.

My voice came out gruff. "Hi." *Killer opening.*

She brushed a strand of her gorgeous hair back, tucking it behind an ear and shooting another quick peek at her friends who were huddled together like two witches at their caldron. "Go on," the blonde mouthed.

"Umm," her voice trembled, "I've...we've been enjoying your playing." She gestured to the pair lurking more closely now.

My nerves made my jaw so tight my words were clipped and, yes, extremely awkward. "Thanks."

"Uhh...well...that's all I really wanted to say. Have a good night."

With that she spun and hurried toward her friends. She took hold of both of their shirts as she moved between them and pulled them with her as she took big strides away from me.

Good job. The girl gets up the nerve to talk to you, and you become Neanderthal Man. What an epic fail.

After fighting my way to the bathroom, I returned to the stage, where Phoenix and Dakota were strapping on their guitars.

"So?" Phoenix asked. "Did you talk to her?"

"Yep," I replied shortly.

He glanced at Dak. "And...?"

The expectant fashion in which they peered at me made me mad for some reason. "And we hit it off. We're getting married next week and plan on having five children." I huffed out a breath. "Leave me alone, would you?"

Phoenix whistled. "All righty then."

As we started the next set, I discovered the girls were back. And this time when Sophie stared at me, she didn't break eye contact. Her dancing style also had become looser, her hips swaying more freely. I smiled and her smile grew bigger.

I'd put money on there being a shot of liquid courage poured into her.

Her shaking it had me incredibly turned on. The blonde's earlier risqué dancing moves paled in comparison to the raw sexiness of the woman before me. I don't know why I did what I did next—maybe I was trying to encourage her, maybe I was hot-dogging, maybe it was the alcohol—but I stepped forward, to within feet of her, and amped up my playing. She seemed appreciative, biting her bottom lip and inching even closer. Phoenix chuckled through his next lyrics, and I twisted to see what was so amusing. Apparently, it was me, as he and Dak were looking at me and grinning. Dak gave me a little nod. So her crew was pushing her, mine was shoving me...it seemed this match was meant to be. But I needed to act less like the Tin Man without his oil can when talking to her, or this was going nowhere.

CHAPTER TWO

Sophie

I don't know what it was about him. He was totally not my type. Normally the whole Mohawk thing would have turned me off, but it was like I could see past that and recognize the chiseled features, the sharp blue of his eyes, the sexy smile he had on his face as he concentrated on his playing...he was totally hot. Other than a small, crescent-moon-shaped scar above his lips, he was perfect.

Probably got it in a bar fight when they were first starting out.

I felt like such an idiot with Savannah and Paige pushing me toward him, but as the night went on and the drinks came more quickly, I began to think maybe a guy like that could be interested in me. And the way he was playing his guitar right in front of me seemed encouraging.

He can't help but play guitar in front of you. You've parked your ass right in front of him.

Still...

Then my mind drifted back to our earlier exchange. He hadn't seemed real interested at that point. In fact, he was curt to the point of rudeness. I got the sense he was annoyed with me. But it was fun for the moment to pretend a guy like him could be into me.

I couldn't understand why I'd let Savannah and Paige coerce me into talking to him. I didn't even say anything to them about how attracted I was to him, but they somehow seemed to know. And once they knew, they became irritatingly persistent. I guess it was such a rarity—me mooning over some guy—they were jumping at the chance to help me to find my "happily-ever-after," although I was far too well-aware no such thing existed. Happily-ever-after was for stupid girls who believed every honeyed lie that dripped off their fiancé's lips. I think my friends were desperate to bring me out of my shell, which I'd only shrunk deeper into after Steve. I knew they meant well, but part of me really wished they'd leave me alone. People were always trying to make introverts more extroverted, but we never tried to make extroverts more introverted. Why was that? Is there something intrinsically wrong with wanting to spend time alone? Why couldn't I stay at home, where I felt safe, and if not happy, at least at my happiest?

But part of me knew this was good for me. I knew I needed to return to the dating world. To stretch myself beyond my comfort level. But it was so exhausting.

"He's playing for you," Paige hummed in my ear like a seductive gnat. It was so easy for me to trust her words. Because I wanted to.

But Mohawk Guy wasn't going to pay attention to Plain, Old, Brown Hair, Brown-eyed Girl. He'd be searching for Mohawk Girl, or at least Tattooed, Lip-pierced Girl, or a girl with pink hair or some other exotic color. He wasn't interested in a book nerd. He was looking for someone with a job in the music industry, or an artist, or fashion designer. Someone whose career was a bit more exciting than the Dewey Decimal kind. Of course, I realized I was making some huge assumptions. He could be into someone people would deem elegant, who played classical piano, or someone like Savannah, a power-suit-wearing, strait-laced accountant. He certainly wasn't interested in me, unless he thought I was the quickest target for a one-night stand, which I probably appeared to be, since I was drooling over him. But in that he'd be disappointed. I sighed.

Savannah tapped me on the shoulder. "Paige is hitting the bathroom. And I'm getting another drink. Do you need something?"

"Yeah, but I'm not sure what I want. I'll go with you."

I trailed after her, determined to leave this useless flirtation behind and maybe find a reason to bow out early and get home to my TV shows and a bowl of ice cream.

Caleb

After the next set, the boys zoomed in on their prey.

"It's getting late. You have to talk to her before they decide to leave," Phoenix urged.

"Who? The brunette?" Levi interjected, a little late to the party.

"Yeah. He refuses to talk to her," Phoenix replied, sounding irritated.

"I didn't refuse to talk to her. I just...didn't have anything to say. I mean...what do you say to a girl like her?"

"Say hi to her," Levi offered. "Be yourself."

I snorted, putting my guitar in its stand behind an amp. "Be myself. Like discuss the art of playing guitar, or geek out over some book?"

Levi frowned. "Oh, yeah. Good point. But you can't pretend to be someone you're not for an entire relationship. It's hard to keep that up. It's better to be honest from the start."

Phoenix shook his head. "No, dude. He doesn't even know if he wants to be in a relationship with her yet. There's time for that honesty crap later."

Levi rubbed his chin. "Hmm. Maybe you're right..." He focused on something beyond my shoulder. "What do I know about relationships?" He clapped Dak and Phoenix on the back. "These are the guys who have experience with women. See you," he added. I followed him with my gaze as he hopped from the stage and hurried to Remi's side. Sure, Dak and Phoenix knew a lot when it came to women, but Levi was the only one who seemed to be involved with someone.

Phoenix and Dak began moving off too. Phoenix paused and caught my eye. "Talk to her. Buy her a drink. I don't know. Ask her what her name is."

"You already told me her name."

"But she's not aware of that. Come on, man. Get your shit together."

And with those encouraging words, he left.

I inhaled and exhaled. *Ask her what her name is. I can do that.*

This time it was she turning from the bar as I approached it, holding two drinks.

"Hi," I said quickly. "Can I buy you a drink?"

"I...uhh..." she lifted the cups higher. "Already have one."

Dumbshit. "Oh, yes. I see that now." I stuck out my hand. "I'm Caleb. You are...?"

Her friend gawked at me but took a drink from Sophie so she could shake.

Oh, yeah. Her hands were full. Can I get any more awkward?

"Sophie. Sophie Lockhart." She glanced around. "I'm surprised your friends didn't tell you about me."

I tilted my head. "Should they have?"

"No," she said quickly. "It's just..." she seemed to have trouble choosing her words, "we went to school together. I've known them forever. I thought...they may have...said something. So...are you here for long?"

It felt like she was trying to change the subject, but I left it alone. "Only until the end of the week."

"Oh."

Did she seem disappointed or was it my imagination?

A bartender had come over and was looking at me with a question in her eyes.

"Water, please?"

She scurried off, but the interruption gave me enough time to think of another question. "So, you grew up with Levi, Dak, and Phoenix, which makes you from Last Chance Beach..." *Duh.* "Do you like it here?"

A shadow crossed her face, and she blinked a couple of times without answering. "Yes..." She swallowed and dropped her gaze briefly. "Yeah. I do."

She didn't elaborate, so I offered, "I'm from New Jersey, myself. Born and raised." I nodded as if proud of the fact, but the truth was, my hometown was a dump. "Much nicer here," I added to fill the silence. "The weather's been...great."

"It has, hasn't it?" she said pleasantly.

Her friend stepped in to rescue us. "Have you been able to get out to enjoy it much?"

I smiled, relieved someone else was taking the conversation somewhere. "No. I've actually been inside a lot re-ah-rehearsing. Yeah. Rehearsing."

Oh, crap. I almost said reading. They don't need to learn what a nerd I am.

Sophie's friend cocked her head with a frown. "You guys rehearse that much?"

"Oh, yeah. All the time." I needed to change the subject. "I'm sorry. I didn't get your name. I'm Caleb." I extended my hand.

"Dude. You're Caleb Winthrop. You don't exactly need to introduce yourself."

I shrugged. "You never know. Not everyone is a fan."

"Everyone who's breathing is."

I chuckled. "Well, thank you. Your name is..."

She gave me a firm shake. "Savannah. Savannah Drew."

"Nice to meet you, Miss Drew."

"Savannah, please."

"Savannah." I returned my attention to Sophie. "Are you guys staying for the next set?"

Sophie nodded. Then she looked at her friend. "I mean, I am. I'm not sure about the others..."

"Well, since you drove, I guess that means we're staying too."

"Oh. Oh, yeah. Did you want to go home?"

My gaze flashed to Savannah.

She laughed lightly. "No. I'm kidding. We're staying until they throw us out." She stared at something over my shoulder. "Which, with the way Paige is behaving, could be any minute. Hold this for me." She shoved her drink at Sophie and took off, marching across the floor to where the third member of the trio was trying to hike herself onto the stage, one leg laying on top of it, her tank riding up to reveal a tramp stamp above her low-cut jeans.

I grinned. "She seems to be a handful."

Sophie released a long breath. "You have *no* idea."

I grunted. Suddenly, even though the noise level was booming, an uncomfortable silence settled on us. It was like we needed Savannah to speak to each other, like she was an interpreter or something. Not wanting to make a complete ass of myself, I searched for an escape route. "Well, I better get going. We're starting our next set soon."

"Oh, wow. That was a short break." She seemed relieved. I know I was.

"Will you let me buy you a drink during my next break?"

"Well, I think I'll be switching to water after this..."

My face fell.

"...but I'd love to talk to you some more."

The smile was back. "Sounds good. See ya in a bit."

Since I had time to kill before we actually played again, I headed to the bathroom. On the way, I ran into Dak. "Dude. I need your help."

"Well, I can give it a try. But playing two guitars at the same time may be difficult even for me."

"No, a-hole." I punched him in the arm. "I need some...advice."

"*You're* asking me for advice? You're the brainiac who reads all the time. What could I possibly tell you that you haven't already mastered?"

"Well...umm..." I licked my lips.

"Oh." His face brightened. "Is this about Sophie?" He searched the room behind me.

I pushed him closer to the stage. "Yes, it's about Sophie, and I don't need you broadcasting it to the entire bar."

"No problem," he said with an impish smirk.

I looked at him sternly, "Dak...I mean it."

He laughed. "Okay. Okay. What do you want to know?"

"Uhh...well...to start with...what kinds of topics do you discuss with a girl? I get in front of her and blank out."

To his credit, he was able to restrain the laughter pressing on his lips. He rubbed his chin. "Hmm...well, generally not sports. I learned that the hard way."

Thank God. The sum total of my sports knowledge could be balanced on my guitar pick.

"You can ask her what her favorite kind of music is. Does she have a big family? ...I'd think of three solid subjects you can hit on ahead of time so you'll be prepared."

"Yeah. Yeah. I like that. I'll do that. Thanks."

He put his hands on my shoulders. "Good luck, dude. Sophie's a..." His gaze roamed again and he hesitated to finish the words. "She's a real sweetheart, man. Be good to her."

"I intend to be." That seemed like a weird thing for Dakota to say.

"Good. I'm going to get a water really quick, but I'll be on stage in a few minutes."

I moved toward the short stairs to the platform we were performing on, deep in thought.

Okay, so...ask about her family, what kind of music she likes, and...

I felt like such an idiot. All I could come up with were the ideas Dak had given to me? How lame was that? But as the set neared the end, I found the third thing we could discuss. I could ask her occupation. That was a reasonable question. I was so excited I practically leaped off the stage. But after a thorough search of the room, I couldn't find her.

The place had cleared out pretty quickly after our last number, so I flopped onto one of the vacant stools at the bar and ordered tequila. She'd left without saying goodbye. Maybe she wasn't as interested as she'd seemed.

Or maybe she had been at first, until I opened my mouth and gobbledygook spewed forth and she began to have second thoughts. I was doomed to be a loner my entire life. Sometimes I thought that would be okay. Other times I wanted someone to share my life with.

After a few minutes, Dak approached. "Did you get to talk to Sophie?"

"Boner," a bartender called before I could answer. He was coming from the storeroom with a case of beer. "Sophie Lockhart told me to tell you her friend's heel broke off her shoe and she turned her ankle. They're taking her to urgent care."

My eyes widened. "Oh."

"Well, that sucks," Dak said succinctly.

"Yeah." But at least she thought enough of me to leave a message. Maybe there was hope.

Dak frowned. "Oh, yeah? If it sucks so bad, why are you grinning?"

I pushed my empty shot glass away. "Must be the tequila," I replied jovially. I stood and clapped him on the back. "Come on. Let's go."

CHAPTER THREE

Caleb

The next night, we were playing at the biggest dive on the island, The Shellfish. The gigantic neon sign above the door, however, read "hell ish," as the S and f had burned out. The logo was shaped like a crab. It was appropriate enough, as I'm sure more than one customer had gotten crabs from the people who hung around there. The first time I'd played with the boys it had been at the "hellfish"—before the f was fried. Seeing the place, I'd almost turned and left. It was such a pit.

I blinked as I entered, my vision compromised by the dim lighting as I came in from the sunshine. My shoes stuck to the floor as I moved forward. Despite the fact that indoor smoking had been banned for a couple of years, smoke seemed to constantly hang in the air and coat the windows so no light could get in. Although rundown and seedy, the joint was actually pretty big. Four truck tailgates hung on the walls for people to either sit on or to give them a place to put their drinks. The bar was long and L-shaped, giving the bartenders ample room to work. Beyond where the shorter part of the L was, another spacious room opened up. Booths lined half of two adjacent sides, and a smattering of tables filled the space between them. In front of these tables was a huge dance floor and the stage. One thing that made this bar distinct was the cages on either end of the stage. I don't know if the owners had gotten them from a strip club or some go-go hangout, but girls loved to dance in them. Especially drunk girls.

The idea of girls dancing conjured images of Sophie swaying as she had the previous night. I hadn't thought of Sophie all day, counting it a fluke, an anomaly that she'd shown some interest in me. But now, as I assessed the surroundings, half of me wanted her to stay away and be safe, half of me wanted her to show. It was stupid and silly to even consider the possibility, so I wiped it from my mind.

So it wasn't like I was watching the door in hopes of seeing her; I simply happened to be looking that way when she and her friends entered. Sort of. They shelled out the cover charge—all going to charity. Our gazes connected across the dance floor and she smiled widely. Her friends seemed to be calling

14

her back to the bar to get a drink before hitting the dance floor, but she kept walking toward me.

"Hi," she mouthed. Or she may have actually said it. It was hard to tell above the cacophony of guitar, laughter, and conversation around us. I nodded.

Is she really here, or am I imagining things? And could she have actually come just to see me?

I was crazy to think so, yet there she was, staring straight at me. Once our set was finished, I swung my guitar off and crouched to speak to her, subtly wiping my sweaty palms on my jeans. "Hey." Then I couldn't help it. "What are you doing here?" As soon as I said it, a new slick of sweat poured from my skin, and I rubbed my hands vigorously on my pant legs.

Shit. That sounds rude. The girl can be anyplace she wants to be.

She smiled coyly. "Well, you owe me a drink, don't you? I wasn't going to let you out of that."

"Oh, yeah. True." I jumped down beside her. "I should probably get that." But I didn't move. We were so close I could smell the intoxicating fragrance of her perfume. Something soft and sweet with a bite of sexiness. Like her.

You hardly know this girl. Don't get all gaga over her, you idiot.

She was the perfect height. A foot or so shorter than my 6'3". All I'd need to do is raise her chin a little bit to claim those full lips of hers. Or I could lift her and press her against the wall...

"What's going on?"

Slowly I turned my head. It was as if my neck was no longer functional or pliable. Her friends were standing next to us and one handed Sophie a drink, shifting her focus from Sophie to me and back again.

I shook myself. "Looks like I'm too late again," I said with a frown.

Sophie stepped nearer and ran her fingers along the edge of my vest where it buttoned, causing my heart to race and breath to shorten. "Oh, I'm not letting you get off that easy."

Her mentioning getting off almost sent me into orbit.

"Oh, boy," her friend Savannah said, rolling her eyes. "Here we go." She took a sip of her drink, her gaze wandering about the place, but returning to us on occasion.

The other friend was wearing one of those boot things. "I take it you're the one who had to go to the emergency room last night?"

"No," Savannah mumbled. "That would have been all three of us."

The boot-wearer socked Savannah in the arm. "Yes. But I'm not letting a little sprain slow me up. I'm Paige, by the way."

I shook her hand. "Paige. I'm Caleb."

"Yeah, I know." She was shaking her ass to the music playing through the loudspeakers, but she lost her balance. Savannah and I both caught an elbow before she went down completely.

Savannah frowned at her. "I'm *not* taking you back to the E.R. tonight. You'll have to Uber it if you get yourself hurt."

Paige smirked and elbowed Savannah in the ribs. "Oh, relax, Savvy. Nothing's going to happen."

Savannah surveyed her darkly. "Like I haven't heard that before."

Finger Eleven's "Paralyzer" came on and Paige's face glowed. "I love this song! This is a great song. Come on. Let's dance."

Savannah laughingly protested, but let Paige drag her off a few feet so they would have room for her to flail around. Sophie and I peered at each other and gave half-hearted smiles. She tucked a section of hair behind her ear and glanced at her friends.

"Come on, Caleb," Paige hollered. "Let's see you dance."

My throat became dry. "Oh...uh...I don't really dance."

"Bullshit," she countered. "I've seen you dance with your guitar."

"That's different," I protested, looking at Sophie desperately.

"Come on," Paige wheedled. "You can do it, Mr. Rock Star. Just shake that fine ass of yours."

"Paige!" Savannah chided.

Sophie frowned at her, then laughed. "You might as well do it. She'll badger you until you do."

I held my hands up. "But I really don't—"

Sophie crooked her finger at me. "Come on. Follow what I do."

Suddenly, dancing became a whole lot more appealing.

She placed my palm on her side. "Feel the rhythm," she murmured quietly enough that no one could hear except me. I was entranced. The warmth of her touch on my hip seeped through my jeans. We extended our opposite arms and laced our fingers together. She began to dip and swirl her hips in a steady backward and forward motion. My body naturally melted into hers and it was like my hips were moving of their own accord, mimicking hers as she was pressed against me. We were fluid and it was intoxicating. I grinned as I peered down into her face.

"What are you doing to me?"

The corners of her lips rose mischievously. "I'm only dancing."

It didn't feel like only dancing; it felt like a lot more.

"Thatta boy!" Paige yelled.

I glanced at her then back at Sophie. I sensed her being a bit forward gave me permission to do a little more than I would normally do with a complete stranger. I dropped my other hand to her opposite hip, and she put her hers on my neck, caressing it. I used the opportunity to take the lead, continuing the same motion, but stronger, and more deliberate on my part. She was singing the lyrics.

"Boner, come on, man."

I lifted my gaze. All three of my bandmates were on stage. I realized a different song was playing. I must have zoned out. I looked at Sophie and her face fell. "You've got to go."

"Uhh..." *Did I? Did I really have to?*

Sophie took a step away, and her fingers trailed along my arms until she reached my hands and gave them a squeeze. "Go ahead."

I moved toward the stage. "You're sticking around?"

She nodded.

I turned, and Phoenix reached down to haul me up. He latched onto my forearm and I onto his. "You better not dump me on my ass, man."

He had on one of those wicked Blackstone smiles that made people's heart rate accelerate in fear. I said a quick prayer as he raised me. It was impressive, as he was long and lean and I was tall and solid; I had to have at least fifty pounds on him.

"Thanks."

For the rest of the set, it was like I was playing a private concert for her. At one point, two guys approached her group, and I caught one ogling her ass when she wasn't paying attention. The hair on my neck bristled. I covered my microphone.

"Hey." He looked at me. "Step the hell off." I glowered at him.

He put his hands in the air. "Okay. Fine." He and his friend left.

After our last song, I crouched to speak to her. "Can I get you that drink now?"

"Yeah. Thanks."

"What do you want?"

"Tequila," she said right away.

I raised my eyebrows. "Tequila, huh? Why don't you come to the bar with me and we'll do one together."

"Okay." She followed along on the floor as I walked the length of the stage and descended the stairs.

"Should I get your friends one too?" I searched the crowd. "Where are they?"

"Oh, they took off. Savanah and Paige came together. I met them in the parking lot so we could all walk in together." She shrugged. "I wasn't sure if we'd all want to leave at the same time."

Did she mean because she wanted to stay to talk to me?

I hope so.

Crossing to the bar, I asked, "So, is tequila your shot of choice?"

"I like all sorts of shots, but tequila's my go-to."

I pulled out a stool for her. My parents might not have taught me much, but they did teach me proper manners. That is to say, pounded it into me.

"Oh, thanks," she said as if surprised. Wasn't she used to men doing that for her?

While we waited for our drinks, I reached for my questions to head off any uncomfortable lapses in conversation. "So, Sophie...you obviously know what I do for a living. What do you do?"

"Well, my family owns a bookshop in town, Beach Reads. I work there doing everything from unloading trucks, to working the cash register, to cleaning the bathrooms."

"That's cool." *Her family must have money like mine. Good, maybe she'll understand then. That is, if anything goes beyond tonight.*

"Which part is cool, the unloading trucks or the bathroom cleaning?"

I chuckled, then a commotion over her shoulder drew my attention. A guy in an Astros cap had turned from the bar and bumped another guy, knocking his drink.

"Son-of-a-bitch!" the wronged party exclaimed, shaking beer from his fingers. He glared at the guy who jostled his arm, taking a step forward. "You spilled my drink."

His outburst and his threatening tone made Sophie spin, and I got up to place myself between her and the arguing parties, in case something were to go down.

The other guy paled. "Oh, hey, man. I'm sorry. Let me buy a drink for your whole party."

There was a tense second of uncertainty, then the guy relaxed. "Cool," he said lightly. "You a 'Stros fan?"

I moved back to my seat, laughing a little and mumbling, "A bumper of good liquor will end a contest quicker than justice, judge, or vicar." I'd seen it a hundred times before.

Sophie's jaw dropped. "Did you just quote Richard Brinsley Sheridan?"

I blinked. "You've heard of him?"

"Yeah. I work in a bookstore, remember? But you're a rock star." I hated that term. "Where'd you learn of him?"

"Uhh...well..." I had accidentally waved my freak flag, and now she knew what a nerd I was. This was probably finished before it had even begun. I sighed. "I read. A lot."

Her face glowed. "You do? Who's your favorite author?"

Maybe it wasn't over. "Uhh...Steinbeck." I held my breath.

"Steinbeck? Eww. What? Like *The Grapes of Wrath*?"

I couldn't help but to defend myself. "Yeah. That's a great book."

"I'm not sure about great. Good, maybe. But great? However, had you said *Of Mice and Men,* I could have maybe agreed with you, but *Grapes of Wrath*? It's so dry."

I let go of my last shreds of worry. "Well, what's your definition of great?"

"I mean...Shakespeare, Dickens...Fitzgerald. I love *The Great Gatsby*."

"Well, *Gatsby*'s cool, but *The Last Tycoon* sucks."

"Yeah, but Fitzgerald never finished that. It was one of his friends who completed it after his death."

"Huh. I didn't know that."

And what followed was the nerdiest of nerdy conversations, with both of us proposing good authors and defending our opinions with examples.

"Faulkner? He's worse than Steinbeck. He wrote a sentence once that was five pages long."

I tilted my head. "I'd like to see that. I think that's an exaggeration."

She laughed. "Okay. Maybe it was a little bit of hyperbole, but it had to be at least three pages."

"I'm not talking *Absalom, Absalom* here. Have you ever read *As I Lay Dying*?

"No. That's one I've never read."

"Oh. You've got to read *As I Lay Dying*. It's told through various characters, some of whom have questionable sanity, and—"

"Excuse me," a bartender said. "Sorry to interrupt, but I gave last call a while ago and we're closing."

"Really?" I scanned the room, realizing for the first time that it was nearly empty. Across from the front door, on the lengthier side of the L-shaped bar, were Phoenix and Dak, jawing with one of the waitresses. In one of the booths a couple appeared to be involved in a knockdown drag out. A female bartender was sweeping the dance floor and another guy was collecting empty glasses from tables into a tub balanced on his hip. "Oh, okay."

"Oh, my gosh. It's almost 2:30." Sophie was looking at her phone. "I've got to be in at seven to do inventory." She slipped off her stool.

"Uhh...can I walk you to your car? It wouldn't be safe at this time of night to go alone."

Her eyes lit up. "Sure. I'd appreciate that."

I put my hand on the small of her back as I escorted her toward the door.

"I've really enjoyed talking to you, Caleb."

"And I've enjoyed talking to you. I don't often get to discuss books with people."

"Well, I have to say, I'm pretty impressed with the amount you've read."

"Thank you."

"Even if Steinbeck is your favorite author."

I chuckled.

"Sophie Lockhart," Dak hollered as we approached. "How the hell are you?"

She ducked her head a little. "Good, Dakota. And you?"

"Darlin', if I was doing any better, I'd get arrested for public indecency."

Sophie's cheeks became flushed. "Oh, well..." She obviously didn't know how to handle Dak's odd comment. "I guess it's good you're not doing better then."

He laughed loudly. "I'm not so sure."

Sophie glanced at me and shifted her weight.

"We were just—" I tried to excuse us, but Dak would have none of it.

He spun until he was more square to us. "I see you've met the token anal retentive member of the band."

"And by that he means the guy who keeps us out of the poor house," Phoenix interjected, slugging Dak's arm.

Sophie studied me. "Oh?"

"Oh, yeah," Phoenix continued. "He's a whiz at investing. Learned a thing or two from his dad."

"He did?"

"Yeah. You know his dad is—" He broke off midsentence, staring at me with his brow furrowed.

I was waving to get his attention and shaking my head. Sophie noted Phoenix's strange reaction and whirled. I lowered my hand and acted like I'd been rubbing my neck. "Anyway," I said hurriedly, "I'm walking Sophie to her car, so..." I prayed they wouldn't give me a hard time about it.

Dak appeared ready to say something, but Phoenix swung his arm to the side, knocking his brother in the chest hard enough to make him exhale. "Oh, great. It was nice seeing you again, Sophie," Phoenix said sincerely.

"Nice seeing you too, Phoenix." She gave him a smile and looked at Dak. "Dakota."

"Okay, so I'll be back in a minute." I tried to usher her away.

"Wait," the guy wiping the bar said. "I'll have to let you out." He hurried around and turned the lock. "Just bang on the door when you're ready to be let in," he said to me and he locked it behind us.

The door bumped closed, the lock clicked, and it was suddenly very quiet.

"I'm over there." Sophie pointed to a pair of cars parked on the street opposite a mostly empty parking lot.

I nodded and we continued on in silence for a moment. I contemplated kissing her goodnight. How I would do it and even whether I should or not. I'd merely had a couple of hours' conversation with her, after all... But hell, I'd gone to bed with girls without so much as a three sentence conversation. But that was different somehow. Sophie was different. She was beautiful, intelligent, sweet...I'd probably said more to her in one evening than I'd said to everyone else put together all year. Talking about books, I was on my turf. I was comfortable discussing writers, themes, and all things literary.

Her question derailed my thinking.

"So, you're good at investing?"

I rolled a shoulder, peering in front of us. "Ehh...I've made a few lucky guesses on stocks. Phoenix is the one who keeps all the books and pays the crew. Most bands have a manager, but we never have. He's very...meticulous."

"Ahh. I see." She chewed this over. "It surprises me, but it doesn't surprise me. I had Phoenix in a few classes. He's very intelligent."

Hmm...maybe Phoenix has his own freak flag...

We raised our heads as three loud, drunk guys stumbled out of another bar across the street, near her car. They turned to their left and ambled up the block, laughing and shoving each other. By the time we got to her car, they had disappeared around the corner.

"So which one's yours?"

"The blue one."

I checked shadowy doorways and places the streetlights didn't reach while she searched for her keys.

She unlocked the door then spun to face me. "You've kept me safe on the way to my car, but who's going to keep you safe on the way back?"

I was a little offended. "What? You don't believe I can handle myself?"

Her gaze danced across my chest and shoulders. "Oh, I've no doubt you could handle yourself..." I felt redeemed. "But if someone were to have a weapon..."

I took her arms. "I'll be fine. I assure you."

She looked toward The Shellfish then at me, narrowing her eyes.

I smiled and released her, sticking my hands in my jeans pockets. I shuffled my feet in loose gravel and broken glass. "I'm glad you came tonight."

She exhaled. "Me too."

"I enjoyed our book literary debate. I don't get to do that much. I think I spoke more tonight than I ever have."

"I'm sure I did too. I usually struggle to find things to talk about, to be honest."

I nodded. "I'm like that too."

But even discussing our joint awkwardness, we had difficulty in finding the right words. I didn't know where to take the conversation from there, and apparently, neither did she.

"Well, umm...I guess I should be going. It's late. And you probably have another show tomorrow."

"Actually, it's a day off. Phoenix has to rest his pipes."

"Oh." She leaned her backside against the car. "What will you do with your free time?"

"Probably sleep." I chuckled. "And finish that Grisham book."

"Umm. Well, if you run out of reading material, there's this really great bookstore in town..."

"You don't say? It wouldn't be Beach Reads, would it?" I wanted her to be aware that I had been listening earlier when she'd discussed her job.

"Why, yes," she said in mock surprise. "You've heard of it?"

"Yes. This pretty lady told me about it," I replied, sidling closer.

"Hmm." I tried to read her body language. I didn't have a lot of experience doing that, but I knew it was important, especially in a situation like ours, where both parties lacked communication skills. She smiled and her lips twitched expectantly, but she dropped her gaze and searched the ground. She was nervous. I was making her nervous. I needed to ease up.

"Can I get your door for you?"

"Uhh...yeah. Thanks." She stepped to the side, and I opened the door for her.

"Be safe."

"Yes. And you." She nodded at the building in our wake and got seated behind the wheel.

"I will." I closed the door, but the *thud* of it shutting had such a finality to it, it made me desperate. I knocked on the window. She jumped and fumbled with the buttons to lower it. "Sorry. Uhh...I was just wondering if you might want to join me for dinner tomorrow? You could maybe suggest some other reading material for me," I added.

She hesitated for less than a second. "I'd like that."

"Great. Pick you up at...six?"

She thought. "Why don't I meet you there? We could try the new place downtown, if you'd like?"

"Sure. What's it called?"

"Up On The Roof...or Up On The Rooftop, or something like that...?"

"Okay. I'll get reservations and meet you there at six. Maybe I should get your number in case they're full?"

"Sure."

I got my phone out and she rattled off the number. "Okay. I'll text you so you can get a hold of me if something changes."

She gave me a big smile. "Sounds good."

"I'm looking forward to it." I retreated a couple feet. "Be safe and I'll see you tomorrow."

"See you tomorrow, Caleb."

I walked backward a couple of yards then stopped to watch her drive away. So, I had a date tomorrow. The thought thrilled and terrified me equally.

CHAPTER FOUR

Sophie

So, I was going on a date with Caleb Winthrop. No big deal. It's normal to sit across the table from the guy *Rolling Stone* had called "one of the best guitarists of our time." Yeah, maybe I hadn't shared a bottle of wine with a member of a Grammy-winning, multi-platinum record selling band before, but...whatever. I had a lot of Girl Scout badges to my name. That's impressive.

Right. I rolled my eyes at myself.

But in my mind, I wasn't having dinner with that person. I was dining with Caleb. A sweet, sexy man who was nearly as nerdy as I was. Smooth he wasn't, but still...there was something about him...the seductive hum of his voice, his rock solid body, the way one side of his smile rose higher than the other when he was amused, his gentle laughter, his sexy—

"Why are you smiling like that?"

My brother's voice made me jump. He dropped a box of books too close to my feet. I drew a book from the box he'd brought from the stock room earlier. "I don't know what you mean." I shelved it, pretending to be too busy to converse.

He reached over and pulled the book I'd just shelved out, flipped it, and reshelved it correctly. "Uhh-huh." He crossed his muscly arms and leaned against the bookcase studying me.

I did my best to ignore him.

"You've got a secret."

I froze with a book half in place, then slowly pushed it the rest of the way in and turned to the shelf behind me, contemplating it.

"You do." He moved so he could see my face. "Dish."

I glanced at him and my stupid lips lifted despite my efforts to hold my smile in. "If I told you, it wouldn't be much of a secret, now, would it?"

"Ahh-hah. So you do have one. Tell me."

I whirled around. "Okay. But you can't tell anybody. Not even Trudy." His girlfriend. "Especially Trudy." The girl would have the news splashed across town before I even finished work.

"Deal."

"And not Mom and Dad."

"Ooh. This must be good." He quirked an eyebrow. "It may require hush money."

I waved a hand and refocused my attention to the historical fiction area. "Never mind then."

"No. Come on. Tell me," he wheedled. "I'm bored to death. I've lugged roughly 165 cases out, and you know how much I hate inventory."

I ran a finger down the spine of the book I'd just put in place. "I have a date tonight."

"No way!"

I hopped across a pile of books and covered his mouth. "Shh!" My mom glanced up from the reference desk she was manning with a frown. I shook my head at her to show my equal disdain for the outburst.

Gabe stared over my shoulder at her and lowered his voice. "With who?"

"No one you know." I smiled to myself. "Personally, anyway."

"What kind of cryptic answer is that?" I didn't elaborate, and he scowled at me. "It isn't Steve, is it? If you're getting back together with that son-of-a-bitch, I'm gonna—"

"Shh!" I checked to see if Mom was looking, but luckily a customer had her occupied. "No, it's not Steve. I'd rather...freaking eat those gumdrop cookies Mom made than do that."

He grimaced. "Those were awful."

I laughed at the face he'd made. "God awful. I can't believe you ate a whole one."

"She was watching! And don't remind me." He put a hand on his stomach.

I turned to my work.

"Who then?"

"You're not letting it go, are you?" I muttered.

He grinned. "Not when it's this juicy."

"Fine," I huffed. "It's Caleb Winthrop."

"Caleb Winthrop."

"Yep."

He folded his arms again. "As in the lead singer from Insatiable Fire?"

"No."

He stood straighter. "Another Caleb Winthrop?"

"The lead *guitarist* from Insatiable Fire."

"Lead singer, lead guitarist, whatever." He stared at me. "Oh. So you've got tickets to a concert."

"Nope." I chuckled.

He growled.

I quit pretending to be wrapped up in my work and turned to him. "We're having dinner right after work."

"You and Caleb Winthrop from Insatiable Fire."

"Yes! Is it really that hard to believe?" I asked, a little insulted.

"Wait. Is he the one with the Mohawk?"

"Yes." I cocked a hip. "Don't you know who the members of Insatiable Fire are? Half of them we grew up with."

"*You* grew up with. You were all at least three years ahead of me. And I like country."

I scrunched my face. "Don't remind me. I can't believe we're even related."

He buzzed and pulled his phone out of his pocket. "Dad. What a tyrant. I've been talking for like thirty seconds and he—"

I frowned at him. "It's been more than thirty seconds."

"Okay. Forty then."

"And that tyrant pays you much more than you deserve."

"Yada, yada. They've brainwashed you, sis." He pivoted to march away but had only gotten a few steps before he spun around, grinning like the Cheshire cat. "I can't wait till they see you with Mohawk-man. You have to make sure I'm there to see their reaction."

"I'll do my best. I'd hate to deprive you of the opportunity to see me squirm."

He absolutely glowed, imagining me, the good child, being the one in hot water for a change. He twisted to leave then did another about-face. "He's the one they call Boner, isn't he?"

I frowned. "Yes."

"This is gonna be great." With that, he hustled off, but he left in his wake a warm feeling. He was a goofball, but he was my brother.

Approximately fifteen minutes later, as I was really getting into the groove with my shelving, a customer addressed me.

"Excuse me, ma'am? Can you tell me where to find a copy of *The Kama Sutra*?"

My cheeks flushed, and I turned to find Caleb leaning with one forearm against a shelf, his legs slanted to one side and crossed, with the cutest, cockiest little smirk on his face.

I moved closer to him. "What are you doing here?" I asked in a rough whisper.

He lowered his voice too. "What? Are we not supposed to talk in here, like a library?"

I glanced over my shoulder. My mom was occupied, but we would be in her line of sight if she looked in our direction. "Come here." I took his arm and led him to a spot behind a bookshelf where my mom couldn't see us. "I thought I'd be seeing you at the restaurant."

He grimaced. "Yeah. About that...I can't meet you."

A chill washed through me from my hair down to my toes and my stomach tightened. He was like all the rest. He wanted to use me, but he found someone hotter, and now he was bailing on me. At least he had the good grace to come and tell me instead of simply failing to keep the date.

"Oh," I said shakily. I drew in a breath to steady myself and attempt to act mature. These things happened. In fact, they'd happened to me big time. I stared at his boots. "I understand. Well, it was nice talking to you the other night. I appreciate you coming to tell me, rather than standing me up." To my embarrassment, tears welled in my eyes. I blinked and peered off toward the front windows, trying to will them away.

He gently put a fist under my chin and moved my head to face him. "First of all, I would *never* stand you up. Well, I wouldn't do that to anybody, but especially you. Second of all, I have *no* desire to not see you this evening. Actually, I have great desire *to* be with you." He lingered over the word desire and brushed his thumb along my bottom lip, following it with his gaze and wetting his own lips with a sigh. I turned to goo and had the strongest urge to kiss him right then and there, and may have done so if a customer hadn't passed us, apparently oblivious to the fact that we were having a moment.

My hands fell to his hips in the most natural way, and we both seemed to draw closer to each other. I furrowed my brow. "What do you mean then?"

"Uhh...yeah. I didn't say that clearly." He inhaled, then the words came hurriedly from his mouth. "It's just Levi has this thing he wants me to do. He's making some kind of treasure hunt or something for Remi, and he asked me to wait for her at The Black Pearl and give her some clue."

My interest was piqued. "What's the clue?"

"I don't know. He hasn't given it to me yet. And he told me I can't read it before she does." He frowned. "He's being very particular and mysterious. It's not like him." He brightened. "Anyway...could you possibly meet me *there* at 6:50 or so?"

I exhaled, releasing the tension I didn't realize I'd been holding. "Sure."

He clapped once. "Great." Taking my hands he added, "You know, I wouldn't have changed things on you...it's only...this seemed very important to Levi, for some reason. And I promise, you will have me all to yourself for the rest of the night." He leaned closer. "*Every* inch of me." His voice was a low rumble that gave me goosebumps, in a good way. He was acting much more intimate than he had as yet. Could he have been thinking as much about me as I had been about him? And it wasn't a turnoff either. Normally a guy responding to me so familiarly in such a short time would have sent me running. This had the opposite effect. I wanted to run to him. Melt into him. Discover what it'd be like to be in his embrace.

My lips lifted, and I shimmied a little nearer to him. "I'm looking forward to that."

He slid his arms around me, and I laced my fingers behind him. "Six-fifty seems so far away."

I laid my cheek on his chest and gave him a squeeze. "I know."

He exhaled and another customer approached. We separated a bit and gave the guy a smile, both saying hello to him. After he passed, Caleb returned his gaze to me. "I'd better go," he said forlornly. He bent in and gave me a kiss on the forehead. "Six-fifty?"

"Six-fifty."

"Okay." He took a breath and whirled to leave. "You're watching my ass, aren't you?" he called over his shoulder.

I was. "What? Of course not."

He chuckled, twisted at the door, gave me a grin, and pushed it open with that fine ass of his before taking off up the street. This was going way better than I could have hoped for.

Caleb texted me an hour later.

SO, APPARENTLY THERE'S A FUNCTION AFTERWARD. NINE O'CLOCK AT THE SANDS. AND...IT'S DRESSY. I'M SORRY. I SWEAR WE'LL JUST MAKE AN APPEARANCE AND THEN BOLT.

After clarifying "dressy" didn't mean full-length gown, I chose a simple turquoise dress for the evening. It was V-neck with a bodice that crisscrossed and wrapped around the back, where it was tied. The A-line design was uncomplicated, but the fabric had a flow, and wearing it felt luxurious. I went with an equally simple thin chain that skimmed along my collar bone with a tiny, sideways cross. I was a little bolder with my earrings, donning a chandelier style and sweeping my hair into a loose bun.

I was nervous and confident alternately. Nervous because we were going on our first date. Confident as I thought about the things he had said to me at the store. Likewise, while getting ready and checking the mirror I thought, *hey, I look pretty good.* But seconds later I'd feel totally inadequate.

He's a rock star; I work at a bookstore. He's traveled the globe; I've been as far as Summerville. He parties with famous people—actresses, models, the rich and beautiful...how can I ever compete?

But thinking of Caleb purely filled me with warmth and a desire to be with him again. We'd just met, yet, oddly, I felt like I could be who I was in front of him, even more so than some of my close friends whom I'd known for years. I'd always been the quiet one. The nerdy one. The oddball.

Savannah, as uptight as she was, could hang with the "popular kids." Somehow brilliant without being nerdy, she was a highly successful lawyer/ CFO at a big law firm in Summerville. She'd made partner at a younger age than any other person in her company and had her name in giant letters on the side of the building, for heaven's sake.

Hali was...Hali. Superstar. Grammy-winner. Her concerts sold out in minutes, yet she still somehow managed to be the same old Hali, a slightly older projection of the flannel-shirt-wearing girl who hung around the smoking area in school.

Paige? Well Paige was also an oddball, but in a cool way. She was unreserved, energetic, and fit in with any crowd, like a social chameleon.

I was awkward even with my own friend group. Although they included me and loved me, they didn't understand me in the same manner Caleb seemed to. I loved them to death, would give my life for any one of them in a heartbeat. But with Caleb I had an affinity. A recognition that we were of the same species, *bookwormus misfitinus*. It was like I had found my place. I had found home.

Oh, good grief. First guy I've interacted with since Steve and I'm already imagining some mystical connection with him. Will I ever learn?

As I peered into the mirror, I envisioned a different Sophie. One with tear-stained cheeks and a veil upon her head. I'd been ready to give myself to Steve. Share my life with him. All the while believing he felt the same. Like really *believing* that with every fiber of my being. Knowing it. But I was an idiot with blinders on. My only solace was that he'd fooled everyone else too. No one truly knew him or foresaw what he would do. They were as shocked as I was. And I was shocked. Rocked to the core. It was like nothing made sense anymore.

I picked up my phone and almost used that number Caleb gave me to blow him off. But I couldn't imagine saying those words, knowing they had even the slightest potential of hurting him. Sure, he'd undoubtedly shrug it off and move on to the next girl who interested him. But I'd agreed to meet him. He needed a date to this thing he had going on later. And I enjoyed his company, so why not? I could play the game too. I could keep my heart out of it.

Right.

Sighing deeply, I stared at my phone. Then I slipped it into my little beaded purse and left my place. Caleb had "sent a car" for me, so I assumed the nicely dressed man leaning against the sleek, black sedan pulled to the curb was my driver.

"Hi. Are you...umm...my driver?" For a second, I imagined he was someone else, waiting for his date to arrive, insulted I called him a driver.

"If you're Sophie Lockhart I am," he said with a smile.

Shoo. How can I make even a small exchange like this so bumbling and awkward?

It was super strange being in the back, with him riding in front, but sitting next to him would have been weird too. He made small talk, and I answered politely while wondering just how hurt I'd get jumping from a vehicle at thirty miles per hour. I rolled a loose bead on my purse as we conversed, making it looser. He ignored my little snafu earlier, which most people would choose to do. It made things easier.

We arrived at the Ocean Pearl. The restaurant where I was supposed to meet Caleb was inside the resort. The driver came around to open my door, and as I stepped out, I realized I should maybe tip him. I fumbled with my purse and attempted to hand him money. He waved me off. "Oh, no miss. I've already been taken care of quite generously."

"Oh." I returned the bills to my purse.

"Right this way, miss." He walked me to the door, which was about three feet away and was a revolving door, so there wasn't even a need for him to open it for me. "Have a nice evening."

"Thank you," I mumbled, proceeding into the portal. Exiting on the other side, I was disconcerted for a moment. I took in the opulent white furniture, royal red carpeting, and the ornate fireplace, with a fire going, although it was a mild night. My gaze traveled over glass and mirrors, sculptures and paintings, vases with fresh flowers, tastefully displayed, and continued up, up to the lofty ceiling. I felt incredibly small.

"Excuse me." A man had entered behind me, and I was blocking his path.

"Oh. Sorry." I moved aside and still stood gawking until I noticed the fancy gold scroll announcing The Black Pearl restaurant. I drifted slowly toward the door, as though being held back by some tractor beam. My brow furrowed as I read the sign on the door. UNAVAILABLE DUE TO PRIVATE PARTY. ACCESSIBLE TO PUBLIC AT SEVEN. SORRY FOR ANY INCONVENIENCE.

Could I have gotten it wrong?

And another thought tumbled free:

Could this all have been a joke?

I didn't think Caleb would do that. Then again, I didn't suspect Steve was capable of the things he had done either.

I was startled by the door opening suddenly, and a young woman stuck her head out. "Oh, hi. Are you Sophie Lockhart, by any chance?"

"Yes?"

"Oh, good. Then follow me."

"But the sign on the door says—"

"That sign doesn't apply to you."

"Oh."

It was dark in the room and my eyes hadn't quite adjusted, but I spotted him as the girl guiding me stepped to the left and waved her arm toward his table. Caleb, who was wearing a tux, was getting to his feet. He moved to the other side of the table and pulled out a seat.

I sat. "I'm feeling a tad underdressed here."

"Don't." He bent to speak so his lips brushed my ear. "You look...amazing." He returned to his seat.

"Are you sure? I mean, you're wearing a tuxedo."

"Oh, this? This is all Levi's deal." He ran a finger behind his collar. "You'd never catch me in something like this otherwise. I may be allergic to formality."

His complaining amused me. He was like a petulant schoolchild who didn't like wearing his Sunday best. I leaned in. "You wear it well."

He dipped his head. "Thank you." His gaze shifted to the doorway. "We only have a few minutes before the rest of the world intrudes. How was your day?"

"Good. Busy but—"

"Uhh-huh. Who was that guy you were talking to?"

"Where? At the store?"

He nodded curtly.

"My brother Gabe."

He exhaled. "Brother." He rolled his eyes and chuckled.

I smiled. "Why? Who did you think it was?"

"Another suitor, perhaps."

"Suitor?"

We were interrupted by the girl who let me in. She set a plate down between us. I was hit by a heavenly, savory, sweet fragrance. "What is this?"

"He said salmon patties with a ginger sauce. It's excellent."

He took a bite and I crossed myself, bowing to say a quick prayer before following suit.

I raised my head, and he was staring at me with his mouth hanging open. "I guess that cross you wear's for real."

"Oh...umm...yeah...I guess..."

"Don't worry about it. I'm Catholic too. I just haven't darkened a church's doorstep in...well, quite a while. It's not like I'm against it or any-thing. I simply don't have the time." He frowned. "Actually...that's a lie. You make time when something is important to you." He paused with a thought-ful expression. "Hmm. Anyway, I was thinking—"

"Oh, my gosh!" I couldn't help but say. "These taste as good as they smell. *So* good."

"I know, right? The chef from The Sands is guest cooking here tonight. Another part of Levi's sinister plan."

I leaned forward confidentially. "What do you imagine Levi's up to?"

He shrugged, cutting into a patty. "No clue. I stopped trying to figure out Levi a long time ago."

"Well, from my experience..." I said slowly, remembering the night Steve proposed to me at The Sands, "a guy doesn't go to all this effort unless it's something big. So, he's either asking her to prom or..."

He'd ceased eating and was listening attentively. "Or what?"

Wow. It seems pretty obvious to me. "Or he's proposing."

"Proposing?" He gaped at me then sank back in his chair. "Proposing. I bet you're right. That makes complete sense."

I had to laugh. "Yeah." I shook my head. "Anyway, I interrupted you ear-lier. What were you going to say?"

"Uhh...oh. I was saying that after dinner we have some time before we have to arrive at the...party, or whatever. We could go to The Sands, but we don't have to be there until nine. They'll have drinks but...I was considering maybe we could grab a drink at that restaurant you talked about and then move to The Sands. What do you say?"

"It sounds like a great idea."

CHAPTER FIVE

Sophie

I loved Up On The Roof. It had tables, couches, firepits, and those tall heaters. It was the closest thing Last Chance Beach had to those big city bars. It was a beautiful night, and from the railing of the balcony we could see all the way to the ocean. As I stood there observing it, Caleb shifted behind me, placing his arms on either side of my body and gripping the rail. He brushed his lips over my ear.

"What are you thinking about, pretty lady?"

I trembled and melted into him. "Well, I can't think of anything now."

His laugh was a low rumble. "Dance with me."

I twisted my head. "I thought you didn't dance."

"Oh, I didn't. Until I got lessons from an expert." He released the rail and separated from me so I could turn.

I snorted. "I'm hardly an expert."

He took my hand and held it aloft for me to spin under, then gently tugged me to the dance floor. He brought my knuckles to his lips and his palm to my lower back as we swayed together.

I glanced about, feeling self-conscious. "We're the only ones dancing."

"Good. It gives us more room to show our *style*." With the last he eased me into a dip. I laughed and threw my other arm around his neck, holding tight to keep from falling. "I'm not going to drop you," he murmured. When he brought me to vertical, our faces were inches apart. Peering into my eyes, he swallowed, brushing his fingers along my cheek. "The moonlight on your skin...You are so beautiful, Sophie."

I chuckled nervously, a little uncomfortable with all of his compliments. "You're such a smooth-talker."

He looked amused. "That's the first time anyone's called me that." He paused. "Well, is it at least working?"

"Oh, *yeah*. It's working all right." And without thinking, I pressed my lips to his nice full ones. I'd been staring at them all night wondering what it would feel like to kiss him, so I guess it was only natural.

He seemed surprised by the kiss; I know I was. He pulled me closer, and I laid my head on his chest. "Man, am I glad you danced in front of me the other night."

The earnest way he said it made me laugh, and I squeezed him. The music changed to "Careless Whispers," and Caleb altered his movements to better synch with the flow of the ballad. I made the mistake of listening to the lyrics of the Wham! song, about a man caught cheating, and I was taken back to that day.

After months of preparation, it had come down to the big moment. I stood shaking, my arm linked with my dad's, behind the big wooden doors my bridesmaids had passed through. I hated being the center of attention. The two ushers flanked the doors, grasping the big iron handles, prepared to open them up when the music switched and the "Wedding March" trumpeted from the organ pipes. My dad looked at me.

"Are you ready, baby?"

I gazed at him and gave him a trembling smile.

I can do this. As long as Steve's at the end of the aisle, I can do anything.

I nodded and the ushers slowly pulled the heavy doors open. As my view of the inside of the church widened, it was immediately clear something was terribly wrong. While everyone was standing, focused on me, the entire wedding party was staring at the side door exit from the church. The sunlight streaming in from the opening faded as the door closed. Chase Michaels sprinted past gaping bridesmaids and exited the church by the same door. I thought maybe it was his fiancée, Emily, who left, but I saw her standing next to Paige and Savvy, appearing to be as shocked as everybody else. Ironic as she had done the same thing to Chase years ago.

My dad leaned in. "What's going on?"

"I don't know." My first thought was someone had gotten ill and ducked out. I was alarmed, wondering who the person suffering could be. I scanned the group standing before the altar, now whispering amongst themselves. One-by-one they turned to look at me, and I realized the person missing was my groom. It didn't dawn on me at the time that my cousin Clarice was gone too. As the organist continued to play in the choir loft, oblivious to the drama unfolding below, and the guests beamed at me expectantly, Chase re-entered the church like a zombie, holding a bridesmaid bouquet. Gabe, the best man, moved in the direction of the door but saw Chase shake his head. My brother twisted and walked slowly toward me. My dad's arm stiffened. By this time, those in the front of the church seemed to realize something was off, and a commotion rose from people asking each other, "What happened?"

I was slow putting the pieces together, or perhaps I didn't want to know. "What is Gabe doing? He's supposed to stay up there."

"I'm not sure, honey."

Before Gabe reached us, I yelled at him. "What's going on? Where's Steve?"

He opened his mouth, but no words came out. The organ music came to an abrupt end. I could still remember the way the words sounded when Gabe finally found his voice. "He's gone."

"Gone? Gone where?"

He echoed my dad. "I'm not sure."

I released Dad and staggered back a few steps. "He left?" Gabe didn't have the heart to tell me, but I could see it on his face. I lifted my skirts and escaped through the entry. The door closed behind me, shutting out the noise, making it easy for me to detect the high-speed whine of a motorcycle. Dirt rose from the long lane leading to the country church. And then I spotted them as they turned onto the paved road. A man in a tux driving the motorcycle, and a woman in a bridesmaid dress clinging to him. The door creaked open, and I pivoted, spying the heel, dyed to match the bridesmaid dress, sitting in the grass beside an empty parking space. My gaze became riveted on that. The voices calling me became garbled, and my knees were weak. Luckily, Gabe and my dad caught me as I collapsed, as I might have bashed my skull in on the stone stairs of the church...

Mixed with these voices was Caleb's. "Sophie? Sophie? Are you all right?"

Sometimes I wondered if I would ever be all right again. "I-I...need air." It was an absolutely ridiculous thing to say as we were outside. I broke from his embrace and stumbled toward the exit, blinded by the tears that had suddenly appeared in my eyes. I yanked the glass door open and ran to the elevator, slamming my hand on the down button.

"Sophie, what's going on?" The sound of my own voice from that day echoed in his. He stood with a bewildered expression, halfway through the door, trying to catch his breath. Of course he was confused. The girl who had been dancing with him moments ago, who had *kissed* him, had run off like she was insane.

I took a step in his direction. "Oh, I'm so sorry." The thought flashed in my mind, unbidden. I was doing to him what Steve had done to me, leaving without an explanation. The tears were covering my face at this point. I'm sure they made me look like the crazy person I was acting like. A sob escaped and I lowered my head. "I'm sorry, Caleb."

"Hey! Hey, now." He crossed the distance between us and took me into his arms. "It's all right." His voice was unsure, like he didn't quite know how to handle this situation.

The man deserved an explanation. I regained my equilibrium and asked, "Can we go somewhere private to talk?"

Caleb

The girl could kiss. Man, could the girl kiss. I was used to certain parts of my body responding to a kiss, but this was like my blood was warming, surging through my veins, bubbling over like champagne.

Then she just left.

My mind, still abuzz from the kiss, registered she was gone, and I ran after her. I burst into the hall and she turned from the elevator. Her face clearly showed the anguish she was in. Strangely, in some ways, it was a relief to me, because I had been wondering what I did wrong...did I have bad breath making that kiss horrible for her? But I knew I'd done nothing to cause this sort of pain.

Somewhere private to talk... My first thought was my hotel room, but I knew enough about women to know she didn't want anyone to see her like this and there was a chance we'd run into Levi. I couldn't exactly suggest we go to her place. And, besides, she'd told me she had a studio apartment nearby, and if I got her into a bedroom, even if that bedroom was also a living room, I'm not sure I could resist taking that kiss further.

"Why don't we head to The Sands—that will optimize the time we have before we need to be at Levi's thing—and we can walk along the beach and find a spot to ourselves if there's anyone out there?"

"That's perfect."

I led her to a black, luxury sedan and opened the door for her and waited for her to get situated before I closed it. Things were awkward when I got into the car. No surprise there, considering the two parties involved, and chit-chatting seemed inappropriate in light of her previous tears.

She broke the silence. "Uhh...did you rent a car for the week?"

"No. Levi again." I started the engine, put on my blinker, and pulled into traffic. I fumbled around for more conversation. All I wanted to do was comfort her. Whatever had set her off must have been a doozy. Hesitantly, I patted her leg. "You doing all right?"

She gave me a quivering smile. "I'm fine, Caleb," she said unconvincingly. Then she added, "I'm not usually this dramatic."

"Dramatic?"

"Breaking into tears and taking flight on you. I usually have it more together." She seemed to rethink that. "Sort of."

"Don't worry about that. We all have those moments."

"Somehow I don't see you bursting into tears and running out of a restaurant."

"That's because—me man," I said in a caveman voice, trying to lighten the atmosphere. "I'm supposed to be stoic or whatever."

"Hardly seems fair," she commented. "Do you mind if I use the mirror to check my makeup?"

"Go right ahead. But you still look fantastic." *Gorgeous. Amazing. Electrifying...*

A pretty blush colored her cheeks. "Thank you." She pulled a tissue from her purse and dabbed at her face, but I got the feeling she wasn't so much fixing her makeup as trying to compose herself further and think through what she wanted to tell me, so I remained quiet.

We reached The Sands, and I maneuvered around to the back lot, sliding into the perfect spot next to an opening to the beach. I took its vacancy as a good sign. I switched off the ignition then turned to her. "We could stay in the car if you prefer."

She squinted at the waves crashing on the beach. "No. The ocean always calms me."

I gave her a smile. "Okay then." She grasped the door handle. "Wait. I'll get that."

"Oh. Okay."

I exited and hurried to her side, again wondering why she wasn't used to men doing that for her. I took her hand and helped her out, then brushed my lips over her knuckles as I peered into her eyes. I reined in my surging testosterone.

This is not the time. Cool it.

She seemed mesmerized for a second, watching me. Then she stirred. "Oh, Caleb. What about your tux?"

I led her forward with a grin. "A little sand won't hurt anything." Once at the front of the car—which was luckily pristine—I rested my ass against it and bent to untie a shoe. "I'm ditching these, though."

"Good idea." She mimicked me, sitting on the hood and lifting her leg, twisting to try to undo her shoe strap.

"Let me get that. It'll be easier for me." I squatted in front of her and undid the dainty strap so she could slip it off, noting her feet were as perfect as the rest of her, smooth and sexy. Clearing my throat, I closed my eyes momentarily to regain control, then returned to my former position to finish ridding myself of my shoes. I stowed mine and hers in the car, locked it, took her hand and stepped into the sand. I'd tried to roll my pants, but the fabric wouldn't hold in that position.

The beach was pretty much empty, except for a fire about ten yards away where three people were sitting—a couple on a piece of driftwood, and another guy sitting in the sand with his knees bent, one leg on top of the other at the ankles. He was lazily throwing things into the flames as they talked.

"Want to walk by the water?"

"Won't your pants get wet?"

I examined them again, silently cursing the fashion industry, and bent to give rolling another try. I reverse rolled them, to the inside, and hoped they would stick. I looked like some idiot, or a clam digger, or some idiot clam digger, but I didn't care. We strolled silently, which didn't feel strange for some reason. She stopped at one point and turned to peer out over the waves. She crossed her arms and ran her hands along her biceps.

I wrapped myself around her. "It's cold here by the water." I thought again of asking her if she'd prefer somewhere else, but she melted into my embrace and the words stuck in my throat.

"Thank you for bringing me here," she murmured, low enough that no one but me could hear.

We stood there for some time, the wind tugging at her hair, trying to pull strands from her bun, and failing altogether to displace mine. Gobs of product had its benefits. She stirred and straightened, parting from me.

"Do you want to talk now?" I asked.

She nodded.

The threesome was well out of earshot, and we'd only passed one couple on our walk, so we seemed to have made the right choice from the privacy standpoint. I led her from the shore's edge to a spot of grass jutting into the sand, which offered both shelter and back support. The area was lit from some resort above us. I removed my jacket and laid it down for her to sit on. She looked at me nervously.

"It's just sand," I repeated softly. We sat, copying our standing position, she in front, me behind, with my legs around hers. I kissed her hair then put my cheek next to her soft one. We again listened to the hiss and gurgle of the waves as they hit sand, stretched, and then were reluctantly dragged away again. A few sandpipers hopped along near the tideline, pecking at whatever it was the swelling waters had washed in.

She sat forward abruptly, finding a decapitated sea oat to fuss with while she talked. "The reason I asked you if Phoenix and Dakota had told you about me was...I have a reputation on the island."

I couldn't have been more surprised. I cleared my throat. "Well, I can hardly judge you on that. I'd be the last person to think poorly of you. Don't—"

She twisted her head and slapped my leg with a smile. "Not like *that*, silly."

"Oh."

What other reputation could she have?

Well, if you'd shut your trap and listen, you might discover the answer.

I zipped it and waited for her to speak again.

"I'm widely known as *that* girl." She sighed. "*That* poor girl Steve ditched. *That* foolish girl who accepted every slimy lie her fiancé gave her. *That* girl who began to walk down the aisle in her fancy dress but found her groom had left with her cousin." She took a deep breath. "They apparently ran off to Hollywood."

Ouch. What a douche bag.

Even though no one was there to take it out on, my gut tightened, my blood simmered, and I clenched my fists.

Why would someone do that to Sophie? The asshole. And the cousin. Family like that makes me glad I'm an only child.

"And that song..."

What song? I wracked my brain for what had been on at the moment she bolted.

"It hit a little too close."

"Careless Whispers." Oh, I get it. No wonder Dak told me to be good to her.

She covered her face. "It just snuck up on me. I didn't expect..." She twisted her torso to put a hand on my cheek, her focus concentrated on one of my eyes and then the other. "I'm sorry, Caleb. So sorry I ran out on you. I—" Her voice tightened in the end and she couldn't speak. A lone tear trickled down.

"Shh-shh-shh." I wiped her tear away with a big, clumsy thumb then cradled her chin. "Sophie." I fought to find the right words. "*I'm* sorry that happened to you. You don't deserve that."

She dropped her gaze. "And sometimes I feel that's true. But sometimes I wonder. I mean, clearly, I wasn't giving him what he needed. Maybe if I'd...I don't know...been different somehow. More exciting. More beautiful. If I'd tried to please him more..."

Anger toward the asshole who did this to her flared again. "No, Sophie. If he couldn't appreciate the...*amazing* woman who you are, he didn't deserve you. And don't worry about bolting on me. I understand." I kissed her softly.

She studied me for a moment, then rotated and pulled her legs in so she was sitting on her heels in front of me, between my legs.

"Thank you." She scooched closer and angled her head, looking at my lips as she leaned in. Our mouths met in mind-blowing, deep, soft kisses, over and over again.

That Steve guy was an idiot.

Then her tongue began to tempt. Tease. My mind swam, and I wanted to swallow her whole. I wanted. *Wanted.* Wanted like I never had before. Loud laughter had me separating from her.

"Get a room!"

I ignored them, laying my forehead on Sophie's. "Fuck, Sophie. You drive me crazy."

She drew away quickly, her eyes wide. "I'm—I'm sorry. I didn't mean to—"

My brow wrinkled. Her reaction seemed strange. "No." I chuckled. "Don't be."

"Oh." She exhaled and laughed at the same time. The tension left her shoulders, and her features relaxed.

Did she believe I was going to jump all over her for some reason? Did I sound angry? I don't think I sounded angry...

I made sure to gentle my tone. "Honey, you never have to apologize for that."

Her expression glowed. "Okay."

I suddenly realized we'd been gone a while. "Oh, shit. What time is it?" I fumbled around in my pocket for my phone, but dropped it in the sand. I retrieved it. "Shit." I scrambled to my feet and helped her to hers. "Come on." I took off at barely under a run. "We have to be there on time. It's a surprise, and we don't want to ruin it."

She kept up with me and we arrived at the car, both fairly winded. We sat on the hood again to put our shoes back on, after rinsing our feet in the spigot conveniently located near our car. I looked at her as I raced to get re-dressed, still breathing hard. Beside me, she raggedly took in air and grinned. I bookended her face and gave her a quick kiss. "You're as crazy as I am. We walk from here. I don't want you to twist an ankle in those things." I glanced at my phone. "But we walk fast. Let's go." I took her hand and we rushed, planning to sneak in a side door.

As I turned the corner to the wide open area in front of the banquet rooms, Levi and Remi were approaching the door of the party room. I reversed so quickly Sophie ran into me. "Sorry."

"Surprise!"

I scurried out and we entered the nearest door to the room, melting into the crowd. No one would be the wiser. "Drink?"

Her splayed fingers were on her chest; she was still trying to catch her breath. "Yes, please," she said with a smile.

And that was the moment I knew I loved her. For the mere fact she'd been willing to run with me, like a loon, across the beach. I always thought that love at first sight thing was ridiculous and cliché. The stuff of romance novels. But we'd known each other for two days. I guess when one met the right person it simply clicked. Well, it did for me anyway. "I'll be back in a second. Don't go anywhere." I didn't want to lose her in the throng.

I moved off to search for beverages and ran into a waiter with a tray full of champagne. "I can relieve you of two of those." I returned to Sophie, saying, "If you don't like champagne, I can get something else."

With the same ease as she'd shown before, she answered, "Champagne is great." That's what I liked about her; she rolled with it. Someone began to talk over a microphone. She leaned in. "Do you have to play?"

I took her hand and backed toward the stage, dragging her with me. "Not tonight," I said with a huge grin.

"I don't know," she joked, cocking her head. "You know what happened the last time we danced."

"I'll ask them not to play..." I cleared my throat. "...a certain song. Besides, some very pleasant things happened as we danced too." I brought her knuckles to my lips.

"There sure were," she purred.

We were still a couple of feet from the dance floor, but I pulled her into my arms and we spun ourselves onto it. She laughed, and the sound was so carefree and happy. Could I, Mohawk Man, make someone feel that way? But I was more than Mohawk Man, and I sensed I was just discovering that.

We danced until the soles of my rented shoes were well worn in. I caught a few looks from my bandmates, but I ignored them. At one point Dak came over. "Can I cut in?"

I swung her away from him. "No."

That seemed to delight her. When the next slow song came on, she laid her cheek on my chest. "This feels so good."

"What? Dancing?"

She tilted her chin back to peer into my eyes, but she hesitated. "Being in your arms."

It filled me with a swell of emotion, and I squeezed her into my chest again, bending my neck to speak into her ear. "I like it too." She shivered and I almost asked her if she was cold, but another thought came to me. Could she be turned on by my speaking so close to her? The thought had never occurred to me, but I stored that information to test later.

She put some space between us and fiddled with one of the buttons on my shirt. "So...you leave tomorrow?"

I shook my head. "Not tomorrow. Tomorrow night we have the gala. We leave on Saturday."

"Mmm." She nodded and kept her gaze downcast.

It made me realize how precious little time we had together. "Can we meet for lunch together tomorrow? And then we can do something fun before the gala."

"Yes." That earned me a slight smile. But we both knew we couldn't make the goodbye awaiting us go away; we could only delay it. Her expression clouded. "Oh. I forgot. Tomorrow's Gabe's birthday—my brother. We made a special effort to schedule the whole family off for the lunch hour to celebrate, as he's going on a date in the evening with his girlfriend. I can't miss that. Not when they called Chuck in to work some extra hours."

"Oh, okay." I couldn't keep the disappointment out of my voice.

"Wait." Her face brightened slowly. "You can come over for lunch too. Gabe would be thrilled, and you could meet my mom and dad. That is, if you want to. No pressure. I can understand if—"

"I'd love to."

"You would?"

"Yes. It gives us more time to be together."

"Exactly. And we can keep it short and sweet and then do...whatever it is you want to do, after."

"Sounds like a plan." I gave her a quick kiss then looked up to see Phoenix and Dak watching us and going crazy on the sidelines. I may have emitted a growl, but she didn't seem to notice.

"I'll have to prepare Mom and Dad to meet you." She said it more to herself. Like she was creating a to-do list.

"Why's that?"

She was so lost in her thoughts, my question startled her.

"Oh. No offense. It's only...they're used to me dating..." She scanned the room. "See that guy over there?"

She nodded toward the bandstand. A polished—I would say stuffy—male model type was dancing with some girl. He had perfect teeth. Perfect hair. And, I imagined, was perfectly boring.

He wouldn't know Tolkien from Tolstoy.

He was practically making out on the dance floor, which I found tacky, and yet a zip of jealousy hit me as that was exactly what I wanted to do with Sophie.

"Well, he seems taken, but I can ask him if he has a brother." I made a move in that direction, but she grabbed me.

"Don't be silly." She dropped her head. "I shouldn't have said anything. I just wanted you to...you know...be prepared for them."

"Are you sure you don't want me to...?" I again acted like I was going after the guy. That little tinge of jealousy I'd had earlier morphed into something more substantial with the thought of her with other guys. Guys who her parents would approve of.

"Caleb, I'm sorry. That was rude. It's only because I want them to see past your physical appearance and understand what a great guy you are." I frowned, and she tried to backtrack. "Not that your physical appearance is bad...it's solely because...they're conservative. I *love* your style."

"You're sure you don't want a guy who's more like him?" I jerked my thumb over my shoulder.

"No. Absolutely not. I've done that. That's not what I want. What attracted me to you is the way you don't conform to everyone else's standards. And...I'm making a mess of this." She seemed truly dismayed. "Everything I say sounds worse than the last." I cast another glance at the guy, and she gently guided my chin to center so I was looking at her again. "I'm sorry. Can we maybe forget I opened my fat, stupid mouth?"

I sighed and pulled her into my chest again. "Your mouth is neither fat nor stupid." But the conversation left me wondering. Was I merely a walk on the wild side for her? A little fling to show people she didn't care that idiot, Steve, was fool enough to leave her? I could feel that iron shield rise again.

The one she'd slid back with her first smile. I had no desire to be hurt again. I suddenly needed to be away from that atmosphere, out of the celebrating mob—because she had been right, Levi proposed to Remi and she'd accept-ed. Big changes were afoot for Insatiable Fire, and I wasn't sure how I felt about that.

"Do you want to go?"

She nodded and followed me to the door. Just as we were ready to take off, I caught Phoenix's and Dak's gazes again. They gave me two laughing thumbs up. They obviously thought Sophie and I were a good pair. I hated the idea that I might disappoint them.

The ride to her place was pretty quiet. I parked, cut the engine, and start-ed to exit to come around to open her door, but she touched my arm.

"Caleb. I'm sorry for what I said. You're not some...monster my parents have to be forewarned of. I—"

I covered her hand with mine. "I've forgotten all about it."

Liar.

"Are we still getting together tomorrow?"

"Of course. You didn't believe I'd let you off the hook that easily." I turned again to the door.

"But—"

I faced her.

"Will you still come to Gabe's birthday lunch?"

That one was a little harder to answer. I sighed. "Of course."

I got out and opened her door for her. She'd told me she had a studio near the bookshop. She took a step up on the long staircase leading to her door, then spun around. "Thank you for the dinner, the cocktails, the danc-ing, and for being such a good listener on the beach."

"My pleasure." I looked at her door. "Aren't you going to show me your place?"

"Umm. I don't think I should. Tonight."

I shuffled my feet. "Okay."

"It's just...if I got you in there, I probably wouldn't want you to leave and...we only met the night before last. I've made mistakes in the past—not that you are a mistake—but I need to be more careful and...not jump into anything."

I exhaled. "I understand." She was a good girl. She wouldn't merely sleep with me for the thrill of bedding a well-known guitarist, and part of me respected that. But, to be honest, part of me was crushed. "Okay. I'll watch and make sure you get in then."

She stared at my toes. "So you're not giving me a kiss goodnight?"

"I'd like to, but I wasn't sure how you'd feel about that."

"Caleb..." she said softly, like she was scolding me. She pressed her lips to mine in a heart-stopping kiss.

We stood on the bottom of her stairs for several minutes, wrapped up in each other, our passion increasing until we were on the verge of taking it further. I reluctantly pulled away, clearing my throat. "Uhh...you should probably go now."

"I probably should." She smiled, hesitating. "I'll text you my parents' address tomorrow. Can you come around 11:30?"

"Yeah. Sure."

"Great. I'm looking forward to it."

But as I drove back to The Sands, I wondered. Could this be some attempt to rebel against her parents? Bring the bad boy home and flaunt it in front of them to piss them off? But she was a little old for that kind of behavior. Still, I didn't really know her; maybe she'd do something like that. By the time I got to our suite, I had worked myself into a state. Walking in and finding all of my band members, plus Remi, there, didn't help much.

"Hey!" Dak bellowed. "There he is."

Phoenix launched in immediately. I guess there was no need for any preliminaries. "How'd it go with Sophie? It seemed like you guys were getting pretty cozy..."

I cut in before he could get any farther, marching to my room and avoiding eye contact. "I don't want to talk about it."

"Sophie Lockhart?" Remi whispered as I closed the door behind me. She sounded shocked. Of course she was. I was not the type Sophie hooked up with. I was a freak. An anomaly.

I wanted to chuck my keys across the room, but I didn't need to give them cause to question me anymore, so I dropped them on the dresser. With a huff, I bent, stretching my arms wide and grasping the edge of the dresser tightly. I raised my gaze to the mirror. With late nights and partying, I'd aged more than the years that had passed. I looked too old to be sporting a Mohawk. I'd gotten it after I was released from prison. Not so much to enrage my parents, although that was a bonus, but to distance me from them and mark a change in me. I left New York in my dust, along with my parents and the girl who had trampled on my heart. My Mohawk had become such a piece of me, my disguise from the world. I turned away in disgust.

I no longer had any desire to go to this the stupid birthday party I'd been invited to, but I'd promised Sophie, and I wouldn't break that promise. I threw myself onto the bed, laced my fingers over my chest and stared at the ceiling. I then had to plan our date—our "fun date" as I'd said—that would now undoubtedly be awkward, no surprise there. My debate should have kept me awake, but I was exhausted and fell asleep. I woke around three. It was quiet; Dak and Phoenix, at least, must have left. After flopping for forty minutes like a catfish lying on the bank in July, I rose to pace my room. Eventually I wandered out to the kitchen area and found some crackers and cheese on a room service tray. The cheese was already hard on the edges, but I ate the crackers and some grapes.

I sat on the couch and watched the sun rise above the ocean without the appreciation I should have had for that. I laid down and must have fallen asleep for a second, but the creak of Levi's door woke me. I lifted my upper body to see over the back of the couch. Remi.

"Hey," she whispered, shutting the door gently behind her.

"Did I wake you?" I said, my voice gruff with sleep and not having spoken in hours.

She shrugged. "I'm a light sleeper."

"I'm sorry."

She waved in front of her. "Don't be. I needed to get up anyway. I have to go relieve poor Wyatt. My daughter is no doubt crawling on top of him while he's trying to sleep, demanding Fruit Loops." The smile on her face showed how fond she was of both of them. She sat in a chair near me. "You wanna talk? About...whatever happened last night?"

My initial, knee-jerk reaction was to say no, but she was so earnest, and I'd really come to like her. I swung my legs to the floor and sat, grateful I'd pulled some shorts and a T-shirt on before leaving my room. Resting my forearms on my thighs and clasping my hands, I shook my head. "I don't know... I like her, like *really* like her, but..." How did I explain how Sophie's comment had hurt me and not come off as a cry baby, or unmanly?

"But...?" she gently prompted.

"I don't know..." I repeated, scratching the back of my neck. I tried to gather my thoughts, but they didn't even make sense to me, so how could I explain them to her? And sharing myself wasn't something I did. It was so foreign, I didn't even recognize the language. Verbalizing our emotions wasn't something the Winthrops did. In fact, I sometimes wondered if my parents had any feelings at all; they were so intent on playing the part of the rich and famous, they didn't seem to have time for such nonsense. "Do you think...Sophie and I would be good together?"

She inhaled deeply, reclined a little more, and stared out the window. "Well..."

I looked too. We were too high to see the ocean, but the strokes of pinks and oranges on the vibrant patch of blue sky were hard to ignore.

"I've known Sophie for years. She's a real sweetheart. *Unfortunately*, some people take advantage of that." The anger in her voice made me turn to study her. "From what I've seen..." she twisted to face me "...you're a real sweetheart too."

My cheeks warmed. "Thank you."

"You're welcome," she said matter-of-factly. "Levi told me you like books, and that's *right* up Sophie's alley."

"Yeah. But you can hardly build a relationship on that."

"True. Levi also said you met in jail, when he was taking the fall for Wyatt, and he said you were taking the fall for your girlfriend."

Levi has loose lips.

Remi continued. "She was making a scene at a club and they called the cops. They searched her and found drugs. You told them they were yours, is that right?"

I nodded.

"And Levi said you're from a wealthy family, and they refused to pay your bail."

I crossed my arms over my chest. "Just how much time do you and Levi spend talking about me?"

She gave a sly smile. "Oh, you're the subject of probably ninety percent of our conversation."

I chuckled. "I am?"

"Oh, yeah," she joked. "No. To be fair, I badger him until he tells me things. It's part of our dynamic."

"Good to know. That badgering, is it something like what you're doing to me right now?"

"Oh, hardly. This is mild."

"I see."

"Anyway...he said—" I could tell she was choosing her words carefully. "—you found out she was cheating on you with a friend."

More like I walked in on the two of them and discovered later it was more than one friend.

She continued. "And you took a girl to prom in high school and overheard her saying she'd only said yes to you because she wanted to piss her boyfriend off."

She told some girl she chose to flirt with me because I was the nerdiest kid in school and she knew that would really tick him off. Talk about a blow to the ego.

"Wow. He really showed you the highlight reel of my dating life. Cool."

She put her hand on my arm. "Please don't be mad at him. He purely told me because I wouldn't let it go."

"Why do you even care?"

"Because." She sat straighter. "You're one of my boys now, and the solo one I don't know. I wanted to get the lowdown on you. And last night you seemed so upset..."

"Yeah." I chuckled. "I was upset." I avoided her gaze, scanning the glass coffee table and noting it reflected the streaks of pink outside.

"The sole reason I'm telling you all this is because...Sophie's been in a...similar situation."

"I know. She told me how the douche bag left her at the altar."

She exhaled. "Good." She paused. "It was an awful thing to witness. She was so crushed, and I don't think she's totally over it. Honestly, it rocked us all. I was so happy for her. He seemed like such a nice guy. I'd known him forever, and then to pull a stunt like that..." Shaking her head, she added, "We were all floored." She glanced at her phone. "Shit. I need to get going." The thud of Levi's feet hitting the floor had us both turning to stare at his door. "He's awake. I was being too loud." She took a deep breath. "Anyway...to be truthful, when they told me you and Sophie were...interested in one another, I was astonished. You don't seem like Sophie's type."

"So I've heard."

"But...the more I analyze it, the more I realize you are perfect for each other." To my surprise, she took my hands. "Whatever happened last night...don't give up on Sophie. She would never hurt you on purpose. She would *never* cheat on you. She's got a heart as big as yours. She's funny. She's smart."

I laughed. "Okay. I'm sold. Besides," I said with a wink, "she's one hell of a kisser."

"Well, I wouldn't know about that. I'll have to take your word on it." She stood and stretched. "Now," a wicked gleam came into her eyes, "I'm going to tell Levi goodbye before I leave."

As she went to pass me, I grabbed her wrist and lifted my gaze. "Thanks."

She grinned. "Any time."

She'd given me a lot to mull over.

CHAPTER SIX

Sophie

My nerves were frayed. It was hard to know if it was due to the absurd quantity of caffeine I'd drank, or due to the fact that I wasn't sure how this little meet and greet with my parents was going to go. I'd sat them both down this morning and told them about Caleb.

They both gawked at me open-mouthed, then stared at each other. My dad was the first one to find his voice.

"Has he offered you any drugs?"

"Dad? *No*. Did you not listen to a word I said?"

"No. To be honest I tuned out when you said the word Mohawk. Honey, are you sure this is the kind of person you want to be involved with?"

I exhaled and plopped into one of the nearby chairs. "No. Okay, Dad," I snapped. "I'm not sure of anything concerning men, and I'm not sure I ever will be, thanks to Steve. But...I can't exactly vet my dates. And even if I did, honesty isn't something that is revealed on a credit report. There is no certification for faithfulness." I swung my gaze from my dad to my mom and back. "I have to try again. I'm lonely. I can't keep coming over here for Netflix binging and popcorn." They had been great support for me, but I'd come to the conclusion it was sort of an unhealthy relationship. A twenty-six-year-old shouldn't hang with their parents as much as I did.

"Oh, we don't mind," my mom interjected.

"I know, Mom. And I appreciate that. But...I believe it's time for me to spread my wings a little. Don't you think? I'm twenty-six. Most of my friends are married and raising children and I'm..." They both watched me carefully. Like they did right after my botched wedding, as if ready to collect the shards of me when I fell apart. They thought I was losing it. "Well, I'm not."

They again exchanged a look, and my dad took the lead for the second time. "We're...not against you seeing someone. In fact, that would probably be good for you. But a guitarist in a rock band? Is that the best place to start?"

"I don't know if you noticed, Dad, but it's not like guys are banging on the front door or lining up outside to joust or something for the favor of my hand. Besides, I like Caleb, and you will, too, *if* you give him a fair chance."

The staircase creaked toward the top. I closed my eyes with a sigh. "You might as well join us, Gabe. That way you won't miss anything."

He slunk down the stairs, seeming a tad sheepish, but not sheepish enough.

I frowned. "Did you catch it all? Do you need for us to repeat anything?"

He grinned. "Nope. I got it all. I especially loved the part where Dad said he quit listening after the word Mohawk. And you, sis, you did pretty good, too, with the guys lining up on the porch stuff."

I almost turned to my parents and said, "Make him stop." It seemed whenever we came home, we took on our old roles, perpetually ten and thirteen. I gritted my teeth. "I'm glad we could amuse you. Now sit and shut your piehole."

"Ooh, touchy, touchy." He scooted quickly to avoid being slugged and sat in the chair opposite me. He leaned back, lacing his fingers behind his head, like he was a god watching his creatures for entertainment. "Well? Go on."

I gave him a final death stare then focused on my parents, taking a deep breath. "Look, I'm not asking for much. I'm only asking for you not to judge Caleb by his appearance. Can you do that?"

My dad started to say something, but my mom cut him off. "We'll try," she said uncertainly. "Won't we, Alan?"

My dad gaped at her for a long moment, then begrudgingly agreed. "Yeah. Whatever."

That was probably the best I was going to get. I slapped my hands on my knees and stood. "Good. I'll finish getting the cake iced." As I passed Gabe, I glared at him and shook a finger. "You're lucky it's your birthday."

I'd nearly escaped the room when my dad called to me. "Sophie."

I sighed, closing my eyes and gathering myself before turning. "Yes."

"If he did offer you drugs, what would you say?"

Gabe sputtered and burst into laughter.

"I'd say how much and what kind?" I answered sarcastically. "Give me a break, Dad." I wheeled around and slammed through the swinging door to the kitchen.

As the door shut, my dad sniped at Gabe. "What? What are you laughing about? This is a serious subject."

An hour later, I was loitering in the living room, pretending to read a magazine, so I could be sure to be the one opening the door. If he was going to be attacked, he wasn't going to endure it alone. I jumped at the knock on the door. Gabe came racing down the stairs and beat me by a hair. I slapped at his hand on the doorknob. "Don't you dare." I glanced out the frosted window in the door. Someone in a dress shirt and nice pants stood on our porch. "It's not him anyway."

"Oh," Gabe's face fell, and he headed into the kitchen.

I opened the door. "Hi. Can I help—" My breath caught in my throat. "Caleb?"

He smiled. "Yeah. Were you expecting someone else?"

"No. I just...didn't recognize you."

"Didn't recognize me?"

Dad picked this auspicious moment to make his entrance. He frowned. "Who's this?"

Gabe hung behind him.

I pulled Caleb in, then turned to stare at him again. He'd lost the Mohawk. Instead, he wore his hair in a conservative—but still totally sexy—way. And instead of blue, or red, or purple, his hair color was a very nice dark blond. He looked sharp in dressier clothes, and he even seemed comfortable in them, despite his complaining about the tux yesterday.

"This is...Caleb?" I said uncertainly.

My mom rushed in, wiping her hands on a towel. Spotting Caleb, she froze.

"But I thought you said he had a Mohawk. Was that a joke?"

"No, sir," Caleb answered for me. "I did have a Mohawk a few hours ago."

"Oh." My dad didn't quite know what to do with that information.

My mom broke the odd pause in conversation. "Well, welcome to our home, Caleb."

"Thank you." He produced a bouquet of dark pink roses—which he'd been holding behind his back—lilies, astromelia, and some sort of small purple flower. It was stunning. "These are for you." He passed them to my mom and said from the corner of his mouth, "Yours are in the car."

My mom actually blushed. "How thoughtful of you. These are gorgeous. And in such a lovely vase too. Thank you. These will make the perfect centerpiece." She put them on the table, and we all followed her for some reason. She set them in the middle and fussed over the ends of the ribbons, draping them on the tablecloth appealingly. She straightened, viewing it with an appraising eye. "There. That's nice."

My dad was still studying Caleb and had his head cocked as he rubbed his chin, glaring at him like he was some sort of imposter. An imposter with a weapon ready to mow down his family.

"He really is Caleb Winthrop," Gabe gushed.

"I told you." I intertwined my fingers with Caleb's, emphasizing our togetherness.

He turned to Gabe. "You must be the guy whose birthday we're celebrating." He stuck out his hand, and Gabe stared at it for a second, as if unsure what to do, then shook it vigorously. "Gabe, right?"

"That's right." It was like I could see the excited *He knows my name!* in his irises.

"This must be for you then. It has your name on it." He slid an envelope from his pocket and gave it to Gabe, then faced my mom. "Do you need any help with anything, Mrs. Lockhart?"

"Oh, no, dear." She hesitated. "It's pretty simple...just some sandwiches and cake. And fruit salad. I made fruit salad."

He smiled. "That all sounds wonderful."

"Holy shit! Is this what I think it is?"

"Gabe!" my father barked.

"Gabriel Thomas!" my mom said at the same time.

He ignored them, continuing to pull things from his envelope. I could see he had concert tickets with backstage passes. I tried to see what they said. I didn't realize any of their events this week required a ticket. "Plane tickets?"

I looked at Caleb in shock.

"And there will be reservations for you at the Marriott Marquis, if you choose to go. I wasn't sure what you'd like, so I thought maybe this would work."

I couldn't believe what I was hearing. "Marriott? Where?"

"New York," Gabe and Caleb answered simultaneously.

"Oh, man." He didn't seem to know what to say. Which was a first. "This is awesome. Trudy's gonna flip when I tell her. I don't know how to thank you."

"You just did." He spun back to my mom. "So...I understand there is a birthday cake, so let's eat so we can get to it. Sophie said you were a wonderful cook."

My mom blushed again. "Oh," she waved a hand, "I don't know if that's true."

My dad relaxed enough to comment. "Her cheesecakes are out of this world."

"Well, now..." My mom seemed uncomfortable with the praise. She wrung the top of one of the chairs.

"And she makes a killer German chocolate cake," my dad added.

My mom seemed ready to deny it, then she grinned. "I do sort of make a killer German chocolate cake."

"No sort of about it." Dad even worked up a smile.

My mom pressed her fingers to her lip briefly. "Anyways... Let's get the food before it gets cold." She took a few steps toward the kitchen with my dad trailing after her. "Oh, wait. It's supposed to be cold. Except the cheesy potatoes. I forgot the cheesy potatoes."

"Are you sure you don't need any help?" Caleb called as they disappeared behind the door.

"No, thank you. We've got it. You all visit."

I leaned on the top of one of the dining room chairs. "Tickets to New York, huh?"

Caleb grinned and shrugged.

"That's gonna make the book I got him look pretty skimpy."

"No, it won't," Gabe said cheerfully, surprising me by his proximity. "It'll be great on the *plane*." He waved his tickets around. "I can't believe this. I'm going to call Trudy real fast."

"Trudy the girlfriend?" Caleb asked.

I nodded and sighed as we overheard Gabe saying, "Guess what?"

"He's twenty-three going on twelve."

"Seems like a nice kid," Caleb commented.

"Sure he does. He's all about you now that you've given him tickets."

He sidled near to me and bracketed my face with his hands. "That's funny because I'm all about his sister." He laid one on me that could have melted the china on the table if we'd been any closer. A sound made us jump apart.

My dad stared at us both in turn, then plopped the fruit salad on the table with a bang and retraced his steps.

Caleb's expression fell. "Shit. I blew that, didn't I?"

As I opened my mouth to respond, shouting rose from the kitchen.

"Nice? Nice? Of course he seems nice. He's trying to butter us up before breaking our daughter's heart."

"Your daughter is a woman. She's twenty-six years old. She gets to decide what to do with her heart." I guess that stymied my dad, because no reply was offered. "Honey...I know how hard it was to see her in those first few months after Steve destroyed her world, but you can't protect her forever. No matter how much you want to."

"Well...that sucks."

"I know it does." Whatever was said in response must have been in a lower volume because all we caught was muffled conversation.

Still, Dad was sullen during lunch. And he continued to eye Caleb like he was an enemy. My palms began to sweat when my dad said a prayer, but Caleb bowed his head respectfully, and I relaxed my breathing. Despite my dad's glowering, the rest of us were having a great time. Gabe had asked Caleb about the craziest thing a fan had done, and he told us just this week a fan had scaled the fence at The Sands and struck and knocked Remi Boyd—soon-to-be Cannon—to the ground. He said Levi hired a security firm to watch over her, which made me worry less, but it was still kind of scary. Then he launched into a much less serious story about a woman who snuck backstage and into Phoenix's dressing room, where he found her waiting for him, completely nude.

Dad broke in with, "You've been with a lot of women, haven't you, Caleb?"

The laughter died on our lips. Caleb turned stiffly to face him, his jaw tight and his gaze intense.

I wanted to crawl into a hole. "Daddy! That's not an appropriate question."

"No, it certainly is not," my mom seconded, looking pretty steamed herself.

Caleb raised a hand. "No. It's okay. I'd rather have this out in the open than hide it. Or excuse it." He straightened his spine. "Yes, sir. I've been with a lot of women. Not as many as Phoenix and Dakota, but still." He drew in a breath, staring at the table and trying to find his words. "However, it was clear to each of those women I wasn't planning to be in a relationship with them, and *they* approached *me*. Maybe I shouldn't have taken them up on their offers, but I assure you, I've never cheated on anyone. Nor would I. I've had that happen to me before, and I know how painful that can be."

My dad squirmed, but held fast to his animosity. Caleb was being so polite, and Dad was acting like such a jerk. "Have you been tested for STDs?"

"Dad! Stop!"

"I'm smart with that," Caleb said carefully. "And...I was tested a few weeks ago, and I haven't been with anyone since."

I'll admit, as insulting as the question was, the answer did take a load off my mind.

"You do drugs?"

"Dad! You can't just pry into his life." I addressed Caleb. "You don't have to answer that."

He was focused on my dad. "No, sir."

Dad scoffed.

"I'm not saying I haven't ever, but I didn't like the loss of control they gave me or the fact that they were so inconsistent in their effects. Phoenix and Dak don't use anymore either. And Levi never did, beyond some pot in high school." He folded his hands on the table. "Do you have any other questions?"

My dad tilted his chin up and peered down his nose at Caleb. His lips twitched. "Not for now."

"I want to make it clear that—" Caleb replied evenly, glancing at me. "—I realize we haven't known each other long, but your daughter means a lot to me, and I don't plan to do anything to jeopardize that." He turned to me. "Sophie, I know this must be uncomfortable for you. Do you want me to leave?"

My answer came without me even thinking. "Not unless I'm going with you."

He smiled. "All right, then." He pushed away from the table. "Gabe, I hope you don't mind us missing your cake..."

"No, man. I get it," Gabe responded, appearing a little shell-shocked by all the fireworks.

Caleb slid my chair from under the table so I could stand. "Thank you, Mrs. Lockhart," speaking to my dad, his voice tightened, "and *Mr. Lockhart*, for including me in your lunch today. Especially as last minute as it was." He dipped his head in my mom's direction. "Everything was wonderful."

He took my hand—as I had gotten to my feet—pushed my chair in, and patted Gabe's shoulder as we passed him. "Happy birthday again, bud. I hope the rest of your day is awesome."

"Thanks." His face brightened. "I'll see you backstage then, I guess."

He peered at me. "Well, I hope to see you again before then. But definitely backstage. If you come."

"Are you kidding? Of course I'm coming."

"Good."

My mom started to rise.

"Oh, we'll see ourselves out." Caleb gestured toward the table. "You enjoy the rest of your meal."

Not saying another word, we left the house. As soon as the door closed behind us, I voiced my thoughts. "I am *so* sorry for that. If I'd had any idea he would act like that, I never would have subjected you to his—"

Caleb swung in front of me, slid his fingers beneath my hair and used his thumbs to tilt my chin up, seducing my lips with his full, skillful ones. "Don't worry about it," he said with a husky voice as we parted. He glanced at the house. "I will say, though, that kissing you on his lawn felt *pretty* good." He gave me another peck. "Come on. Let's go have some fun." He'd texted earlier, and we'd agreed to go scuba diving. We walked hand in hand toward his car. He looked at me from the corner of his eye. "Your swimsuit under there, or are you changing?"

The hunger in his voice made a smile tug at my lips. "Both."

He chuckled. "Both? How does that work?"

"I have my swimsuit on, but I'm going to pop this T-shirt off and use my cover-up when we get on board."

"Cover-up? Why would you want to cover up?" he teased.

But it struck me. The fact that he was a rock star and had seen plenty of women who weren't covered up in the slightest. I felt backwoods-ish and like a prude. Although I hated it, my dad's question echoed in my head. *"...you've been with a lot of women, haven't you?"*

"Sophie?"

I blinked. We were in a parking spot near Sink & Swim Scuba Adventures.

Caleb studied me with concern. He probably thought I was going to fall apart on him again. Poor guy. "You kind of zoned out there. You okay?"

"Oh, yeah. Sorry. I was...thinking."

"And what was it that had so much of your attention?" he asked patiently.

"Oh, nothing, really." I tried to brush it off, but he made no move to exit the Jeep. "How my dad was treating you." Partially true. "You were being so polite, and he was being such a jerk."

He put a hand on my knee. "It's no big deal. He was only being protective of his daughter. If I had a daughter as beautiful as you are, I'd never get a night's sleep worrying over all the guys who came around."

"But I—" I was on the verge of saying I didn't have a bunch of guys coming around, but he interrupted.

"I respect the way he was caring for you. I wish my parents had given a damn about me." Before I could delve into that, he left the vehicle.

As we strolled toward the building, I asked, "Where does a New Jersey boy learn how to scuba dive?"

"Well, we are on the ocean."

I elbowed him in the ribs, relieved I'd managed to steer the conversation away from my thoughts of his sexual history. "I know. But New Jersey isn't the first place that comes to mind when you think scuba diving."

He tilted his head. "True. And I didn't actually learn to dive in Jersey. Did you really believe I could work with three Last Chance Beachers and not learn to scuba dive? They insisted my education wasn't complete until I'd learned how to scuba dive and surf, despite all the money my parents had thrown at private schools."

We reached the building, and Caleb held the door open for me. Sadie Lawson rushed out as I entered. "Oh, hi, Sadie."

She nodded coldly. "Sophie. *Boner*." Her voice and eyebrows rose at the end.

"Sadie," Caleb muttered, his face coloring.

What the hell was that about? And then it occurred to me that maybe Sadie was one of the many women Caleb had been with. Lord knew she'd been with half the population of the island, and ninety percent of the men.

My gaze widened. "Did you and Sadie—?"

"Why if it isn't Miss Sophie Lockhart." Jared Wilson was one of my favorite schoolmates. He treated strangers like friends and accepted everyone. "What the hell are you doing here, darling?" He gathered me into a big bear hug.

"Quit smashing the girl, you brute." Chase Michaels thwacked Jared in the shoulder and he backed away. "Let me do it." The next thing I knew, Chase was lifting me off my feet and swinging me around. I couldn't help the giggle that escaped.

He set me down and Caleb cleared his throat.

"Oh, fellas, I want you to meet," I swept my arms dramatically in his direction, "Caleb Winthrop." For some reason, Caleb didn't seem very happy. I studied him as Chase extended his hand.

"Welcome to the island, Caleb. You're one hell of a guitar player."

"Thank you," he said begrudgingly.

Jared stuck himself between the two men. "Jared Wilson." He beamed, pumping Caleb's arm until I'm sure it was sore. "I'm a huge fan. I have all of your guys' albums. I grew up with your bandmates, and Sophie here."

Chase jostled him out of the way. "Me too."

Caleb finally smiled. "Thank you for your support."

"Sophie, how did you two meet? Through Phoenix, Dak, and Levi?"

"Well..." I slid my gaze to Caleb. Saying we met in a bar sounded so low-class.

"Actually," Caleb put his arm around me. "I noticed Sophie in the crowd and knew I had to meet her." He squeezed me tightly against him. There seemed to be some silent communication going on between the men.

"Oh," Jared and Chase said, both with oddly high pitched voices. They looked from him to me and back, then at each other.

"Oh, I see," Chase said thoughtfully.

"Huh," Jared continued to consider us in turn. "Interesting."

Chase snapped out of it first. "Jared, why don't you take...Caleb, here and...you said on the phone you've dove many times before?"

Caleb nodded. "That's right."

Not taking his eyes off Caleb, Chase spoke from the corner of his mouth. "Take him to sign the release papers and get whatever gear he needs."

"Huh?" Jared stared at him stupidly for a moment, then shook himself. "Release forms. Yes. Of course." He gestured to the counter. "Right over here."

I started to follow, but Chase touched my arm. "Sophie, it's good to see you." His brow wrinkled. "How are you?"

Are people going to see me that way forever? With both concern and sympathy, like watching a bird with a broken wing, worried by its flapping around that the injury will never heal? I'm not like that anymore. I'm stronger.

Then I recalled my running from Caleb on the dance floor at Up On The Roof.

Do some hurts never end? Are you permanently scarred from them?

I didn't want to be that person. Forever the victim of other's cruelty. I wanted to rebuild my life and try again, even if it meant being hurt again. I glanced at Caleb. He was leaning against the counter, his body twisted in my direction, answering Jared's questions with his gaze on me. My heart zinged, and I got that sensation people get in their stomach when first descending a hill on a rollercoaster, the lifting and dropping sense of both fear and excitement. A smile eased across my face so naturally, like it had been hidden, yet always waiting for this moment. Always waiting for him. His lips rose, too, his eyes dancing with a comforting warmth.

I turned back to Chase. "I'm good. Really good."

"Really?" He opened his stance and looked from Caleb to me. "Good. That's good to hear, Sophie."

His genuineness boosted me further, and on impulse I kissed his cheek then flew to the other side of the room, my gaze on Caleb. His grin wavered at one point as he watched me approach.

"Hey," I said softly.

"Hey," he said in the same intimate tone.

The bells above the door crashed and in strode Hali, Savannah, and Phoenix, as Dakota held the door for the group. Hali and Savannah had their heads together and were giggling about something. Dakota was loudly razzing Phoenix for having been scared of the water as a child. My heart soared, and I ran to throw my arms around Hali.

"Oh, my gosh! What are you guys doing here?" I squeezed Hali extralong. It wasn't often she got away these days to do something frivolous like scuba dive. Not to leave Savannah out, I hugged her too.

"Well, when you get a special invite from someone to spend the afternoon with one of your best buds, how could I resist? But where's Boner? I thought he was going to be here."

Caleb cleared his throat, coming up from behind me and lightly grasping my shoulders. Hali blinked. "B-Boner?"

She checked with me for clarification. I nodded.

Her gaze widened. "Holy shit!"

I glanced over and both Dakota and Phoenix were transfixed, gawking, wide-eyed, with their mouths hanging open.

"Oh, wow!" Savannah smiled brightly and nudged me, for some reason.

Dakota was the first to recover. "Wh-what happened?"

Caleb laughed. "What do you mean?"

Dakota gestured vaguely toward his head. "I mean...I mean...what happened...there?"

"I got a haircut, man. It's not like it hasn't happened before."

"Not like that, it hasn't. I mean..." He crossed his arms and came forward to have a closer inspection. "Will you still be able to play?"

"What?" He peered at me, his eyes dancing. "It's not like I've had an amputation."

Phoenix squinted harder, and Dakota appeared like he was about to argue the point. He circled Caleb slowly, as if he had somehow hidden his Mohawk somewhere. "It's just not...Boner." He switched his focus to Phoenix. "You know what I mean?"

Phoenix nodded, then seemed to regain his senses. "It looks...good, man."

He said it in such a doubtful way Caleb responded with a chuckle. "Well, that sounded convincing." He glanced at one brother, then the other. "Come on, guys. It's only hair."

Dakota was stunned. "It's not only hair, it's who you—"

Phoenix interrupted him. "It's great. It really is."

Savvy grabbed my hand. "Let's get changed." I let her drag me across the room to a set of doors styled like shutters and we each took one.

Alone in my little room, I grinned at my reflection. He'd called my friends. This was turning out to be one amazing day.

CHAPTER SEVEN

Caleb

As soon as Sophie was on the other side of that door, they jumped me.

"You and Sophie have something going on?" Dak started.

Hali brightened. "Is that why you cut your hair?"

Phoenix chuckled. "Dude."

I lowered my voice, speaking to Dakota. "Yes, we're seeing each other." Then I spoke to Hali. "No, I didn't cut my hair for her. More for her parents. And me too. I needed a change, and I want to quit hiding behind a persona and be myself."

Phoenix just wagged his head. "Dude. You've got it bad."

"No. I've got it good, and I'd like to keep it that way. So, if you guys could kind of...chill, a bit, I'd appreciate it.

Dak straightened his back. "Chill? I'm always chill."

Phoenix and Hali rolled their eyes, saying at the same time, "Yeah. Right."

A door creaked and I turned. Sophie was coming from the stall, clutching the sides of her top to hold them together. Didn't make a difference. My heartrate kicked up a notch merely knowing she had a swimsuit on under it. She smiled at me tentatively. How could she be both cute and sexy as hell at all at once?

Jared clapped his hands together, then rubbed them quickly. "All right, gang. Are we ready to go?"

"Savannah's still getting her suit on," Sophie said as she came to me.

Jared's brows rose. "Oh."

I slung an arm across Sophie's shoulders and pulled her into me, unexpectedly warmed by the pride of knowing she was with me.

"Here I am. Here I am," Savannah called as she came out. She was wearing a swimming suit that was more like a tennis dress, white with navy geometric shapes on it, and was sporting a big hat. "Anyone need sunscreen?"

Dak clucked his tongue. "We don't need sunscreen. We're rock stars."

Looking him in the eye the whole way, Hali sauntered over to Savannah and took the offered sunscreen. "I'm pretty sure being a rock star doesn't make you impervious to the effects of the sun." She tossed it at him pretty hard, hitting him in the stomach and forcing air from his lungs. "Slather up," she ordered.

One corner of Dak's mouth quirked. "I love it when you talk dirty to me. And all commanding too. Whoo." He shivered exaggeratedly.

She sashayed to him slowly, wickedly. Lifting his chin with one painted fingernail, she murmured seductively, "In your dreams, big boy." Then she walked past him, and he turned to watch the sway of her hips.

"Yes. That goes without saying," he said haltingly.

Phoenix whistled. "Man! That was hot!" He sidled next to his brother and spoke in a low voice. "You and she have a thing going on?"

"Who? Hali?" He glanced around. "Nah. She's a wreck. I'd never get involved with that." Dak said it in a way I was sure he thought was quiet, but his voice had a tendency to carry. I was almost sure Hali was listening because her body became stiff in a wave, rising from her waist to her head.

I moved in her direction, pausing as I passed Dak. "Keep your voice down."

"What?" He flinched. "You don't think she heard that, do you?"

I didn't answer because I was now closer to Hali than to him.

Of course she heard you, you moron.

"Hey," I said softly to Hali, then I struggled to find something to say to her. She was showing Jared her diving license. I could tell he'd taken in Dak's comment, too, as he was focusing on her with sympathy in his eyes. "So...uhh...how long have you been diving?"

She blinked rapidly, not looking at me. "Umm...I've been doing it since the moment I could fit my foot into the smallest size flipper."

I lifted my gaze and caught Jared's attention. He was standing with his mouth open like he was hoping that alone would make words come forth. So, I wasn't the only one who was tongue-tied. Sophie strolled up from behind us and slipped her arm over Hali's shoulders. "Hey there, Siren." Apparently, it was a nickname. "Are you ready for our adventure on the high seas?"

Hali smiled at the nickname. "Ready when you are, Rebel."

Rebel, huh....

Jared released a breath. "Okay. Right this way then."

He crossed to a door at the rear of the shop and held it open for them. "All aboard, folks," he yelled at the rest of us. One by one we filed out after them.

I watched Sophie as she descended the steps built into the hillside and leading down to the dock. She and Hali were laughing at something. The wind was playing with her sheer cover-up, making it billow. At one point, a sudden gust raised the back to almost waist high. Sophie whipped her arm around to tame it. I chuckled to myself. The juxtaposition of her modesty and Hali's brazen suit—merely strips of fabric crisscrossing in front of the important parts, fire-engine-red on one side, black on the other—amused me. Then there was Savannah, in conservative attire she wore with confidence, like the wind wouldn't dare mess with her because she had ordered it not to. The three friends couldn't be any more different. The only thing they had in common, it seemed, was their love for one another.

By the time I reached the gangway, Jared, Chase, and Hali were in the boat. Chase must have snuck off at some point earlier to make some final preparations for our excursion. My focus was on Jared as he took Sophie's gear, then her hand to help her aboard. I knew it was an innocent gesture, meant purely to keep Sophie safe, but something about her hand in his made me bristle. Unwillingly, I flashed to the memory of finding Heidi, my ex, in another man's embrace in a much more intimate location, my shower. I tried to shake it. This was not Heidi; this was Sophie, and Sophie wouldn't do that to me. At least I didn't think she would.

Then again, I never thought Heidi would.

But I asked myself sometimes if I really didn't know Heidi was capable of it, or had I simply chosen to ignore the fact. I threw myself headlong into that relationship wanting it to be, and trying to will it to be, something it was clearly not.

Although I made an attempt to talk myself down from the ledge, I still held a zing of hostility toward Jared. I mean, wasn't he being a little too chummy with all the women? Granted they'd gone to school together and knew each other well, but still....

I wanted to give him some strong eye contact upon getting into the boat, but he was peering first at the deck, then up the hill at the others trailing me.

Hmm...I noticed you didn't take ahold of me and help me into the boat.

My unease and resentment subsided when Sophie grabbed my hand. "Isn't this a beautiful boat?"

I took my first look around. It was big and stylish. Not like any dive boat I'd been on. The bench seats were light beige with darker beige accents and even the back support was cushioned. The flooring was teak, with slits in it for the water to escape through. "Boat? More like a yacht."

Jared interjected, "Some might consider it a yacht, because of its length and luxury, but we prefer to call it a boat, because we use it to work, and she works hard. We use *Emily's Sanity* for sunset cruises, fishing trips, scuba diving...and of course, the occasional cocktail party."

I bet. I'm sure it impresses the ladies.

As he helped Savannah aboard, I asked, "How big is it?"

Chase appeared from the bow of the boat; whether he'd been in the bow or the cockpit, I don't know. "It's a little over forty-two feet. And has a ton of options." He sighed. "On a day-to-day basis, Emily's pretty frugal. But when it came to *Emily's Sanity*, all practicality flew out the window."

"And far away," Jared added with a grin. "This thing is equipped with *four* outboard motors, the biggest head you've ever seen, and it even has a grill. The girl likes the glitz."

"What can I say?" Chase asked, placing his hands on his hips and pushing his chest forward. "She always wants the best."

Jared rolled his eyes. "Yeah. But she settled for you."

Chase gave him a faux snarl. "There was no settling."

Once everyone was on board and had stored their gear, Chase and Jared stood in front of the cabin to address us all. Bench seats lined both sides, and one folded down in the stern making a U-formation. Phoenix and Dakota were on the back bench, Savannah and Hali the starboard bench, and Sophie and I—thankfully—on the port bench. Although it was so cushy it would have been better labeled a sofa than a bench. Chase started. "Welcome aboard *Emily's Sanity*. She is a Boston Whaler 420 Outrage. I'll be your captain today."

Jared waved dismissively with a comical expression. "And I'll be your dive master. But feel free to simply call me master."

Chase grimaced. "We'll be underway shortly, and then the dive *master* here will go over your dive plan details with you. There's water and soda in this bin. Please help yourself."

I needed a moment alone with Sophie. I was beginning to regret asking people to join us for the first part of our date, but I'd wanted a sort of conversation buffer, to ward off any awkward silences we might have had. "Mind if we take a look at the cabin?" I asked Jared and Chase before they left.

"Please," Chase answered. "You're our guests. Roam at will."

I took Sophie's hand and led her as we descended into the darker interior of the cabin. Darker than in the bright sunlight, but illuminated with blue track lighting, I discovered. The inside was equally as nice as the exterior, with a TV, leather seats in the same light beige color, a microwave and a shower head that rained from multiple holes in its wide, square surface.

"Man! I need one of these yachts."

Sophie laughed. "Oh, yeah. Me too."

I took her hips and drew her toward me, my front to her back. I bent to speak into her ear. "I really didn't bring you down here to examine the luxury options on this beast." My voice was a low rumble.

She spun in my arms, languidly lacing her fingers behind my neck. "You didn't?"

"Nope. That girl Emily didn't know what she was talking about. This boat is making me insane because I wanted so badly to get you alone and kiss you silly."

She ruffled my hair. "Because it's been...what? Twenty minutes since the last time you kissed me?"

"Forever."

She was laughing softly as my lips covered hers, but I lost myself in the kiss, going under without my scuba gear. Feeling movement "below deck," so to speak, I tried to curb my desire so as not to embarrass myself. This girl was driving me crazy. I wanted to swing her around and explore the forward berth, test to see if it was as comfortable as the rest of our surroundings. Who was I kidding? I'd take her on the teak deck. Or in the shower....

She abruptly pulled away, clearing her throat and nodding toward the doorway over my shoulder. Clearly someone was there. And if someone was there, it was no doubt—

"Well, if it's not our little Sophie raising Boner's mizzen mast," Dak bellowed.

My jaw twitched, but I didn't give him the satisfaction of looking in his direction. "You know, for a musician you have awful timing, Dakota."

Someone smacked him and said, "You are so crude! Why don't you sit your ass down." Hali. I love that girl.

"Oh, you want me to sit by you? All you had to do was ask, honey." I'm not sure what happened next, but Dak disappeared and Hali giggled.

I half-twisted to follow what was transpiring above. "And they call *me* Boner," I grumbled. "He's the biggest bonehead here."

Sophie turned my face back to her. "We'll have time together later."

"You promise?"

She gave me a sly smile. "Ohh, yeahh!"

Well, that sounds encouraging.

She made her way to the stairs but pivoted when I didn't follow. "Aren't you coming?"

"Uhh. I need a few minutes."

She came toward me. "Is something wrong?"

I held my arm out to stop her. "No."

She froze.

"Dak wasn't all that wrong about...my mizzen mast." I shrugged, heat rushing to my cheeks.

"Oh," she said matter-of-factly. Then, "Oh!" Her gaze dropped to the area in question. She smiled brightly, gave a noise of delight, spun on her toes and scrambled through the hatch.

I grinned but listened to make sure Dak didn't say anything I'd have to smack him for. Luckily, I heard nothing. The moment I came topside, Dak zeroed in on me. He opened his mouth to speak, and I gave him a dark look. "Stick a sock in it, Blackstone."

He lifted his bare feet from the deck—having stowed his sandals—his eyes twinkling menacingly. "But I'm not wearing any."

Hali, who was sitting on the bench next to him, jabbed him in the ribs. "You know what he's saying. Put a lid on it."

I continued to glare at him but took my seat next to Sophie.

It was a beautiful day, so I couldn't stay irritated for any length of time. Seventy-five degrees, a light breeze skipping over the water, the sun warming our skin...couldn't beat it. I was in one corner of our seat, twisted slightly, and Sophie was stretched out, leaning against me. My hand trailed lazily along her arm while we listened to the others talk, her skin softer than my worn, favorite jeans, and those were like butter. Once she had relaxed, she forgot to hold her clothing together, and her suit was smoking, the top in a solid peach color, the bottom the same color, but with palm branches, pineapples, and large, white tropical flowers. The cover-up had fallen off her shoulder and was halfway to her elbow; it matched the floral design of the bottom of her bikini. The top sort of crisscrossed in the middle, not that I was examining it intently...but I was. Hell, the polish on her fingernails and toenails was even the same shade of peach as the suit.

I am one lucky guy.

The wind blew her hair into my face, and it smelled sensational. When I didn't think anyone was paying attention, I bent to give her head a quick kiss. She snuggled closer. We alternately listened to the hum of conversation around us and gazed at the ocean.

"Uhh...Boner. Could we just have a chitchat for a second?" Dak asked during a lull in conversation.

It took me a moment to react. "Yeah. Sure." I extricated myself from Sophie. "I'll be back in a minute."

She nodded.

"What's this about? Band shit?" I asked as they led me over to the steps going down to the cabin.

"Something like that," Phoenix replied vaguely.

Once below deck, the two brothers squared off opposite me, which made me feel kind of ganged up on. A wave of cold ran along my arms.

What the hell is going on? Are they firing me?

I looked from one to the other. My mouth was suddenly dry. "Why do we need to have this little rap session?"

They stared at each other, then Phoenix burst out with, "You've got to talk to the girl."

"Who? Sophie?"

He made an exasperated noise. "Yes, Sophie. You haven't said anything in twenty minutes. You like her, don't you?"

"Well, yeah, but..."

"Don't you guys have anything in common?" Dak interjected.

I straightened my shoulders. "We have a lot in common."

Why am I defending myself to them? I don't need to defend myself to them, her parents, or anybody. Why is everybody all in our business?

Phoenix gestured with his hands like one of our old high school teachers. "You see, to have a relationship, one needs to...well, *relate*. Do you want her to get bored and dump you?"

"Of course not," I said indignantly.

"Well then, do something!" He stormed up the steps muttering and shaking his head, "Aye yi yi."

Dak poked one of his big, fat fingers in my chest. "Relate." Then he disappeared too.

I sighed, gripping my hips and staring at the floor. It was true; I hadn't spoken in a while. But that's how I was. Still, as much as I hated to admit it, they might be right. To get close to one another we had to get to know each other and to do that I'd have to share myself with her. Verbally. But...what should I say? I looked at the light pouring through the hatch. Where I had been feeling light and breezy earlier, now it was like I'd been weighed down with stone. I thought for a little while longer then returned to the deck.

"Hey." She sat so I could reclaim my seat and she could lie against me once more. "So...have you—"

"What is—?"

We were talking over each other. We laughed. "You go first," I offered.

"Oh, no. You go."

"Okay...well...I was going to ask if you've ever been on a boat like this before." As soon as I said it, I wanted to pull it back in. "Wait. That's a stupid question. Of course you have. You've dived in the past."

"No. That's not stupid. I could have done my diving from offshore."

My eyebrows rose. "True. Well, have you?"

"Not on anything this nice."

"Yeah. No kidding." A few seconds passed while I desperately searched for something to say. Then I remembered she'd been asking me a question. "What did you want to ask me?"

"Uhh..." She glanced at Savannah and Hali. I peeked myself and they seemed to be mouthing her encouragement. But catching me looking at them, they closed their lips tightly. "I was going to ask what's it like living in Jersey?"

"Oh, uhh...I haven't really lived there for a while. My folks moved to New York, so I have an apartment there."

"I see..." She kept nodding her head. She wasn't acting like herself. What was up?

"So, Soph," Savannah called. "How's Gabe doing?"

"Oh," her face brightened, "he's doing well, thank you. Actually, today is his birthday."

"Oh, it is?"

"Yep. He's twenty-three. Nearly a quarter of a century."

"Really? Please tell him happy birthday for me, and I'll bring him over some of those cookies he likes next week."

"That's sweet of you. He'll love them." The conversation lagged again.

Phoenix huffed out a breath, slapped his hands on his knees and stood. "Anyone else want to investigate the rest of the boat?"

"I would," Savannah said sunnily.

Hali rose too. "Mind if I tag along?"

"Not at all." Phoenix stood aside so the girls could lead the way, and he took a few steps behind them, with his torso twisted, staring at me with a frown. He mimed the word *talk,* while making his hand look like a mouth opening and closing then turned away.

I sighed. "I'm sorry if I'm not saying much. It's not that I'm...disinterested. I'm simply not much of a conversationalist, as my friends were nice enough to call my attention to," I added, disgruntled.

She laughed, which irritated me initially, but she seemed to notice and immediately reassured me. "I'm not making fun of you. It's just that the girls were all over *me* for not engaging you more. I do enjoy our conversations...but I'm also happy that I don't feel stressed about finding topics to discuss with you merely for the sake of speaking. I'm comfortable in our silences. I hope you are too...?"

"Absolutely." I grinned. The guys didn't get me, but she did. I relaxed and basked in that knowledge.

They were gone quite a while, and when they returned, Hali wasn't with them. I'd managed to get in a few sentences of conversation in their absence.

"So, what did you think?" Dak asked. I realized he'd been unusually quiet in their absence.

"It's sweet," Phoenix pronounced with a tilt of his head.

"The bow has a conversation area with a table, and benches that can convert to chaise lounges." Savannah swung into a seat. "I could definitely live on here."

"You could not," Sophie countered. "You'd be lost if you didn't have your laptop."

"Oh, my laptop would be on board, of course. Because, you're right. I can't live without it."

Dakota got to his feet and stretched exaggeratedly. "I'm going to ask Jared a question. See ya in a bit."

I watched him as he left, but he didn't stop at the front of the cockpit where Jared and Chase were sitting in some cushy Barcaloungers. Even the captain was comfortable while he was working. Go figure. My money was on Dak wanting to check on Hali and possibly attempt to apologize for acting like an asshole at the dive shop.

But Hali came charging across the deck minutes later, looking shaken.

Sophie straightened. "Is everything all right, Hali?"

"Yeah. Yeah," she muttered dismissively. "How much further do you think we have until we reach the dive spot?"

"Twenty minutes." Jared said from behind her. "I was just coming to give you a warning and ask you to suit up." Dak trailed her, wearing a hangdog expression. If he'd made an apology, it hadn't gone well.

Everyone pulled out their dry bags, organized their gear and put their wetsuits on. We stowed the bags again after we'd finished, to keep from mixing our stuff or having it become a hazard. Before we knew it, the engine was winding down and then was cut completely. Chase bustled about doing captain-of-the-ship stuff, and Jared turned to us.

"If you're ready, I'll take Phoenix, Dakota, and Savannah to the front to do a giant stride entry. Hali, you, Boner, and Sophie prefer back roll entries, right?" She nodded. "You'll do those from here, but wait for Chase to come help you. He'll be here momentarily." With that, they were gone. It was unusual to have a dual entry like this, but the way the boat tapered to the stern made it perfect for a back roll entry, and the height of the bow was ideal for stepping off.

Sophie padded in her fins over to Hali. "Are you sure you're okay, Hali?"

Hali took a deep breath, then lifted her gaze. "I'm fine, Soph." She put her hand on Sophie's cheek. "You worry too much."

Sophie lowered her chin. "I know. I—"

"And that's why we love you." She pulled Sophie's head down and gave her a kiss on the brow. "Now let's do this."

Chase appeared. "All right. It sounds like Hali wants to go first."

Hali nodded, giving Sophie a wink, then hiked herself onto the gunwale. She secured her mask and put her regulator in her mouth, then gave Chase the okay sign. Chase stood ready to help her if she slipped or had any issues. Hali's fingers were splayed to hold her mask and her regulator on one side, the others were on her mask strap to both protect her skull and make sure the mask stayed where she desired it to be. She took one last look over her shoulder, presumably to make sure the area below was clear, then drew her knees in, fell backward, and disappeared with a splash. Chase watched for the okay signal then twisted to us. "Who's next?"

Sophie peered at me with a huge smile on her face.

"You can go," I said with fake reluctance.

She clapped her gloved hands together. "Goody!"

She moved forward, repeated the sequence Hali did, flipped back, and was gone.

My turn. "Are you ready?"

I exhaled. "I believe so."

I'd be lying if I said I wasn't a little nervous. Diving was an amazing experience, but it could also be dangerous, even if one paid attention and followed all the rules. The resulting rush was exhilarating. As I got in position, I glanced to my left, catching Phoenix at the moment he took his step off the boat, like Wylie Coyote after he was tricked by the Road Runner and ran past the edge of a cliff. I half-expected a cartoon cloud to rise from the waves upon his entry. I made sure all my hoses were streamlined and close to my body so they wouldn't get tangled, took a couple of breaths to make sure my regulator was working, went through the routine as the others had and took the plunge.

CHAPTER EIGHT

Sophie

We all gathered around the anchor line and paired up with our dive buddy. It seemed like Hali and Dak, and Phoenix and Savannah fell naturally together. Curious... Jared would partner with Caleb and me. After checking everything was still secure—tanks, hoses, etc.—everyone gave their hand signal indicating they were ready to go. Once under, I began to release air from my Buoyancy Control Vest via the dump valve to take me down, being sure to equalize the pressure in my ears as I descended by working my jaw to make them pop, like when one was in an airplane.

We reached our dive depth of 110 feet, and I held my pressure gauge in front of me to make sure it was measuring my air correctly, but before I could check it, something hit my mask hard, displacing it. A mullet stopped and stared at me as if to say, *I'm sorry*, then jetted off and I was surrounded by a whole school of his friends. I quickly cleared my mask by holding the top in place and lifting the bottom to break the seal while blowing air through my nose, as I had been taught. The air chased the water out, and I found myself caught in a tornado of mullets. I watched as they swam away. As the school formed and reformed, it was mesmerizing, like the inside of a kaleidoscope.

Caleb, who had been looking back and witnessed my finned friend nailing me, was concerned, signaling with a crooked finger for a question mark, then making the okay sign to ask me if I was all right. I nodded vigorously to reassure him, giving my okay sign in return. This seemed to reassure him, but, to be honest, I was so distracted by the sea turtle beyond his shoulder I forgot Caleb was even there for a moment. The turtle had emerged from an overhang of coral where he had been getting his shell cleaned by little surgeonfish and plecos. He swam up between us, as elegant as an ice skater. It was the first time I'd gotten that close to a sea turtle, and I was enthralled. He was huge, probably almost three feet long. But the graceful way his flapper-shaped feet cut through the water belied his bulk.

I was hit, once again, with the beauty of scuba diving. A diver enters an entirely different world from the one above water, strangely quiet, other than the rhythmic sound of one's breathing. The sense of being weightless is freeing, and everything seems to move in slow motion. The sea whip coral undulates, beckoning one in for a closer inspection. The variety of shapes and colors of the reef fish was mind-blowing, but my favorite was the seahorses, latching onto coral with their tails like a horse on land, tethered to a hitching post. Such unusual creatures.

Thinking about seahorses, I better rein it in.

I tended to get so captivated at the beginning of a dive, I had to tell myself to focus, to check my gauges, to check my dive partners. Caleb was within feet of me, so I knew he was okay. I searched for Jared. He was hanging back roughly seven yards, probably trying to give us some privacy. I checked my gauge. Three thousand PSI. Normal. I returned to my observation of the nearby marine life. Then it struck me.

Wait. I had three thousand PSI at the outset. It should be lower. Odd.

I shrugged it off for the moment, knowing I'd had a full tank initially, but vowed to check it often. But a few minutes later I was finding it difficult to bring in air. Something was wrong. Caleb had swum a little beyond me, exploring the reef. I remembered his worried face when the fish bumped me. I knew the worst thing I could do was panic, and seeing him with that expression again might send me over the edge.

I'll get Jared's attention. He's a professional. He'll remain calm and that will help me to keep it together.

But by the time I was halfway to him, things were looking strange, colors seemed to intensify, shapes shifted and became less defined. Jared was nothing more than a two-dimensional swipe of black on a squirmy, riotous background. Why was I even swimming toward him?

I became acutely aware of the lack of the sound of my breathing. There was no sound at all. Was I even real? Had I passed on to some other dimension?

I shook my head and concentrated.

I can't panic. Panic will increase my rate of respiration.

Thank God, Jared had seemed to sense something and was coming to me. He repeated Caleb's earlier signing, crooked finger followed by okay sign.

No. I'm not okay. Something's wrong. But what is it...

Somehow, through the brain fog, the answer came.

Oh, yeah. I have no air. That's bad.

My thinking had become very simplistic. But miraculously my body was moving, bringing a hand to my neck and making the slashing gesture. It was like I was outside looking in.

Jared's eyes widened in his mask, and he hesitated a fraction. Then, exactly like me, it seemed, he went on autopilot. He reached for his backup regulator and gestured between us before locking one hand on my arm, below the elbow. I gripped his arm in a similar manner. That little touch, to actually touch another human being, almost made me come undone with relief. He passed me the regulator, and I sucked on it hungrily, forgetting to clear it and inhaling some water into my lungs. I coughed and he hit the purge button on the front of my mask to clear it for me.

He asked me if I was all right again. I pushed down the continuing urge to clear my throat by coughing and signaled, indicating I was fine.

Other than the blinding migraine which just started.

Jared signaled up and added air to his buoyancy control vest. Despite my head being heavy and the urge to sleep, I managed to do the same. We began to slowly ascend. In the back of my mind, I registered the fact that someone was with us. We rose at a speed that seemed needlessly slow—like we were working our way through a pool of oatmeal—although I was aware it was necessary to give our bodies time to adjust to the changing water pressure. Then Jared signaled to level out for a decompression safety stop. By the time our three minutes had passed, everything inside of me was scratching and clawing with a need to surface. As we came to the anchor line, Jared took it and tried to shake it. Then he beat on the hull of the ship.

Upon reaching the top, I snatched my regulator from my mouth, wanting to breathe normally.

"What the hell happened?" Caleb shouted, fear ringing in his voice.

At the same time, Chase looked over the side of the boat and asked a similar question.

"Her air supply was depleted."

"Depleted?" Chase said as if Jared had just announced he was the Man in the Moon.

"I'm fine." I managed to say. I separated from Jared and started to swim toward the ladder.

"I'd rather you let me..."

The sound of his voice fizzled and things got fuzzy again.

I don't know how long I was unconscious, but it could only have been a few seconds as Caleb was holding me, but I didn't seem any closer to the ladder. "I've got her."

Jared shoved him away. "I said I've got it," he snapped, finally seeming to lose his cool. He slid his hands under my armpits and propelled us in the direction of the boat.

"I'm okay," I mumbled. "Stop fighting."

I remember, briefly, an awkward struggle to get me aboard, and the next thing I knew I was stretched out on one of the bench seats, and Chase was putting an oxygen mask over my face. "You told me you checked the canisters," he growled.

"I did!" Jared insisted. He examined what I presume was my pressure gage, then turned it toward Chase. "See. 3,000 psi." He frowned and checked it again. "3,000 psi? That's what we started with. It should be lower than that."

Chase ignored him, smiling at me and speaking gently, which was a sharp contrast to the way he'd spoken to Jared. "Just relax, Soph. Everything is going to be all right. Breathe in deeply. Good."

Dak padded aboard, followed by the rest. "What happened?"

"She ran out of air," Caleb explained, glaring at Jared, who was too absorbed looking at the pressure gage to even notice.

"This isn't one of our gauges," he muttered. Then, "Hey, this isn't one of our gauges!" He looked up. "It looks similar, but it's not the same model."

Chase frowned. "Are you sure?"

Jared rose to show it to him. "See, it has the depth and psi gauges, but no compass like ours have."

"You're right."

"What do you mean?" Dak said, standing there dripping with Hali, Phoenix, and Savannah right behind him. He reminded me of a giant, black frog.

Jared looked at him in wonder. "Someone switched our gear for their broken gear."

"You mean they were trying to steal it?"

"Maybe," Jared scratched the stubble covering his cheeks. "But why replace it with their broken one? Why not just take the one you want and hightail it out of there?"

Hali frowned. "What are you saying? That someone was trying to kill Sophie?"

Jared shrugged. "Maybe. It's the most logical conclusion."

They all stared at me.

Phoenix flipped some of his wet hair back. "But who would want to kill Sophie?"

I shifted my focus to Caleb. His jaw was tight, his brow furrowed in anger, but his eyes were wide and wet from worry and he hadn't taken his gaze from my face.

I pulled my oxygen mask off. "I'm fine."

"Leave that on!" Jared, Chase, Dakota, Hali, and Phoenix shouted.

"Geesh." I replaced it.

CHAPTER NINE

Caleb

I peered down at her, trying to get a full breath myself. She was so pale, and her lips had a bluish tint. Despite all her exertions, she was fine; I could see she was scared, her eyes wide as Chase stretched the oxygen mask around her head. When she'd passed out in the water, my heart dove back to the bottom, where I'd first seen her with Jared and realized something was wrong. I wasn't going to lose her before we could explore what we had between us, was I?

The ride to the shore was much more subdued than when we'd been on the way to our dive location. I sat on the deck near Sophie while she rested. I was a nervous wreck. I wanted her to relax, but if she was too still, I worried she'd lost consciousness again. I would occasionally twist to verify she was okay, and she would touch my shoulder, reassuring me she was all right. Phoenix, Dak, and Hali all crowded together on the bench across from us and, like me, Savannah sat on the deck, her knees tucked within the circle of her arms, her focus solely on her friend.

My anger at Jared had waned since he spoke about checking Sophie's gear preceding the dive. It reminded me that, as her dive buddy, I had inspected her equipment too. Had I missed something? Had I been concentrating more on her than on her pressure gauge?

The boat had relatively decent speed for such a big craft, and as it bounced over the waves, Jared and Chase took turns coming to check on her, one taking her hand as he chatted, one squatting next to her. Eventually, we pulled alongside the dock, and they busied themselves with securing the boat. Sophie promptly removed her oxygen mask and sat up.

I scrambled to my feet. "Whoa. Don't sit too fast."

She swung her legs over the edge of the bench. "I'm fine."

I tried to talk sense into her. "Sophie, you went without air..."

"For a couple of seconds. It's not that big of a deal." Her color was better; still...

Attempting to give her a stern expression, I argued, "You passed out."

She played it off. "I think I was just hungry."

Chase and Jared rounded the corner together. "I can drive," Chase was saying.

"I'll drive," I insisted, a bit aggressively.

"My Rubicon is roomier than your truck," Jared countered as if I hadn't spoken.

Chase tilted his head. "True." He looked at Sophie. "How are you feeling, hon?"

"Good. But I'll feel even better after Caleb buys me some lunch." She raised her eyebrows hopefully as if begging.

Like she would have to beg for anything from me.

Jared smiled at me. "Oh, I'm sure he'll do that after we get you examined at the hospital, won't you, Caleb?" He nodded to encourage me.

I sighed, glaring at them for a moment before putting my hand on her leg. "Anywhere you want."

"I'm not going to the hospital," she spouted.

Everyone stared at her, Dak crossing his arms with a frown.

"You guys..." She glanced from one to the other, searching for someone to back her.

We weren't having it.

Her grip on the bench loosened and tightened in turn. "You are all blowing this way out of proportion."

"Maybe," Chase said, coming to her side and helping her to her feet. "But we'd feel better if they examined you and cleared you to resume normal activities. We'll take care of the bills, of course." He didn't give her room to fight him. "Here we go. Watch your step." He helped her onto the dock.

"But...this is ridiculous," she sputtered as Chase dragged her reluctantly forward.

"Oh, I know it is," he returned as if coddling a small child. "Jared, bring your car around."

"I can drive," I said again, but everyone ignored me.

"I don't need him to bring his car around." She yanked her arm from his hold. "I can walk just fine."

Chase withdrew his hands. "Fine," he conceded, letting her win this small battle. But he gave Jared a pointed look and he jogged off.

His concession seemed to have worked. Sophie straightened her spine proudly. "It's not like I was bitten by a shark," she muttered.

"I know. I know," Savannah said reassuringly. "It's only...we all love you so much... You understand that, right?"

Sophie blinked rapidly. "Yes. And I love you. But—"

"We would simply feel a whole lot better to hear a medical professional tell us you're all right."

Jared screeched to a stop at the end of the gangway, hopped out, and circled it to open the passenger side front and rear. Sophie didn't seem to realize the car had been brought even though she'd insisted it not be. Savannah kept talking to her which distracted her. Even as she climbed into the back, Savannah was keeping up a running commentary.

"I'll get in on the other side." Savannah scurried around, leaving me the seat next to Jared.

I'd wanted to sit by Sophie, but now hardly seemed the time to throw a fit. We'd been in the waiting room of the hospital for twenty minutes, and no one had called Sophie's name.

"I'm starving," Sophie said to the girls. "Aren't you guys starving?"

Hali and Savannah looked at each other and hesitated. They had to be hungry. It was five o'clock and none of us had eaten lunch.

"No. No. Not too bad," Savannah said.

Hali added, "Yeah. That whole eating thing is overrated."

They laughed. But my nerves were about shot. And I was dying of hunger. I kept re-seeing her limp body sinking under the water. I shot out of my seat and paced in front of Phoenix, Dak, Jared, and Chase's chairs, pinching my lips.

A nurse came and we all gazed at her hopefully. "Calvin Hooper?"

Some little old man and his little old wife rose and hobbled over to her.

Those in our group who were seated sighed and sank into their cushions.

"Y'all don't need to stay," Sophie said for the millionth time. No one even bothered to answer her this time. She turned. "Chase and Jared, why don't the two of you get back to your shop, at least."

Another ten minutes passed.

"What the hell is taking so long?" I said under my breath to Phoenix and Dak, but Sophie must have had ears like a bat.

"They're busy, Caleb."

I glanced around. The place was sort of hopping. And Sophie hadn't helped matters by telling the triage nurse she didn't have any pain. She even said her headache was gone, though I'd caught her wincing occasionally and rubbing her temples.

Dak stood. "You're right. This is ridiculous. I'm going to talk to somebody."

Oh, Lord.

The man returned in less than a minute, chatting up a nurse. They paused in the doorway.

"Sophie Lockhart?"

"Oh." Sophie rose hurriedly. "Hello." She greeted the nurse with a smile.

"Thanks, Kathy," Dak said. "See you later." He turned to us, took a dramatic bow, then announced he was seeking out "the little boys' room," and left.

Hali peered at Phoenix. "Did he know that girl?"

He shrugged. "I doubt it."

Her gaze narrowed and her lips became tight. She whirled around, giving us a view of the back of her head. Phoenix and I exchanged a look. A few minutes later, Nurse Kathy returned. "Sophie can have two visitors."

We all sprang to our feet.

"*Two.*"

Hali stared at the hall Dak had disappeared into. "You go, Savvy. I can switch with you."

No one challenged me for my spot. They wouldn't have dared. Kathy walked us through a set of doors to an area sectioned off by curtains. How they could keep track of who was in which room was beyond me, but she walked directly to one on the right and held the curtain so we could enter.

We walked in, and I was surprised to find Sophie on her left side with the bed tilted up at the bottom, making her slant downward. They already had an IV in her arm, and a nurse was taking her blood pressure. I checked the monitor near her bed, which was stupid, because I had no idea what the numbers were supposed to be. Her positioning must have caught Savannah off-guard too, as she exclaimed, "Oh. Interesting."

Sophie's laugh was muffled by her oxygen mask. "Come here."

We crossed the end of the bed so we could see her face. She had lowered her mask. Seeing us, her eyes warmed. "Hi."

Before I could respond, someone called, "Knock, knock. Everybody decent?" The warning didn't mean much because he was already in the door. He wore faded jeans, a Hawaiian shirt, and a white lab coat, unbuttoned.

Great. Who's this clown?

He came over to our side, and we moved back to give him room. He was a shorter guy with curly red-blond hair and a beard. "It *is* you, Sophie Lockhart."

She squinted, her forehead wrinkling. "Rick? Rick Schneider?"

"Yeah." He rubbed his chin. "I didn't have this facial hair in high school. I didn't know if you would recognize me."

"It did throw me for a moment. Good to see you. How are you?"

He pulled a stool to her bed and straddled it. "Apparently better than you. Ran out of oxygen? How'd that happen?"

"A faulty gauge. But it was really no big deal."

"How long were you deprived of air?"

"Oh, only a few seconds. I got to Jared quickly—we were at the Sink Or Swim—and we buddy breathed. My friends are overreacting. I feel fine."

"I'll be the judge of that," he said sternly. He glanced at his clipboard.

No iPad? Maybe we need to take her somewhere more state-of-the-art. Get her a specialist...

"It says here you have no headache?"

"Nope."

"That's highly unusual." He scrutinized her. "You sure you're not lying so you can go home?"

She hesitated and her words came out stilted. "No. Why would I do that?"

"Well, because most people don't like to hang around here. It's giving me a complex." He grinned. "Do you mind if I do a few tests on you?"

"If it will get me home, sure."

He rose and stood beside her. "Ahh! So you admit it then? You're downplaying your symptoms so I'll release you."

"I admit nothing."

The nurse leaned over Sophie, straightening some tubes. "I'm going to bring the back of your bed up slowly so you don't get a head rush." She unhurriedly raised her until she was flat.

The doctor used a little sink and dried his hands before continuing.

At least he's familiar with hygiene.

He mumbled some instructions to the nurse, then addressed Sophie. "Can you turn on your back, please?"

Sophie immediately changed positions.

"Okay. To start off, let's put that oxygen mask on." She complied reluctantly. He lifted the covers and took one foot, pushing to bend the leg at a ninety-degree angle. "Any pain here?"

She gave a negative indication. I watched her face for signs she was lying but detected none. He pressed her leg to the side, against the bed. I would have been in pain if he'd put me in that position, but again she said no.

"Straighten your leg. Now, keep me from pushing your leg down." She resisted the pressure. "Good." He slid his hand under her leg. "Push my hand down. Good."

He moved to the other leg and repeated his tests, and manipulated both arms as well. "Grab my fingers and squeeze as hard as you can. Ouch! Geesh! Let go," he joked, shaking his hands. He raised her arms and examined them, turning them over. "Any rash?"

She shook her head. "I don't think so."

"I'm going to have a look at your torso." He folded the blanket lower, checking her stomach and legs. Sophie squirmed a little, no doubt feeling a bit exposed since she still was in her bathing suit. "I'd say, besides the migraine you're trying to hide, you are asymptomatic. You're a lucky girl."

"Did she tell you that she lost consciousness?" I interjected before he could write the whole thing off.

He turned from me slowly and eyed his patient. "No. She left that out."

She pulled the mask to her chin. "It was only for a second."

"That's long enough," I said gruffly.

"Caleb..." she pleaded.

"Your friend's right. It could be an indication of some hidden damage. Keep that mask on."

"Wait. I just remembered something..." She stared at a spot on her blanket. "I haven't eaten much today. That's why I'm so hungry," she said as if to herself. Then she lifted her gaze. "That's probably why I was...a little faint."

The doctor's brow furrowed. "Didn't eat much, huh? Is that a habit?"

"No, I...I woke up late, and we were going to have a birthday lunch for my brother, so I decided to wait for that. Plus...I was a kind of nervous, so I wasn't sure how the food would sit."

"Nervous?"

"Yes..." She looked at me, but didn't elaborate.

Shit. I made her leave lunch early and didn't get her something to eat. She was no doubt worried about her parents meeting me, and that was a disaster. Maybe I could have said something different...

I realized I was missing what the doctor was saying and tuned in again.

The doctor flipped through his notes. "What was her initial pulse ox?"

"Ninety-two percent. She's now up to..." The nurse checked the monitor. "...95."

The doctor stared off into space, twirling his pen idly while we all waited. "Well, Sophie," he said finally, "it appears you dodged a bullet..." Sophie beamed, probably sensing her 'get out of jail free' card was on the way. I frowned at her. "...but I think, to be on the safe side, we should give you a couple of hours of hyperbaric oxygen therapy."

Her smile wavered and mine grew. "Hyper-what?"

"Some people call it..."

"Decompression therapy," the doc and I said at the same time.

He continued. "Hyperbaric oxygen therapy is putting you on 100% oxygen in a pressurized chamber to create conditions that will help your body to obtain more oxygen than it normally would if you weren't in a pressure chamber."

"Oh. I've heard of a decompression chamber, but I've never heard it referred to as hyperbaric oxygen therapy."

"Ahh. Forgive me. I have this bad tendency of speaking medicalese to people who aren't in the medical profession, using terms only other doctors would use. Please call me on it whenever I slip into speaking like that and ask me to explain if you have questions."

"Are you sure this is necessary?" Sophie whined.

"Sophie…" He put his hand on her arm and inhaled deeply. "I don't want to scare you but…last week we had a 46-year-old diving instructor in here, on vacation, doing a standard dive, ascending slowly afterward… He was healthy and in great shape. He came in here coherent, with minimal pain, simply some shortness of breath and mottling of skin. He died within twenty-four hours. This is serious. I don't think you will have any problems, but I'm not taking any chances." He peered at the nurse. "Diane here will get you ready for treatments and I'll go call the lab and reserve time for us in one of the chambers. I'll be back shortly." Turning, he eyed me again. "You're…"

"Caleb Winthrop," the nurse said flatly without even looking over.

"That's what I thought. Could I…maybe…get your autograph later. I'm a huge fan."

"Sure. No problem."

"Awesome!" He left with a little more pep in his step.

As soon as he was gone, Sophie moaned. "I'm starving. Now I won't be getting out of here for hours."

"I can order a tray for you," the nurse offered. "It's pretty decent, for hospital food."

After that less than glowing endorsement, disappointment was written on Sophie's face. "Okay. Sure."

Savannah spoke up. "Would we be allowed to bring Rod's in?"

"Yes! Oh, please!" Sophie begged.

"Only if you bring me some," the nurse said with a sly smile.

"No problem," I assured her. "Cancel that tray."

"Y'all better hurry and get some. Once I get Miss Sophie here into a hospital gown, they'll be taking her down when they're ready."

"Okay." I moved over to the bed, giving Sophie a tender kiss on the cheek. "You behave while we're gone."

She grabbed my shirt and pulled me to her, slipping her mask off. I thought she was going to kiss me. "I want fries. And a chocolate shake."

I chuckled. "Yes, ma'am. No burger?"

"Of course I want a burger. Are you crazy?" She released me to give Savannah a hug. "Savvy knows my order."

Savannah smiled. "A cheeseburger with everything, hold the lettuce and tomato."

The nurse raised her eyebrows. "Yes. We'd hate to have anything remotely healthy on it."

Savannah squeezed Sophie's hands as they parted. "We'll be back soon. I love you."

The nurse motioned for Sophie to put her mask on. "Thanks," came her mumbled response.

Savannah turned to the nurse. "Can the others come in?"

She looked at Sophie. "Are you up for more visitors?"

Sophie nodded rapidly.

The nurse slid the rail on the side of the bed down. "Tell them I'll come get them in a minute, after I get Sophie changed. Two at a time." We began to leave. "Hey. What about my order? I wasn't kidding."

I grinned. "What do you want?"

"Same as her. Now get going. I'm hungry."

When we returned, we had to kick Phoenix and Dakota out.

Phoenix got to his feet and stretched. "We're cruising back to the hotel to get ready for our gig, Sophie, but if you need anything, let us know."

My face drained. "Oh, shit. I forgot we're playing tonight."

"We got Wyatt to play for you," Dak said as he approached me.

I exhaled. "Oh, thank God."

Sophie piped up. "You really don't need to stay."

I swung around. "I'm staying." I turned away to avoid an argument. The girl needed to save her strength for healing.

Dak knocked my shoulder hard as he went to pass me and leaned in. "Take *full* advantage of your night off, if you know what I mean."

Behind him, Phoenix rolled his eyes. "Of course he knows what you mean. You've got as much finesse as a sculptor working with a jackhammer. And you're twice as loud."

"I'm simply saying he should take her home and..." He thrust his hips back and forth.

Phoenix thwapped him. "Stop!"

Dak was crude, but he was amusing. I gave him a faux frown. "Not in her condition, sicko."

He glanced over his shoulder. "I don't know. She looks like she could handle it. It might be your best chance. In her delusional state, she may mistake you for me and be more open to—"

Phoenix brought his hands down hard on Dak's shoulders, shaking his head. "Come on, bro. Leave them alone."

Capitalizing on my hands being full, Dak opened one of the bags and stole some fries. "I'm just trying to help them out," he said innocently.

"Yeah, yeah. I've heard it all before." Phoenix pushed a resistant Dak forward. "Call us if you need anything," he added to me.

"Thanks, man. I appreciate it."

The nurse bustled in. "Don't you be eating my fries." She slapped Dak's hand.

He withdrew it with a grimace. "Ouch."

Phoenix finally got him pushed through the door. The nurse pulled a freestanding tray to Sophie's bed. "I'm going to raise you the rest of the way so you can eat."

Sophie had only taken one bite when another nurse escorted two police officers in. One I'd seen at The Sands talking to Remi. "Miss Lockhart, do you feel up to answering a couple of questions from the police?"

She sighed and waved them over. "Sure. Why not? Come in."

"Hi, Sophie. You know Sam, right?"

The policewoman next to him nodded at her. "Hey. Sorry to have to meet you again under these conditions."

"It's fine. I'll be just peachy as soon as I finish this baby." She took another bite.

The first officer stepped over, extending his hand. "Hi. Caleb Winthrop, right?"

"Yes."

"Declan Moran, Chief of Police. And this is Officer Samantha Ruiz."

The lady cop lifted her chin. "Hi."

The police chief crossed to the side of the bed. "So, Sophie...Jared described your accident for us, only he feels it wasn't all that accidental." He gestured to the door. "I've already got your friends' takes on it, and they supplied me with most of the info I needed, so this shouldn't take long." The lady cop had pulled out a pen and tablet and was poised to take notes. "Let's start with the obvious...do you know anyone who would want to do you physical harm?"

Sophie finished chewing her bite and swallowed, her forehead wrinkled. "I've been considering that and, honestly, I can't name a soul."

"No run-ins at the bookshop? Irate customers?"

"Not that I can think of. Do you really believe someone would try to kill me because we...ran short of your wife's books?"

He tilted his head with a grin. "You never know. People get crazy due to the littlest things. What about ex-boyfriends?"

"The only one I ever dated was Steve, and you're aware of what became of that. He left me, so he couldn't be upset over how the relationship ended."

"Do you..." The chief cleared his throat. "...know where Steve is these days?"

She shrugged, swiping a fry through some ketchup. "Last I heard he was in L.A., the city of angels...and Clarice and Steve," she said wryly.

"Did you notice anything unusual this morning? See anyone on the docks before you took off?"

"No. No one. I'm sorry."

He patted her arm. "Don't be. You've given us all you know. That's all we could hope for. I'm sure you would have been paying closer attention had you realized someone was going to try to kill you today." He exhaled and looked at Officer Ruiz, then faced me. "Is there anything you can add, Mr. Winthrop?"

I tried to remember. "Only that we ran into Sadie Lawson as we were entering."

"Huh...that would have been a promising lead if Wyatt had been with you. Still, we'll check it out."

"Time to put that mask back on," the nurse commanded.

"But I haven't finished my shake yet."

"I'll stick it in the freezer in the nurses' lounge until you're discharged. They're ready for you downstairs."

I watched them roll her away and wondered over how the girl had me completely knotted inside after merely a few days.

CHAPTER TEN

Caleb

Three hours later, Sophie was given the green light to go home. Chest x-rays and CT scans didn't reveal any air where it shouldn't be, and I breathed a sigh of relief. When we finally left the hospital and I walked out with her, I pressed her against my car, which I'd picked up on the trip back from Rod's.

"You certainly went to extremes to prolong our date."

She smiled, putting her arms around my neck and playing with my hair. "A girl's gotta do what a girl's gotta do." She gave me one hell of a kiss.

"Shit. I think I need oxygen now."

She laughed and pushed me away. "Oh, stop."

I held the door while she got in. "No, I'm serious. I'm seeing stars," I teased.

But on the way into town, we got into an argument. I wanted to drop her by her parents' house, so they could be there in case something unforeseen happened to her. She wanted me to drop her at her studio by the bookshop.

"Rick said I could resume normal activities. Only no diving and no air travel for a couple of days." We pulled to the curb in front of her place, and I switched off the engine, turning to her.

"Yeah, but how much experience does he actually have? He seemed freaking young."

She glanced down at her lap, growing quiet as she messed with the cuff of her shorts. I could tell something was on her mind. "One more day, then you go."

"I believe you're changing the subject, but yes."

She swung around with tears in her eyes. "I'm sorry I ruined our time together."

"Hey..." I brushed hair away from her face. "You didn't ruin anything. It's not like you purposely took a busted tank. Speaking of which," I lowered my head to look to the top of her steps, "another reason you need me here is the fact that there may be someone out there waiting to kill you."

"Oh, please," she said dismissively. "No one's trying to kill me. If anything, they're after one of you guys. They had no idea who would use that specific tank."

"That's true." I rubbed my chin. "I never thought about that." *Couldn't think of anything except you.* I needed to convince her to let me stay, even if I had to sleep in a chair. That way I could watch her and be there...just in case.

Her question cut through my thoughts. "Do you want to see my place?" *Perfect. It'll be harder to say no to me if I'm already in the chair.*

I followed her up the stairs without speaking, going over my options should I meet resistance. She let us in and hung her keys on a hook right inside the door.

She spread her arms wide, with flair. "Welcome to Chez Sophie!" She scanned the area. "Oh, my God. It's a mess." She scurried around, plucking articles of clothing from the floor. It was tight quarters. Twin beds were parked on each side of the room, separated by maybe 4 feet. Between the two was a huge dormer window, which must have let in a lot of light. The ceiling was angled inward above the beds, but there was plenty of clearance. The most prominent thing in view was the easel that sat across from the window, pretty much in the center of the room.

"You paint?"

"Oh, that. Yes. From time to time." She came to whip the painting out of its stand, but I grabbed her hand to prevent her.

"This is amazing." She'd captured a close-up of a sailboat. The sweep of blue in the sky was done with a light touch, and I could almost feel the wind as it billowed the sails, taste the salt in the air. It was so tranquil; I couldn't stop looking at it. She'd somehow made the motion in the scene come alive.

With solely paint, brush, and canvas. It's incredible.

She finally pried it free. "That's just something I..." Her voice faded as she added the canvas to a stack of others at the end of her bed. I knew it was her bed because it was unmade and the other one was not. "So, this is my kitchen." Snapping on a light, she revealed a galley kitchen. Had it not been night, it would have again been a sunny spot, with a long bank of windows practically the length of the room on one wall, under which nestled the sink and countertops. The wall housed the appliances, no dishwasher, merely a fridge and stove with a microwave hanging above it, and another expanse of counter. It didn't give her much cabinet space, but I could see she'd done her best to maximize what she had by housing towels in a basket and pans on hooks under a shelf, where her canisters perched. An apron hung on a single hook on the wall. A tall jar filled with liquid and paintbrushes rested near the sink beside a crock holding her utensils. Her tools then, kitchen and art, were together. A dish rack lay on the other side, with open countertop beyond. She hustled about, whisking a dirty glass into the sink and pushing in a drawer that hadn't shut completely.

She turned around, and I swung my arm over the stack of canvases, having counted nine total. "From time to time?"

She clasped her hands in front of her. "Well, I...umm, maybe do it a bit much."

"May I look at them?"

Her face registered surprise. "If you want to, but don't feel like you have to."

I paged through them slowly. One had three sandpipers walking along the edge of the water, each with forward foot lifted, paused in motion. Again, I marveled at the talent she had for depicting motion, showing the reflection of the sun on the waves, using such vivid, living colors and applying them so gracefully. The next was a fun picture of the bright, colorful umbrellas on the beach, as if seen from a resort balcony. One was simply sunset and water, but the way she had put the sun off-center was unique and captivating.

She came to my side and hovered nervously, making jerky movements—reaching out her hand as if to tear the paintings away from me, then drawing it back. "It helps me relax, even though I know it's a waste of my time and I shouldn't—"

"A waste of your time?" I said, incredulous.

She seemed confused. "Yeah. I mean...it's purposeless." The word hung between us for a moment. "I should find better things to do with my time. And I'm not even good at it."

The manner in which she said it made it sound like she was repeating someone else's words. Had her parents discouraged her?

I straightened. "Who told you that?"

"Huh? Steve. He said it showed how stupid and lazy I was, spending all my time 'dicking around' with paint."

I blinked. "And you let him talk to you like that?"

"Let him? What do you mean? It's a free world. Anyone can say what they want."

"Yes, but that doesn't mean you have to listen to his garbage." I was beginning to get a clearer picture of this Steve guy, and I was not impressed. He'd torn her down. Made her feel small. No doubt to boost his own ego. At the same time, I could make out another voice, across the miles...

"Caleb, why are you always reading?" She took my book and flung it against the wall. "Read, read, read! That's all you do is read. You should be...I don't know...watching sports or something manly instead of being such a wimp. Honestly, it's embarrassing. Do you think I want to be seen with a guy like that?"

I'd let Heidi talk to me like that until the day I caught her with someone in my shower. So why was I so surprised Sophie had done the same?

Because she's beautiful. She can have any guy she wants.

But I knew what it was like. First the manipulator builds their target up with compliments and pretty words, like "I love you." They build a person up so they know the right process for tearing them down and manipulating them. And pretty soon, the victim starts to believe what they are being told, and it all happens so smoothly. So smoothly the pawn doesn't know they are being played. The puppet can't see the puppeteer. The strings are invisible.

"Honey...that's ridiculous. I'm no art expert, but I know if a painting speaks to me." I gestured to the stack. "And these are freaking screaming talent. I mean..." I drew one from the pile. It was of the waves, but one section hadn't peaked yet. It was still climbing to its full height, with just a hint of foam on its tip foreshadowing the crash to come. The underbelly of the wave was so realistic... "How do you even do this with paint?" I pointed to a section. "It's like...3D, like the water is coming out of the picture, about to splash on the floor. How do you make the foam...look like foam? I mean..." I was struck dumb. Each picture I chose was better than the last.

Her whole body relaxed. Color returned to her face, and a smile spread where there had been none. "Caleb," she said, rolling my name off her tongue in a fashion that made my blood heat. "Do you want an art lesson?"

The way she spoke made parts of me move even though I was standing still, mostly from below my waist. "Are you going to teach me?" I responded in kind.

"Uum-hum." She bit her bottom lip on one side and my tingling parts throbbed all the more. She took my hand and walked backward. "This'll be fun." But instead of stopping at the easel, she went beyond it, pulling a teal soda shop chair from near the window to a spot between the beds. "Sit. I'll be just a minute."

I watched her sashay away.

Holy shit! I feel like I'm imploding. Could she get any more freaking hot?

She disappeared into the kitchen, and I could hear some shuffling noises. I leaned to my left, stretching my neck to try to see into the kitchen, but she was too deep in the room for me to see her from my angle.

"I'll be right there," she called.

When she entered, my jaw dropped. She wore the apron, and only her bra and underwear. She'd gone from timid to vixen at the drop of a paintbrush, and I was absolutely loving it. She wiggled her little ass over.

"Excuse me..." She batted her eyelashes. "I just need to get...these." She stooped to pick something up, sticking her tight tush out to within inches of me. She lifted a corner of sheet that was on the floor and retrieved a pair of strappy high heels.

Holy fuck! I closed my mouth to conceal the drool.

She bent to put the shoes on each foot, giving me a clear shot of the curves the apron top was hiding. Then she came around in front of me and draped her hands on my shoulders. Before I knew it was even happening, one of those stilettos landed on the chair between my legs.

She wet her lips. "Do you think you could...maybe...help me with these?" She passed a hand along her shoe's strap.

Huh? My mouth was hanging open again, and I was pretty sure my brain had shut down entirely.

She narrowed the gap between us, her lips hovering above mine. Her breath shimmered with warmth as she whispered, "Please."

Hell yeah! As many times as you want to, baby.

My hands came alive and fumbled with the strap, finally getting it secured.

"Thank you." That foot went to the floor, and the other one came up with a sharp ring as it hit the seat, perilously close to my jewels.

Once I'd buckled that one, she spun and sauntered away. "Let's see..." She took deliberate steps, her hips swaying from side to side in a tantalizing style. The curves of her ass begged to be squeezed. She wasn't wearing a thong, but the scrap of silk between her legs was an even bigger tease. Snatching a big drawing pad from the end of the other bed en route, she crossed to her easel, sliding the paper onto the stand. Taking a seat on a paint-splattered stool, she at first only offered me a view of those legs, one atop the other with the top foot bouncing.

"Hmm...no palette." She seemed genuinely stumped by this for a moment. Leaning around the easel, she asked, "Are you comfortable?"

My throat was too dry to speak, so I nodded.

"Good." She chose a silver tube of paint from her easel, unscrewed the cap, and pressed a dot of paint onto the wrist of the opposite hand. "I'm having to make do," she explained with a smile and a shrug of her shoulders. She seemed a bit embarrassed by this, but the sight of that blob of paint on her wrist, where her pulse was beating, did something erotic for me. Clearing her throat, she picked a paintbrush up from the tray in front of her easel. She had turned herself slightly sideways so I could see her a little better, and she could see me. Her wet lips were parted, and she chewed on the back end of the brush while she studied me. She dipped the brush in the paint and drew a few strokes before slapping the brush down.

"No. This won't do." She grabbed a stained cloth from somewhere and wiped the paint from her wrist as she mumbled. "It won't do at all."

She rose and came in my direction. The closer she got, the more my head lolled backward so I could eye as much of her as possible. "You see," she waved a hand beside her body, "I'm not wearing much clothing, and yet, you still are." She grabbed hold of the edges of my shirt where it buttoned and yanked them apart. A few buttons were forced through their holes. She moved her hands lower and tried to do the same, all the time leaning toward me. The fragrance of her skin enticed me. My hands found their way to her hips and pelvic bone. Having finally touched her warm skin, my anatomy sighed with pleasure.

The bottom buttons wouldn't give so easily, so she carefully worked them free with painted nails, agonizingly slow and methodical. She got the last couple done. "There," she said with satisfaction. She parted the fabric, her hands gliding across my skin. "Much better." She enunciated her words strongly and brought her knee between my legs so she could slide the shirt from my shoulders. Running her hands along my chest, she let out a soft moan. "Much, *much* better."

Part of me wanted to throw her on the bed and take her, but I was so captivated by everything she was doing, I didn't want to spoil the slow build up. Figuring if her hands could explore, my hands could too, I glided them over her nice, round ass, finally finding my voice, although it was rough. "You're driving me crazy, you know."

She laughed in a delightful way, throwing aside the temptress briefly and laying her forehead on mine. "That's what I'm trying to do."

"Well, you didn't have to try so hard." I put my hand on her cheek, fighting for control. I wanted badly to take the reins, but this was her game to play. I nipped her bottom lip. "You had me since the moment I first caught sight of you on the dance floor."

"Oh," she purred. "You know *all* the right things to say."

Our mouths met in a crash, and it was all on. She straddled me, and I held her in my lap, again running my hands across the curves of her rear. I pressed to standing, lifting her with me and taking a stride away from the chair. I stopped and tugged on the sides of her underwear. "These need to go."

She dutifully set her feet on the floor, and I slid them down so she could step out of them. I tossed them on the bed. "Now this." I smiled, yanking on the ends of the bow around her neck, whipping her apron off, and flinging it who knew where.

She pinched her bra strap and peered at me with a question in her eyes.

"No. You can keep that on for the present."

I shuffled her a few feet back and threw a look over my shoulder at her portrait of me. It was a stick figure. "Nice."

She laughed, until I pushed her against the wall and smashed my lips on hers. She kissed me as feverishly as I kissed her. We changed angles and the manner we used our tongues, sometimes nearly swallowing each other;

sometimes playing, teasingly on the periphery. I swung her arms in an arc until they were above her head and held her wrists in one hand, dropping my mouth to her neck and upper chest. She writhed against me.

If she keeps doing that, this won't last for long. And I want it to last. And last. And last. Until we are both too tired to move.

I pulled away and spun her, pressing her stomach against the wall, while again holding her hands up. I put my unoccupied hand on her jaw and twisted her head so I could nibble on her earlobe. This position wasn't giving me much relief as her ass was now against my crotch and every sweet maneuver she made brought me closer to the edge of my restraint. I let her loose, but she kept her hands on the wall, releasing a moan.

"I want you like crazy, Sophie." I found her chest, aroused all the more by her curves and taut nipples beneath the lacy bra. Exploring further, I discovered that magical point where fabric gave way to her silky skin and yanked on the material to expose more of her. I pinched her nubs between my fingers, and she cried out, arching against my shoulder. Then I dove under her breasts where the surface was cool and somehow even smoother, cupping her to fill my hands and feel their weight. She was the perfect size, not small but not overwhelmingly big either. I groaned. "Fuck, you're so damned perfect." I quickly unclasped her bra and she shrugged free of it, casting it to the floor. "So beautiful," I murmured in her ear, placing my hands next to hers for a moment, then using one to outline her body starting at her wrist, gliding along her arm to her side, to the swell of her breast, and the curve of her hip. Then I slid it across her stomach, splayed, to take it all in, and between her legs to stroke her in circles, making her inhale sharply. I worked her up until she put a hand behind my neck, pressing against me even more, her breath stuttering as I pleasured her until she was frantic.

"Now it's my turn to paint." I shifted to find the right silver tube.

She spun, watching me, sucking in air as she waited to see what I would do. I squeezed bright blue cream onto my palm.

"What? Are you going to finger paint?"

Yes. But not on canvas.

I stepped forward and her eyes grew wide. With my clean hand I moved one wrist above her head and the other arm seemed to rise automatically. I trailed my finger across her skin again, only this time leaving a blue line.

Once I reached her ribcage, I quickly spread the paint to both hands and drew parenthesis around her breasts, continuing lower, to trace another set on her hips before traveling to her rear and lifting her. She clasped my shoulders and her legs encircled my waist. I kissed her slowly, taking her to her bed. I was glad she'd left it unmade because it saved me the hassle of tugging the blankets down. Not caring that I was getting paint on them, I ditched the rest of my clothing and joined her, sliding on top. As I rode her in waves, she made tiny sounds of pleasure, fueling my desire for her even more. When her cries changed to a higher pitch, I increased my pace, driving until she melted, and releasing after her, seeming to send further tremors through her body. I stayed for a few moments, trying to bring my heartrate within its normal range, then rolled to the side and flopped onto my back. "I guess I need to get you some new sheets." Blue paint was smeared everywhere. We laughed brokenly, still trying to catch our breath.

I looked across the pillow at her. She wore a wide, loose smile of contentment, and my heart was seized. "Come here," I said roughly and she snuggled under my arm, sighing. I kissed the top of her head and lazily skimmed my fingers along her skin as we lay, each occupied by our thoughts. Several seconds passed. "Sophie?" She pulled away, and my gaze roamed over her face. "Oh, God, Sophie...I think I'm falling in love with you, and it scares the shit out of me."

Her brow furrowed. "You know I'd never do anything to hurt you, don't you?"

I drew her to my side, mostly so she would not see my expression and the doubt I was trying to hide. She would never do anything cruel or on purpose, but the threat still loomed. Then I was struck by a thought. "Shit!"

"What?" she said in alarm.

"I forgot to use a condom. I *never* forget to use condoms," I added in wonder. "I can't believe...I'm sorry. It was so irresponsible of me. I should have never—"

"Caleb," she said calmly. "It's all right. I forgot about it too. It's not your fault."

I was quiet for a moment. "If I got you pregnant, I want you to know I intend to care for you and the baby."

She laughed. "Whoa, whoa, whoa. Aren't you getting a little ahead of yourself?" She touched my cheek. "Everything's fine." She smiled up at me, so confident of her statement.

She fell asleep, and I stayed awake for hours, berating myself. How could I do something so stupid? I didn't know if Sophie was ready for children, or even if she wanted children at all.

If I've done anything to impact her life negatively...

Troubled by my thoughts, it took me a while to fall asleep.

I woke and light was streaming in through the window. I turned my head. It bathed Sophie's serene face in a golden glow.

Oh, shit. I really love her. Worse than ever before. I promised myself I wouldn't go there again, but...what can I do? I rolled on my side and watched her sleep. Eventually I drifted off.

CHAPTER ELEVEN

Caleb

The morning was great. We ate breakfast at a little café and ignored the fact that I'd be leaving the next day. As we walked back to her place, hand in hand, swinging our arms between us, my phone buzzed in my pocket and my heart dropped. I told myself it didn't matter if I answered it or not.

She had become quiet.

I didn't want to ask but I needed to. "Do you have to work today?" I'd already decided I would hang around the shop until her dad had me bodily removed.

She raised her head, peering down the sidewalk; the bookstore was half a block away. "No. I got someone to cover for me."

"And how long do you think we have before your dad sends out someone to arrest me?"

She smiled at that. "I may have bought us some time. My mom texted as soon as the shop opened and D.J. showed up to work for me. I told her I was tired from everything that happened yesterday and wanted to take the day off."

Our footsteps slowed, and I studied her for a moment. The sun made her hair glow like she was crowned with a halo, some celestial being sent to Earth. "Did that worry her?"

Her lips twitched. "Not after I assured her I didn't have a headache, was not nauseous, could breathe well, had no pain..." She stopped abruptly. "Caleb, aren't you going to answer that?"

"No."

She looked away, then back. "What if it's...something important?"

I lifted her knuckles to my mouth to kiss them, wondering for the zillionth time over the softness of her skin. "Nothing is more important than this right here."

Instead of reassuring her, this seemed to aggravate her. She withdrew her hand, wrapping her arms around her middle. "You should answer it."

I stared at her, not sure how to approach her and wondering what could be bothering her.

Like you don't know.

The sharp buzzing continued. Like a fly caught between screen and window.

Who the hell is calling me? You'd think they would have given up by now.

I slid my phone out, read the screen, and hit the button to silence it.

"Wasn't that Dakota?" She must have spied his name.

I brushed it off. "Yeah. It's fine. He'll leave a message." We'd gotten to my Jeep. "Do you want to take a walk on the beach?"

She exhaled. "Sure. Yeah."

I opened the door for her, and she climbed in wordlessly. As I walked around the vehicle, my phone buzzed again. I subtly tried to mute the ringer without removing it from my pocket.

"Did you tell anyone where you were going last night?"

"It's none of their damned business."

"But they might be worried for you, Caleb. Maybe they're concerned something happened to you. You need to answer them or call them."

The only one more persistent than Dakota Blackstone was the beautiful woman sitting next to me. I growled and fumbled to get the phone out. Dak was calling again. "What?" I barked into the receiver.

"Holy shit, man! You need to quit screwing and get back here and pack."

What the hell?

"What are you talking about? I have plenty of time for that tomorrow."

"No, you don't. We're leaving this afternoon."

My heartbeat picked up. "What? Why?" I glanced at her. She had her elbow on the window frame and was looking off to the side, chewing on a nail.

"Because," he said in an aggravatingly condescending tone, "someone activated the sprinklers in the gala's banquet room. Everything's soaked, including some of our equipment."

"But why does that mean..." I hesitated, then twisted away and lowered my voice. "...we have to go?"

"The gala's canceled, and Levi wants to leave town as soon as possible so we can return sooner. Although I don't know how that'll work since our tour dates are set. I think he wants to give Remi space so she can concentrate on fixing everything that got destroyed by the water. Whatever the reason, we're hitting the bricks ASAP, and you need to get your ass back here. I'm done talking to you, now. I need to pack." He disconnected. I dropped the phone in my lap and stared at it, completely numb.

"What did he say?"

I searched for a way to tell her.

"Damn it, Caleb, what did he say?" Her voice was shaky.

I looked up quickly, caught off guard by the anger and desperation in her tone. The tears in her eyes struck me dumb.

"All right. Forget it." She opened the door and got out.

"Hey, wait. What are you doing?"

She slammed the door shut and stood, grasping the frame. "You have to go. So go." She spun on her heels and began to climb the stairs to her studio.

"Sophie." I scrambled to follow her. "Sophie! Wait!"

She stopped but didn't twist to face me. I put a hand on her elbow. "Hey," I said softly. She was still as stone. I climbed two stairs so I could catch her expression. She avoided eye contact, blinking rapidly.

"Caleb, I'd rather not do this here."

"Do what? What are we doing?"

Her gaze finally flashed to mine. "You know, I've already got a reputation in town for men leaving me. I'd rather not have anyone witness another one doing the same."

"What are you saying? I'm not leaving you."

She crossed her arms and cocked a hip. It would have been cute except for her tears. "So you're going to be here tomorrow."

I opened my mouth to speak, but nothing came out.

"Yeah. That's what I thought." She pulled free of my grip and stomped up the rest of the steps.

I didn't turn at first. "Sophie, can we discuss this?"

"There's nothing to discuss, Caleb," she said in a weirdly high-pitched voice.

I spun around. She was fumbling with her key in the door. A wave of panic hit me. I got the feeling if she got behind that door, everything would be finished between us. Finished before it had even really started. I scrambled to catch her. "Come on, let's talk." I put my hands on the door on either side of her. "*Please.*" The fragrance of her hair speared right to my gut and scenes from the previous night played in my mind. Her hair splayed on her pillow, running through my fingers when we kissed, over her shoulder while I was nibbling on her neck...

She sighed. "Okay. Okay. Fine." She opened the door and for a moment I thought she would slam it in my face, but she didn't. She dumped her purse on the made bed and sat on hers.

I didn't know how to approach her. "Can we analyze why you're mad at me? What I did wrong?"

She was staring at my toes. "I'm not mad at you. Only upset. You did nothing wrong. You were honest about the length of your stay, and I knew our time was ending, so it's not fair for me to be angry with you. I'm just sorry it's over."

"Wait...You thought after I left, you'd never see me again?"

She gazed up at me now. "Well, yeah," she said like it was the most obvious thing in the world.

"You thought..." My ire began to rise. "What exactly did you believe went on here last night?"

She smiled. "Some seriously hot sex."

The corners of my lips twitched. "That's for damn sure." I tried to stay focused. "But, did you think I was doing it without feeling? That I'm the kind of guy who would take advantage of you for one weekend, then leave and never look back?"

"Well, aren't you?"

"No!" I said indignantly. I paced, one hand on my hip, one on my forehead, pushing down the headache that was forming. Had I misread everything? My footsteps slowed and then stopped altogether as a thought struck me. I rotated to stare at her. "Is that what last night was for you? Merely a fling with the guitarist from a band?"

"Not on my end."

"But you thought that is what I was doing?" My anger and volume increased as I continued. "Having some weekend affair with a chick just to get my rocks off?" She didn't speak. "When I told you I was falling in love with you, did you judge those to be empty, pretty words?"

"I didn't know," she shouted back. A sob escaped, and it was like a knife to my gut. She covered her face.

I fucked this up. I fucked this up royally.

We'd never discussed any sort of future. I had simply assumed her thoughts were the same as mine. Had I forgotten completely that fool Steve broke her heart?

"Sophie, don't." I squatted before her. "Please, Sophie. Stop crying." I put my hands on the outsides of her thighs. "I didn't mean to hurt you."

She sniffed, drew a deep breath and raised her head. "I'm sorry, Caleb. It's...wrong of me to break down in front of you. I don't want you to feel guilty..." She put her palm against my cheek. "You shouldn't feel guilty about leaving. I knew that was happening from the start." She rubbed her thumb gently over my jaw. "Thank you for a lovely couple of days. I've enjoyed every minute of being with you. ...Except when I ran out of air. That really sucked." She laughed through her tears; then she sobered again. "I don't regret being with you or any of the decisions I've made since." Her gaze strayed to my lips and she leaned in, tenderly kissing me for a long moment.

"Sophie, you've got this all wrong. I intend to return as often as possible. And I can fly you to shows whenever you want to, and I'll call you after—"

She sprang to her feet so quickly she nearly knocked me on my ass. It was her turn to pace, only from the other side of the easel. "Let's not do that. Let's not make promises to each other that we can't keep. Let's just end it on a good note. Be grateful for the time we had together..."

I went to her, stepping in her path and taking her shoulders. "Sophie, I'm not Steve," I said slowly, wanting to emphasize the fact. "I will keep any promises I make to you. I swear."

She studied me, and her face morphed from one emotion to the next and back again. Like someone trying to bring a camera into focus.

I wish I knew what was going on inside that pretty little head of hers.

She finally landed on a neutral expression. "Okay." She became all business. "So, it sounded like Dakota was wound up—"

"When is he not?"

"Did something happen or..."

"Yeah." I looked down. Now I got to tell this girl—who I wasn't sure believed my sincerity about wanting to be with her—I was leaving early. "So apparently someone set off the sprinklers in the banquet room and the gala is canceled. We're actually leaving...today."

She seemed stunned. "Today?"

I nodded. "Today."

"Oh, today." She bobbed her head, staring at nothing in particular. "It's probably for the best—"

"The hell it is. I wanted to spend more time with you." She breezed by that like I hadn't even spoken.

"You probably need to get packed." She walked toward the door. "You'll have to get moving then." She opened the door and held it, smiling stiffly.

"Are you throwing me out?"

She continued in the same sweet-as-honey robotic way. "No. Don't be silly. I just know Dakota is concerned..."

"Yes. I only wish *you* were a little more concerned." She'd left me thrown and irritated. This is not how I'd thought of our goodbye happening. Actually, I hadn't thought about it at all because I didn't want to. Yet here we were. Since she gave me no choice, I strode to the door, stopping midway through to look at her, but she averted my gaze. Feeling I had no other recourse, I crossed the threshold, and she closed the door behind me. Was this how we were going to leave it?

I could see her on the other side of the muted glass, still hanging onto the doorknob. I rapped on the door loudly. She swung it open, and I pushed into the room, grabbed her face, and backed her up to the wall, kissing her long and hard and deep. Still holding her, I spoke. "This isn't over. I love you, and damn it, *we will make this work*. I *will* return." I whirled around and left as quickly as I could, afraid I would break down in front of her.

When I reached the car, I caught a glimpse of the flowers I'd gotten for her on the floor in the rear. The water in the vase hadn't spilled, but they were wilted and lifeless in the supreme heat of the stifling vehicle. I got in and laid my head on the steering wheel, shutting my eyes, trying to collect myself. Then I started the ignition and drove away, more determined than ever that little Miss Sophie Lockhart would be mine someday. I just had to prove to her this could work.

Sophie

I couldn't believe what a complete idiot I was. I had let a guy into my heart again. One would have expected me to have learned something from the whole wedding debacle, but no. I think Caleb really believed what he was saying. He wanted it to work out, *at the moment*. He really was a sweetheart of a guy. Nothing at all like Steve.

Making love with Steve—if you could call it that—was a fifteen minute event, with only one of us feeling fulfilled in the end. I simply thought that's how it was. Never imagined it could be anything like the way Caleb Winthrop made love to me. He was a generous lover, making sure all of my needs were taken care of—again, and again, and again—before his own needs were met. I never knew, *never* knew or imagined it could be like that, my body could respond like that. It was mind blowing. Earth shattering. Heavenly. On all levels.

After he left, I stood in the same position for a long time. Afraid if I moved I would fall apart. Tears trickled down my cheeks, but I did not collapse into a puddle of tears as I desired to do. They grew cold on my skin. The light changed outside. I finally crossed to the bed, where I flopped on my stomach, staring at the sun's rays on my floor, understanding that they, too, offered a false, ever-changing warmth.

My dad was right. A rock star was the last person I should have been getting involved with in a first relationship after Steve. He hadn't said it to my face, but Gabe had loose lips.

I was surprised when I finally looked at the clock to see it was almost three in the afternoon. I got up, took a shower, and with nothing better to do, went to the store.

"Soph? I thought I was supposed to work your whole shift for you." DJ Oates furrowed his brow. "Did I get it wrong?"

"No, Deej. I just wanted to come in. If you have something you need to do, go ahead and clock out. But if you want to work, that's fine too."

"Well, there are a few things I could get done at home..."

"Then go. And thank you for coming in for me. Especially on such short notice."

"Sure. Anytime." He finished sliding a book onto a shelf.

"Go. I've got these." I indicated the box at his feet.

"Okay. Thanks." He hesitated, examining my face. "Is...everything all right?"

"Yes. Why?" But even I could tell my voice sounded fake.

"You seem...off?"

"Oh. Uhh...I'm groggy. I got up from a nap just a little while ago. But getting to work will help." I stepped forward and started shelving books, ignoring his probing gaze.

"Okay. Well, let me know if that feeling doesn't get better."

Fifteen minutes later, Gabe walked by the aisle I was working in and backtracked. "Well, lookie who's here."

I gave him a cursory glance, hoping he would go away, because he had an uncanny ability to read me. "Hey."

He sauntered toward me, a huge grin stretching his face. "I spotted Caleb's Jeep parked in front of your place this morning."

My heart raced. "You didn't tell Mom and Dad, did you?"

He hesitated long enough to make my chest tighten and my throat muscles constrict. "No. I didn't tell them." He put the books on a shelf. He turned, wearing a wicked smile. "And if you want to keep things that way, I'll be needing some concert tickets."

You're out of luck there, bro. "You've already gotten tickets."

"That was for my birthday."

"You're not getting any more tickets," I snapped.

"Whoa." He put his hands in the air. "Easy. You'd think getting laid would have made you less uptight."

I rolled my eyes. "Gabe..."

"I'm kidding." Elbowing me, he queried, "So...how was it?"

I continued to shelve books. "Do I ask you about your sex life?"

"No. But you should. Trudy and I tried this really funky position last night and—"

Abandoning my shelving instantly, I slammed the book I was holding down on top of the ones already shelved and covered my ears. "La, la, la, la, la! I don't want to hear this. La, la—"

He laughed. "Okay. I'll stop."

I didn't trust him and gave him a squinty glare.

"I promise."

Slowly I removed my hands.

"So where is lover boy? You guys hooking up again tonight?"

"No. He's gone." I tried to sound casual, but the words stuck in my throat. "He and the rest of the band packed and left a couple of hours ago."

His mouth hung open. "He left...without saying bye to me?"

"Don't worry. You'll get to see him at the concert in New York." *Which, ironically, is more than I will.* I accidentally put too much emphasis on "you'll," I hoped he wouldn't catch it.

His gaze narrowed. "He said goodbye to *you*, didn't he?"

I avoided eye contact. "Of course he did."

He cocked his head. "You're not telling me something."

"Gabriel Thomas!" We both jumped at the sound of our dad's voice. "Why in the world is it taking you so long to get those books for me?"

Gabe snatched them off the shelf. "They're right here."

"Well, come on with me then, and leave your sister alone." He peered at me. "I thought your mom said you weren't feeling good."

"I wasn't. But I felt better this afternoon and decided to come in."

He lifted his chin. "Oh. Did DJ leave then?"

"Yeah. He had something he needed to do."

"Ahh. Well, I'm glad you're feeling better."

"Thanks, Dad." He was easy to fool, fairly oblivious to anything not right under his nose. Gabe was a different story.

Dad's tone of voice changed, becoming harsher. "Come on, Gabe. I've got something I want you to do."

Gabe turned to me, saying under his breath, "Great."

"Come on. You've been lollygagging half the day. Do something to earn your pay."

I listened as Dad's griping got further and further away. I inhaled deeply and released it, suddenly tired. I drew my phone out to see how much time was left before my shift was over. There was a message notification. Caleb.

I MISS YOU ALREADY.

I opened my phone and scrolled through to check the time the message was sent. About two hours after he left. Part of me wanted to respond.

But what's the point? I don't need to prolong my misery by staying in touch with him.

I stuffed it back into my pocket and focused on my work for the rest of the evening, and pretty soon it was time to close. I stood on the doorstep with my mom while Dad locked the door.

Mom gave me a hug. "Good night, honey."

"'Night, Mom."

I watched them get into their car and waved as they drove off. I really didn't want to return to my place, where Caleb and I had spent an unforgettable night together; but I really didn't want to be in public either.

I should have gone to Mom and Dad's.

A figure crept from the shadows, and I screamed.

"Ha, ha, ha. I got you." Gabe was holding his sides as he laughed.

I smacked him on the arm. "That's not funny. You scared me to death!" I put my hand over my heart, which was thumping out of my chest. "I thought you and Trudy were seeing a movie."

"She didn't feel good, so I needed to take her home."

"Oh. That's too bad. Do you think she'll be all right?"

"Yeah. She was super tired—worked a double today—and she has this weird thing about being exhausted. She gets nauseous."

"Oh, yeah. You told me that. Well, if you were hoping to get a ride from Mom and Dad, they just left."

"No. My car's across the street." He pointed to his prized Mazda Miata. How had I missed that?

"Oh. What are you doing here then?"

"I came to check on you."

"Me?" I said, my voice a little too high-pitched. "Well, hate to disappoint you but the most fun I'm having tonight is crawling into my bed." I couldn't help but think of waking up with Caleb in that bed.

"I want to get the scoop on what's going on between you and Caleb."

"Caleb and me? There's nothing going on between Caleb and me. We went scuba diving yesterday and he left today."

His gaze was piercing. "Which leaves out what happened last night, when he spent the night with you."

"He...didn't spend the night," I scrambled for a reason his car would have been parked in front of my place. "He had a bit too much to drink and took an Uber home. He came back and got the car later."

He rubbed his chin. "Mmm. Almost believable."

"You know, I don't need to stand here and be grilled by you over my personal life. So, if you'll step aside..."

"Not a chance."

I wanted to scream, but people were walking across the street and a couple getting into their vehicle up the block. I narrowed my eyes on him. "Did Mom and Dad send you to spy on me?"

"No way. I'm insulted, ...unless they'd offered to pay me. Then I might have considered it."

I frowned. "Well, it's nice to know where your loyalties lie."

"We're not talking about me here. We're talking about you."

"Well, I'd rather we not be talking at all. It's late, and I want to go to bed."

"It's not late. Come on. It may make you feel better to get it off your chest."

"There's nothing to discuss."

"When are you going to see him again?"

I exhaled, exasperated. "I have no earthly idea. Maybe never."

"Is that what he said?"

"No. He said he wanted to see me again, but we all know that's a line. He's a rock star. Lies roll out as smoothly as bubblegum from a dispenser."

"Now you're sounding like Dad."

"Well, I..." I couldn't think. The way he was pressing me was wearing me down. We stared at each other for a moment. "Come on, Gabe. You know I have good reason to be distrustful."

I got the feeling I'd played right into his hand because he jumped on that. "You can't equate Caleb with Steve. Steve was a douche bag."

"But you didn't know that until he...did what he did."

He looked at the sidewalk, tapping his Nike's on the concrete. "Actually, I always knew he was a douche."

My eyes widened. "Well, why didn't you say something?"

He shrugged. "Because...you seemed so happy with him. I didn't want to spoil that simply because *I* didn't like the dude."

"Why didn't you like him?"

He continued to scratch at something at his feet. "Because I didn't like the way he treated you. He was always talking you down. Belittling you. That is, if he even let you talk at all. Caleb doesn't do that, from what I can see. He treated you well. He treated Mom well. Hell, he even treated Dad well when I wanted to jack him for questioning Caleb like that."

"And, most importantly," I countered. "He treated you well, huh? Of course you're backing Caleb. He gave you a weekend in New York, for God's sake."

"Listen, sis. Just because Steve broke your heart doesn't mean all guys are going to do the same."

"I know."

"Did Caleb ever do anything to make you believe he wasn't sincere about the things he said?

"Well, no, but—"

"So do you think it's fair to judge him on something he may or may not do?"

"Well, I…"

"Is it fair to judge him on *your* past, which he had nothing to do with?"

I stared at the ground and stayed silent. As much as I wanted to, I couldn't dispute his words.

"Is it fair to judge him on what other people in his profession might do?"

I snapped my head up. "No, it's not fair. But maybe I'm tired of being fair. Maybe fair's never gotten me anywhere."

He let that hang there for a moment. "That's not my sister. She always treats people fairly, whether they deserve it or not." He leaned in. "That's one of the many reasons I admire her. Don't let what Steve did ruin that. That's all I'm asking. Give Caleb a try."

I clicked my tongue. "It's not like I ran the boy out of town. He left." *Like Steve left.*

"I'm guessing he had an explanation for that. All I know is the guy who spent half the day at the hospital with you wouldn't leave unless he had a good reason. I saw the way he looked at you whenever you were together. That's not something someone can fake. Do you want to be alone all your life?"

"People don't have to be in relationships, you know. It's fine to live a solitary life."

"I won't deny that. But is that what *you* want?"

I huffed. *Is it really Gabe, goofy Gabe, who's lecturing me on life?* I put my hands on my hips and peered off to the side, unhappy my little brother had backed me into a verbal corner. Finally, I lowered my gaze and took in a long, clean breath, releasing it slowly. Without raising my head, I said weakly, "I'm tired, Gabe. I only want to go to bed. That's all. So, please..."

Then he did the weirdest thing of all. He enclosed me in his arms. I was stiff at first, but I really was tired. *That* I wasn't lying about. I relaxed, leaning into him. He separated from me finally, bending to make eye contact. "Just mull it over. Okay?"

Was he going to let me go now? "Yes. Yes, I'll meditate on it." I doubt I will be able to think of anything else.

"Good. Go upstairs and make sure you lock the door after you." He scanned the vicinity. "It would be easy for someone to keep tabs of your habits and take advantage of you being alone."

Was he worried, like the others, that someone was gunning for me? I studied him for a moment then slipped around him, going to the bottom of my stairs. I paused on the first step, gripping the railing. "Gabe?"

He was checking along the street, his hands in his pockets. "Huh?"

"Thanks for coming by to check on me."

He returned his focus to me. "Anytime, sis."

I climbed to my door and opened it. Once I'd turned to wave goodbye, he finally left.. Striding into the room, I spotted the blue paint on my sheets. He might have been gone, but he'd made his mark. One I couldn't erase. Staring at it, I kicked off my shoes and let them stay wherever they landed. I unbuttoned and unzipped my skirt, wishing it were him doing it. It slipped to the floor, and I abandoned the puddle of fabric, treading on it on my way to the other bed. I undid my bra clasp and worked it free underneath my top then folded the covers down and climbed in. Lying on my side facing my bed, I pulled the blanket up to my chin, tucking it underneath my shoulders.

"Alexa, switch off the lamps." The room was suddenly dark, except for the path the moon made leading to the other bed like a spotlight. Like the spotlight Caleb could have been standing in right now, fingers caressing the guitar strings like they'd caressed me, bringing me to life. I closed my eyes and let the ache for him wash over me. Some fifteen minutes later, I reached for my phone. I'd stashed it on the soda chair, which I'd replaced in its spot by the window before I left for work.

Rolling onto my back, I opened the screen to where it had been stuck all day. Caleb's message. *I miss you already.*

As if of their own accord, my fingers typed.

I MISS YOU TOO.

I flipped to face the wall, dropping the phone on the mattress nearby. It was somehow as if a weight had been lifted.

CHAPTER TWELVE

Caleb

I got on the bus, walking past where the other guys sat, and swung my bag into a seat on my left. I sat in the far corner on the right with my prop, my book, so as not to arouse suspicion. They wouldn't notice anyway. It wasn't unusual for me to separate myself and not join in their conversation.

I peered through the window as the "Welcome to Last Chance Beach" sign flew by, and moments later we crossed the bridge into Summerville. I turned my head to watch it get smaller and fade off into the distance. The bridge to Summerville seemed symbolic, a physical rift to mirror Sophie's and my emotional rift. I picked up my phone to message her, but started a dozen messages before dropping it into my lap with an exasperated sigh. The words simply wouldn't come together for me. I didn't know what to say to her. I stared out the window blankly as mile after mile fell between us. The confidence that I'd had when I'd left her place had waned, and then totally seeped out altogether, leaving me empty inside. As dead as the flowers I'd purchased for her and threw away at the hotel.

I became aware of movement and switched my focus. My bandmates were all walking toward me. Phoenix took a seat beside me, Dak and Levi opposite me.

"Why don't you just go ahead and text her like you want to?" Dak challenged.

I sat straighter. How did they know?

As if reading my mind, Phoenix said, "We could see you back here staring at your phone. And, uhh…" he glanced at the others, "you seem kind of depressed."

To avoid eye contact, I gazed at my reflection in the window, although not actually registering anything I was viewing. "What am I going to say to her? I'm abandoning her exactly like that shithead fiancé of hers."

Levi leaned forward, resting his arms on his knees. "Dude. It's so not the same."

"Isn't it?" The tires slapped relentlessly at the road. "You know, guys, I really do appreciate you trying to help, but, if you don't mind, I want to be alone."

They exchanged looks. Levi sighed and pushed off his knees to standing. "Who wants a shot of something?"

"I'm down," Dak said, following him to the bar in the front.

Phoenix shook his head. "I'm good." He moved to the seat across the aisle, dumping my bag on the floor.

I considered it briefly. "No thanks."

"Okay. But you know where we are if you want to join us."

They walked away, and I returned to studying the passing scenery.

In my mind I could see Sophie in that damned apron...and without it. That had been the best sex I'd ever had, bar none. And, strangely, it was centered more on being able to give to her, not about taking. I saw her face, smiling as I held my hand aloft and she twirled under it at that rooftop bar of hers. I remembered waking with her in my arms in that tiny bed, blissfully happy for the first time in forever. I was more alive with her. She made me alive.

"Boner?" Phoenix said quietly. Dak was being loud up front, so I was the only one who'd be able to hear him. He was lying on his side, now using my duffle as a pillow. He started over. "Caleb," the name sounded odd coming from of his mouth. "Call her. Or at least text her. You'll feel better if you do."

I nodded, but said nothing. I thought on it. A few minutes later, I grabbed my phone and texted the words that kept running through my head.

I MISS YOU ALREADY.

It was ridiculous. We'd been gone only a couple of hours.

Having sent it, I continued to dully stare at the lights passing by the window.

Could I have done something different? Handled things better?

I blinked, and suddenly it was dark outside. Phoenix was snoring softly. I don't know where the hell Dak and Levi were. I checked my phone. Nothing.

Maybe she's working. No, she got someone to cover for her.

Somewhere near Nashville my phone buzzed and I jumped, knocking it to the floor. I scrambled to find the damn thing and about pulled something in my neck and arm retrieving it, but she had responded.

I MISS YOU TOO.

It wasn't much, but it was a reply.

"Huh." With a big smile on my face, I stretched out and relaxed, falling asleep almost instantly.

We were in Boston. In had been nearly two weeks since we left Last Chance Beach, and I was chomping at the bit to see Sophie the next night in The Big Apple. We'd been talking every day, or texting if our schedules didn't mesh, but tomorrow would be the first day I'd see her since we'd departed.

We finished our encore, and I was headed back to my dressing room to hit the shower, a sweaty mess.

"Hey! Caleb!"

I spun and if I'd had dentures, they would have fallen out. *Chris Rider.* I'll admit, my initial response was pure fear. It was only natural. The guy had been the source of my nightmares for all of junior high. He'd lived to torture me, tripping me in the cafeteria with a tray full of chili burritos, calling me to describe all the lewd and violent acts he hoped were done to me, leaving a used condom in my locker...the list went on and on. It culminated in an incident I still bore the scars from.

It was long after the last bell. I'd gotten caught up in a book and probably missed my ride, but as I was hurrying down the empty hall, Chris and three of his Neanderthal buddies rounded the corner. Chris had a baseball bat. He wasn't on the baseball team.

It was the janitor who brought me to consciousness, kind of shaken by it all. He probably thought I was dead at first, that's how much blood was pooled near me. He called an ambulance and insisted I call my parents. I must have turned on his speaker as he passed it to me because my mom's irritated voice resounded in the hallway. It was her bridge day, which was sacred. Just like her tennis lesson day, her ladies' auxiliary meetings, and whenever she was worshiping at Tiffany's or Saks Fifth Avenue, or Bergdorf Goodman...

"Honestly, Caleb," she huffed. "You never give me a moment's rest. Are you sure you have to go to the hospital?"

"Mr. Mier already called an ambulance."

"Fine, then," she spat. "Make sure they take you to Lenox Hill, not that filthy Mt. Sinai. I will meet you there. Do not say a word to anyone about what happened. We don't need this hitting the papers. Tell them...tell them you were mugged. That's easy enough to believe. It happens every damn day in this city. Don't mention those kids, especially Wesley Duggan. His mom is the president of our Lady's Club. Boys will be boys, Caleb. You need to learn to defend yourself." The line went dead. I slowly hung it up. Defend myself against four attackers. I'd have to be freaking Daredevil or some other superhero.

"Son," Mr. Mier said, "I don't normally put down others' parenting skills, because I know I wasn't exactly the perfect father to my kids, but..." he waved a hand in front of me, "that's not boys being boys. That's assault and battery."

By the time my mom got to the hospital, my eyes were nearly swollen shut, but I could see through a slit of light. She was at the foot of my bed, dabbing at her face when the police came in. She railed on them for not doing more to stop what had happened to her "poor son." As soon as they were gone, she tucked her dry tissue in her purse and said, "I need to go now, Caleb. I have a nail appointment. Call Robbie when you're discharged." Robbie was a guy my parents kept on retainer for those occasions they needed a ride and snapped their fingers. He was there four days later, after they discharged me. My parents hadn't visited once. The doctors said I was lucky to only have a few skull fractures, a broken arm, sixteen stitches in my lip and twenty-five in the gash on my head, and three broken ribs. I didn't feel lucky.

Chris had found me the first day of high school and apologized. It seemed he'd had an epiphany of sorts as he, get this, was mugged over the summer. He never bothered me again. Never talked to me again.

Until this moment. He embraced me and I flinched a little. "Good to see you. Oh, you *are* sweaty." He recoiled, wrinkling his nose in disgust. "These are my clients, Keith Mackelroy and Danny Robins. Gentlemen, I give you Caleb Winthrop. They didn't believe we were friends. Tell them."

I glanced from him to them and back. Chris had a sort of desperate, pleading look in his eyes.

I should out him right now. Tell them what a complete dick he was in junior high, and probably still is.

But I was too tired for revenge of the nerds, and I wanted to get to the hotel to call Sophie. "We went to school together," I said flatly.

"See! I told you." He laughed. "Good seeing you again." He gave me a once-over. "You've gotten big. Muscular, you know?"

He had whittled away to nothing. It made me wonder if he was on meth.

"Well, guys. Should we hit the Yale Club?"

One said, "Sounds good. I could use a drink."

But I couldn't let it go at that. "Umm…gentlemen, would you please excuse us? I want to have a little private chat with Chris here. He'll return in a few minutes."

I took him across the hall and out of sight and slammed him against the wall. "I covered for you because I'm not the asshole you are," I hissed so as not to be overheard. "But you get one pass, Chris. *One.* Got it?"

He nodded, looking like he was going to piss his pants, which kind of ruined my fun.

"I never want to catch you backstage again, or we'll see exactly how tough you are without a baseball bat." I gave him one last shove and released him.

I stuck my head around the corner and waved to his clients. "Nice meeting you." Then I did a one-eighty and left.

A half hour later I had my phone to my ear waiting for her to answer. I was in my hotel room, and I yanked the sheets loose from under the mattress, threw the extra pillows to the other side of the bed—where she should be—and flopped down.

"Well, hello, there." She sounded a bit sleepy.

I got the pillow I'd just rid myself of and placed it behind me with the other one there. "Hi, baby. Were you asleep?"

"No. I had to get up to silence the phone anyway."

I smiled and put my free hand on the back of my neck. "Bullshit. You keep the phone right by your bed so you can charge it."

"You noticed that?"

I dropped my voice a register. "I notice everything about you, gorgeous."

"Mmm…you gave me a shiver."

"I'm gonna give you more than that the moment I get you alone tomorrow."

"Oh, stop. You'll get me all aroused and I'll never sleep. Any stories?"

This had become our thing. We'd tell each other whatever interesting tidbits we'd experienced since we last spoke. I filed them in the recesses of my mind during the day knowing I would talk to her in the evening.

I considered telling her the story of my encounter with Chris, but I didn't want to let him anywhere near her, even in conversation.

"Well...Dak's been acting kind of strange."

"How so?"

"Quiet."

"That is strange."

I switched positions, lying on my back, and again discarded the extra pillow. I had taken my shirt off but still had my jeans on. I didn't care. I'd sleep like the dead anyway. I lifted my legs so I could pull the sheets down and slid under them, then rethought the belt and unbuckled it so I could remove it.

"Yeah...and he's been disappearing into his room a lot. He always stays in the living room area until he's ready to hit the sack."

"What do you think is going on?" She sounded more awake. That was my little curious girl who I loved so much.

"I don't know. We've heard him on the phone too, but can't make out what he's saying."

"A woman?"

I hit the switch for the bedside lamp, which left only the bathroom light on. "That's what we're figuring."

"No way! The Great Dakota Blackstone has fallen? It can't be. ...maybe he's a spy devising some nefarious plot, talking to someone in Istanbul."

I grinned in the dark. I loved this woman. We spoke the same language. "I doubt that. I'm sure they hire people who are a tad more unobtrusive and quieter. Although it's perhaps a more likely scenario than him finding a woman." She laughed and I sighed. "I can't wait to see you tomorrow. Remember, I'll be wearing a ball cap and shades, and there will be a gigantic guy with me who looks like he could play for the Pittsburgh Steelers."

"How ever will I tell you two apart?" she teased.

I chuckled. "Yeah, right." Not wanting our time together to end, I searched for something more to say. "Gabe ready to go?"

"Are you kidding? I think he's been ready since the day you gave him the tickets."

"I'm sorry I couldn't get you into first class."

"That's fine. It's no big deal."

"But Gabe will lord it over you."

"Oh, he's *so* going to lord it over me. No question." She yawned.

"You're tired. I should probably let you go."

"It is kind of your fault with all your dirty talk last night. How's a gal supposed to sleep after you get her that revved up?"

A little shiver ran through me. I curled onto my side. "So," I cleared my throat, "what, pray tell, did you do to relax yourself?"

She laughed. "Uh-uh-uh. Don't you start again. I don't want you getting nasty again until you're with me," she added slyly.

I threw myself onto my back with a groan. "You're killing me here. Now how will *I* sleep?"

"Not my concern...tonight."

She was playing with me, and she knew exactly how to do it too. "I can't wait to see you. And...it's not solely because of all the sex stuff." My voice became soft. "I've really missed you."

She became serious too. "I've missed you too. But...if we go to sleep, then when we wake, it'll almost be time."

"Good night, Sophie."

"Good night."

I flirted with the idea of telling her again I loved her, but I figured the ball was in her court on that one. I disconnected and mentally went through our conversation again. And then began over from the first time we'd met. I was both warmed by interacting with her and aching to hold her at the same time. Tomorrow couldn't come soon enough.

The first one off the flight was Gabe.

He waved. "Caleb."

So much for my disguise.

It consisted of fake glasses and a hat saying, I heart New York. Most of the time I could get away with just that. People tended to overlook a guy in a ball cap, chalking him up as merely another tourist.

Gabe was linking arms with a slight blonde who was all of five-foot-nothing. He crossed the carpeted gate area to where I was waiting in the wide corridor with Andy, my bodyguard. He was only around when I was playing at a bigger venue, like Madison Square Garden, where we were playing tonight. Anywhere in NYC, in fact, or any large metropolitan areas. It wasn't like I was concerned about my safety, but it helped keep the chaos under control, for the most part, because people were more likely not to approach if Andy was in the picture. He was actually a really nice guy, but he could be scary as fuck.

"Hey, Gabe." I shook his hand and clapped him on the back. "How was the flight?"

"Great," he said enthusiastically. "I'd like to introduce you to my girl-friend Trudy. Trudy, this is...Caleb Winthrop." He said the last like he was unveiling a statue in a museum.

I dipped my head. "Nice to meet you, Trudy. Welcome to New York."

Gabe had become aware of Andy and was gawking at him. Person after person filed past us. "Lot of people on there, huh?"

"Yes. Overbooked." Gabe hadn't taken his focus from the looming presence behind me.

"But your sister was on there, right?"

He twisted to consider me and blinked. It took several seconds for my question to register with him. "Oh," he half looked over his shoulder, "yeah, she was on there. Sitting back with the riffraff."

But I wasn't listening to him anymore. The object of my attention was one Sophie Lockhart, who had just passed through the doorway and was searching the crowd, even prettier than when I'd left, somehow. I had a sudden urge to check one of the gift shops for paint. Her gaze landed on me, flicked away for a moment, then returned. Her eyes lit up, and slowly a grin spread across her face.

Although I hadn't commanded them, my feet moved in her direction as she moved in mine. Right before she reached me, she dropped her bag and threw herself into my arms. I let out a breath I think I'd been holding since I last saw her, lifting her off her feet. "I've missed you," I murmured in her ear.

"I've missed you too."

"Oh, man. You really should avoid *those people* in Coach. Most unsavory."

Without breaking our embrace, Sophie smacked Gabe. Andy cleared his throat and I glanced at him. He nodded his head to point to a gaggle of three girls who were twittering while studying us. It was harder to get by, sometimes, in New York, as people were semi-used to seeing celebrities and were on the alert for them. Same with L.A. "We better hit the road." Besides, I wanted to get Sophie alone.

When we got to the two SUVs, I opened the door of the first for Sophie, letting Gabe know the second was for him and Trudy.

"Since we're going to the same place, we could ride with you guys," Gabe suggested.

Sophie paled. "Oh. Well..." She looked at me desperately.

"We're actually having lunch first, and, unfortunately, I only made reservations for two." *True, to a point.* They didn't know the hotel was right around the corner from Rockefeller Center—where I planned to eat—and they didn't need to know. Nor did they know that, while I had paid for a room at the Marriott Marquis for Sophie, I was hoping she would stay with me at my place. "I'll send a car to take the three of you to the concert later." I waved and, following Sophie, climbed into the vehicle.

"I thought I'd have time to change before lunch," Sophie said nervously.

"You will." I kissed her. "I want to show you my place. We can change there, then head out to lunch."

"Your place?" she said, inching closer and sliding her hand behind my neck. "We'll never make it to lunch."

I brushed my lips over hers. "That's why the reservations aren't until three. You might want to avert your gaze, gentlemen," I said to Andy, who sat in front with my driver. "It's about to get X-rated in here." I twisted so my back was facing them and took her into my arms, swallowing her up in a kiss.

She surrendered briefly, then giggled and squirmed. "Caleb!"

I reluctantly moved away, glancing in the rearview mirror as I shifted. Amusement shone in Andy's eyes. "Okay. I'll be good. For the moment." She squeezed my hand as I settled into my seat. For the rest of the trip, I played tour guide, wrapping my arm around her and pointing to various sights outside our windows. She eagerly took it all in, and I enjoyed showing her what I considered my hometown.

When we got to my building, the doorman beat me to her, helping her out as I approached. "John Milton, I'd like you to meet Sophie. Sophie, this is John Milton."

He tipped his hat. "Nice to meet you, ma'am."

"And you," Sophie returned. "Oh," she whirled, "my bag."

I urged her forward. "Don't worry about that. They'll get it." As I was speaking, John snapped his fingers and two porters rushed to the car. She watched them over her shoulder as I escorted her into the building. The elevator man greeted us with a smile. "Mr. Winthrop. Welcome home." Even though he was new, I didn't have to tell him my floor, he knew.

On the way up, she clutched my hand in both of hers. "This is a beautiful place."

I drew her arm through mine and kissed her temple. "I'm glad you like it."

A few seconds later, the doors opened at the penthouse, and we entered the foyer of sorts. I tossed my hat on a table near the door. "Welcome to my place." She took a few steps forward, and I paused to observe her. Directly in front of us and down a few stairs was the sunken living room. A fire was going in the fireplace in one corner, doing its best to make the place feel as cozy as it could get with such an open layout. Two large L-shaped couches framed the area, and a wet bar stood off to one end. The New York skyline was the backdrop with a window running the length of the wall, a balcony beyond that. To the left was the dining area, and the kitchen was spacious but tucked in a corner. A wide balcony spanned two sides with some pretty amazing views.

To the right, the bedroom stretched behind a glass wall, visible now as the privacy curtains were open. I could see Sophie's suitcase was already on a stand in the corner. It never failed to amaze me how quick and unobtrusive the porters were. They must have had a separate rocket-speed elevator somewhere they kept hidden.

My gaze raked the area, worried something might be askew, but as usual the housekeeping crew had done a fabulous job. Still, my heart rate accelerated slightly. Why was I so nervous about her reaction? What was not to like? Before I'd met her, I got a little thrill out of showing my digs to women, knowing they'd be impressed...and appreciative. But Sophie...with Sophie it was different in so many ways. Initially her features were bright, but the more she surveyed the area, the weaker her smile became. She took the few steps down to the living room and ran her hand along the top of the blood-red couch.

"What?"

She startled at the sound of my voice and turned to me with wide eyes, not saying anything.

I crossed to her and put my hands on either side of her face, searching her. "What's wrong?"

She rolled a shoulder in a fashion meant to be casual, but I felt her muscles tighten. "Nothing."

I tilted my head, trying to read her. "Don't lie to me, Soph."

"I'm not. I—"

I frowned, and she looked at the carpet, rubbing the nap with her foot. "It's just..." She scanned the room again.

I caught our reflection in the window. I didn't even resemble myself. I flashed back to a time I caught my reflection in my early days, a girl bent over the couch while I fucked the hell out of her from behind. At the time I'd been cocky about it. Now it made me shiver.

"You must think my place is a dump."

"What?" The thought had never crossed my mind.

"To tell you the truth, I'm kind of embarrassed." She took a step backward, dropping her gaze and speaking rapidly. "Maybe this is a mistake. Maybe I shouldn't have come. I—"

"Hey," I said softly, sliding my hand under her chin to lift her face. "Sophie, your place is like the Taj Mahal compared to some of the places we lived in before my dad hit it big on the market. Shit. I named the freakin' rats in the places I grew up in." I shimmied her in closer by her hips. "You are *right* where you should be. Next to me." I kissed her softly and she gradually gave in. "Come on." I took her hands and led her to the bedroom, standing her next to the bed. "Let me show you how much I've missed you."

I pulled down the comforter on the bed. The expensive sheets beneath it might be a playground for our lovemaking later, but at the moment they were the backdrop for my worship of her. I got rid of her clothing unhurriedly, piece by piece, and got some lotion from the bathroom to smooth on her skin. I had her lie on her stomach and took my own clothes off, straddling her back to first massage her, then bringing my mouth into play wherever it most affected her. After I slipped inside her, I moved slowly. Painfully slowly. Until she was trembling with need, clutching me and moaning my name as

I brought her to ecstasy. We napped for a bit, her warm, naked body beside me.

I woke on my stomach, cracking an eye open. She was silhouetted against the frosted glass of my shower wall, like some crazy-sexy peep show. I instantly became hard with desire. She was singing. I concentrated to hear her voice above the noise of the water. I recognized our song and smiled. If other girls had done this, I would have known they were playing me, baiting me, asking me to join them. I would have debated. Am I too hung over? Too sore from the hard sex the night before or my stage antics? Do I even want a piece of ass right now?

With her, I knew she was completely unaware I was watching. I twisted to sit on the edge of the bed for a moment, then padded as quietly as possible across the room. The door squeaked, and she spun to see what had caused it, then turned, seeming to fold herself around her nude figure. Could she be embarrassed?

I guess I should have knocked.

I cleared my throat. "Do you mind if I hop in with you?"

Did I just ask her if I could join her? So weird.

But she made everything new. New and wonderful.

We lathered each other up, and I even knelt so she would wash my hair. When she was finished, she said, "I should get dressed."

"Okay. I'll be through shortly." I gave her backside a swat as she left.

"Hey." She covered it and threw me a fake glare over her shoulder.

I stayed under the hot water another five minutes, then got out and dressed. I was examining myself in the mirror, tugging my cuffs down, when she came from behind me. "You look very handsome." I wore a charcoal gray suit with a startlingly blue shirt. "Is that new?"

"No. I may have worn this to the MTV awards." I frowned. "Or the Oscars?"

"Oscars?"

"*Unbridled Passion* was in that James Bond movie."

"Oh, yeah." She stepped to the side and checked her own reflection. "Well, this dress is new. It has not been worn to any award shows."

I held up a finger. "Yet."

"Yet? What do you mean?"

"I may take you as my guest to the next MTV Awards."

"Oh, yeah? When's that?"

"May, I believe."

She laughed. "May? Aren't you getting ahead of yourself, buster?"

"No." I slid my arms around her and nuzzled her neck. She leaned back against me and we looked at each other in the mirror. "I'm really glad you're here."

"Thank you for inviting me."

I caught the time on my watch. "Shoot. We better get going."

Although it was close, we took a car to Rockefeller Center for our lunch in the Rainbow Room. It was easier to duck in and out without being spotted by fans.

I initially made our reservations hoping to impress her, but regretted that, considering the extravagant accoutrements might make her even more uncomfortable than she had been earlier. We had a table tucked away near the stage, where classical musicians played soft music. Surrounding us were sweeping views of New York City, dominated by the Empire State Building. White linen was draped over the tables which were covered with cut crystal and elaborate floral displays. The bottle of their best champagne was iced and waiting for us as I'd instructed.

After we ordered, we admired and discussed the view. I noted all the places I recognized. Then I raised my glass. "To the beautiful woman sitting across the table from me, to our weekend in New York, and many, many more weekends spent together." She wore a simple but elegant black dress, sparkling earrings with a matching necklace, and she put every other woman in the room to shame.

She drank but chuckled a little as she put her flute down.

"What?"

"I just recognized that this is a far cry from the Shellfish, Mohawks, and ripped jeans. You are a man with many facets, Caleb."

I shrugged. "I want to keep you guessing."

The waiter arrived with our meal. Sophie stared at her plate. "Speaking of guessing...is this what I ordered?"

The menu was filled with dishes that would make a gourmet enthusiast weep, but the elaborate presentation made the food unrecognizable.

I chuckled. "I think so."

"It's too pretty to eat."

"Eat it anyway, you goofus."

After dinner I twirled her around the polished dance floor with its design of lighter and darker wood that reminded me of a compass. The lovemaking or the champagne, or both, had relaxed her, and we were having a blast. We were the solo couple on the dance floor, which was usually used more at night. I was laughing with her, spinning her out to the end of my arm's length, at the moment I spied them. The shock caused me to lose hold of her, which made her stumble a little, but she didn't fall.

"Mother." I kissed her cheek stiffly then offered my father my hand. "Sir."

He nodded, shaking my hand but not saying anything.

"Caleb. Fancy seeing you here. Are you in town with that band of yours?"

That platinum-record, award-winning band, you mean?

I hated how my mom always acted like what I did was just a lark.

"Yes. We're playing Madison Square Garden tonight."

"I see." She arched her brows and stared down her nose at Sophie.

I gritted my teeth. *Don't forget you were a hotel maid once, Mom.*

"Who is this?" she said lightly, but the edge was in her eyes.

"Umm..." I was so caught off-guard by running into them, I was tongue-tied.

She scrutinized Sophie. "That's a lovely dress, dear," she said in a way clearly meant to imply the opposite.

"Oh." Sophie glanced at her dress and brushed a hand over it, color rising in her cheeks. "I wasn't sure...since it was lunch..." She trailed off, apparently as speechless as me.

Dad, in the meantime, was also checking Sophie out, but without disdain, rather, with unveiled lust.

"Well, nice to see you, Caleb. Do stop by the condo sometime. And bring your lovely...friend...here." It wasn't an invitation so much as a challenge. My mom tugged on my father's arm. "For God's sake, David, close your mouth," she sniped as they walked away.

Sophie and I looked at each other. She slowly turned and walked to her seat. I followed. She sat, staring at the tablecloth.

"That was David Winthrop," she said finally.

"You know who he is?"

"Of course I know who he is, Caleb. I'm not that much of a backwater idiot. The man's face has been printed on half of the *Forbes* and *Money* magazines I've shelved." Her gaze pinballed all across the tablecloth. "I can't believe this."

"It's no big deal."

"No big deal your father is one of the richest men in the world."

"Well, I don't think he's quite one of the richest men in the world..."

She planted her elbows on the table and ran her fingers through her hair, dislodging it from the intricate weave of braids she was wearing. "I can't believe this."

"It's really not that big—"

"If you say it's not that big a deal again, I'm going to throttle you," she snapped.

"Oookay."

She looked at me finally. "You should be married to some oil baron's debutante daughter, not with me."

"I don't want—"

"I don't care what you want." She was becoming irrational now. She glanced around. "I don't belong here. You come from a world of silk sheets and chandeliers. I come from a world of paint-smeared sheets and dusty books."

The talk of her paint-stained sheets made me tighten in response. I took her hand across the table and was glad she didn't pull away. "Sophie, I'm the same guy as the one you knew before you found out who my dad is. Nothing's changed." She stared at me but didn't speak. "Yes, my parents had money when I was growing up, but I'm happy to say that hasn't meant a whole lot to me over the years. I'll admit," I tapped a finger on the table, "I brought you here to impress you. But—"

She put a hand on her chest. "Impress *me*? Why would *you* have to impress me?"

I shrugged. "I don't know. I just wanted to kind of...sweep you off your feet." I rushed past that. "My point is...if I never stepped foot in The Rainbow Room again, I'd be fine with that. If I never visited Last Chance Beach again, I'd be fine with that."

She blinked, taken aback.

"But—" I brought her hand to my lips and kissed her knuckles. "—if I never saw you again? That would devastate me. Can't you see that?"

She squinted at me as if trying to see something through a haze. "I—" She tilted her head and lowered her gaze.

I took her other hand and inched forward. "Come on. We were having such a good time. Don't let them ruin that for us."

She exhaled shakily then looked up. "You're right. I'm sorry. It simply—caught me off-guard. Who your father is, and what background you come from, that's not who you are now." She leaned in, and, unbelievably, smiled. "And who you are now is pretty special."

She kissed me and I sighed into it. We'd dodged another bullet. It seemed like that was what we were constantly doing, avoiding fireballs meant to derail us.

"Being with me won't be easy. It comes with a lot of crap, like me being away from you. Fans not giving us a moment's peace... That's part of the reason I came here today. I knew no fan would interrupt us for an autograph here. Everybody here thinks they're far more famous than me."

"You're wrong. Being with you is as easy as breathing. I am more myself with you than with anyone else. The rest, the rest is merely annoyance. We can handle it."

Her swinging back to center, accepting who I was and where I came from, was nothing short of amazing. Where seconds before she was on the verge of losing it, now she was so confident we were meant to be together. She said being with me was like breathing. Being with her was like deeply inhaling fresh air. To have someone who understood me the way she did...we were simpatico. I was no longer alone. "I love you, Sophie."

She put a hand on the side of my face. "I love you too, and I want this to work."

From there on out, she believed in us unwaveringly.

CHAPTER THIRTEEN

Sophie

It came down to making a decision. Did I listen to what society says, to what my own experience said, or did I trust in him, open myself to him, give myself to him freely, no matter the cost. I had to put myself all in and risk losing everything. Put my heart on the line. And I chose to do just that. If being with Caleb was a mistake, then it would be a mistake I embraced fully.

We went back to his place to change our duds, to trade dress and heels for jeans, a black halter top, and short, sexy boots. He morphed from a suit-wearing son of a socialite to a ripped jeans-and-T-shirt-wearing rock star. He even spiked his shorter hair a little to give him an edge. Then we called a car to take us to the Marriott, and I got my key to the room we really wouldn't be using much.

Caleb felt bad for leaving me alone when he went to sound check, but I assured him I'd be fine curled up in bed catching a nap. The excitement over leaving for New York had made it hard to sleep the previous night. An hour later, I met Trudy and Gabe, and we took the car which had been rented for us, along with the driver, to Madison Square Garden. I got out, and Gabe was gawking at the building.

I looked from him to the building and back. "What?"

"It's circular."

I surveyed it again to see if I was missing something. "Yyyes?"

"Why is it circular?"

"I don't know. Maybe to maximize seating?"

"Then why did they call it Madison *Square* Garden if it's clearly—" he gestured "—round?"

I peered at Trudy, and she shrugged with a smile. "You did not just ask that."

"I did," he said indignantly. "It makes no sense."

I shuffled forward with the throng being herded through multiple doors. "You know that song, 'Give My Regards to Broadway?'"

He frowned. "Yes."

"Well, it says remember me to Herald Square..."

"You're not telling me Herald Square is round too?"

I rolled my eyes. "You're hopeless."

Once inside, the buzz of the concert-goers was considerably louder. It was like the whole place was vibrating with expectancy. Like the building had a pulse and that pulse was beating with mine, at a slightly higher than normal rate. I pulled out of the flow of the crowd. "Caleb gave me a number to text when we got here. Some Matt guy is going to come meet us and lead us to a spot right in front of Caleb."

"Sweet! I guess there are some advantages to sleeping with—" Trudy sent an elbow to his solar plexus— "Why did you do that?"

I gave him a baleful expression. "Because she beat me to it. Really, Gabe?"

Over his shoulder, I caught sight of a large man with short-cropped hair wearing a security shirt, headed in our direction.

"I think I see Matt."

They turned to see as I called, "Are you Matt?"

"Yes. You must be Sophie. You look exactly like he described you." I wondered how Caleb had described me as Matt addressed Gabe. "Hi. Nice to meet you."

Gabe shook his hand. "I'm Gabe, and this is my girlfriend Trudy."

He nodded. "How are you tonight?"

Trudy was on cloud nine. "Pretty excited, if you want to know the truth."

"Ahh, understandable. Well, I'm here to take you to a spot by the stage. Right this way." He led us through a curtained area behind us, then addressed Trudy again. "Have you ever seen them play?"

"Yes, but only in a small venue."

We followed Matt, descending some stairs. He and Trudy were having to shout to be heard over the surrounding racket, but, even so, it was difficult to catch their conversation.

"Oh, small venues are the best. But I don't think you'll be disappointed. Insatiable Fire puts on a really good show. Wherever they are."

"I take it you've seen them before?"

"Oh, yeah. I travel with the band. I'm a roadie/security guard/errand boy. Best job I've ever had."

"So they're not prima donnas?"

He burst out laughing. "Oh, hell no. They're as down-to-earth as you get." He lifted his head. "Hey, Lance."

Lance was apparently the guy checking bracelets and letting people on the floor. We didn't have bracelets.

"We never got armbands," Gabe said to me, half in a panic.

Matt caught his statement. "You won't need them." He waved at the opening Lance stood next to. "These three are with me." He stood aside so we could cross through the opening in the half wall separating the seats from the floor.

I'm pretty sure the Rangers play here. This is so cool.

Matt skirted the crowd on the edge, leading us forward quickly until we were near the stage. "Excuse me," he said to two tall guys at the front. "Will you please make room for these V.I. P. guests?"

"Sure," they said with the joviality surely brought on by the twenty-dollar beers they were sloshing about. "Join us."

"This is awesome," Trudy said under her breath to me.

"I agree."

The guys we'd booted back engaged Gabe. At concerts, everybody is your friend. Automatically, there is a shared interest in music. "So, are you here for the opener or for Insatiable Fire?"

Gabe rolled a shoulder. "I like both."

"Have you heard either of them play before?"

Gabe acted casual. "Oh, sure. I've seen Insatiable Fire tons of times."

"This is our first," the taller of the two said. "We were told they put on a great show?"

Nodding, Gabe replied, echoing Matt's—who had now disappeared—earlier words, "You won't be disappointed."

"So how'd you get V.I.P. status? You buy one of those meet and greet things?" the shorter of the twin towers asked.

"Oh, no. We couldn't afford that. My sister here," he jerked his thumb over his shoulder at me, "is sleeping with Caleb Winthrop."

I leaned into Trudy. "I'm going to pound him."

"Who?" one of the guys asked.

"The lead guitarist."

They looked at each other. "You mean Boner?"

"Yes. Ouch!"

I had grabbed Gabe's ear and dragged him off a couple of feet. "If you tell one more person about Caleb's and my relationship, I'll torture you through all eternity."

"Okay, okay. Geesh! I'd imagined you wouldn't be embarrassed of you and Caleb."

"I'm not. I simply don't need my sex life broadcast to everyone in the arena."

He shrugged. "Your choice." He twisted his head. "I need to go work on mine."

Gabe returned to Trudy's side, and I was grateful when the lights went down for the opening band—Just Short of Chaos—to take the stage. Grateful because Gabe and Trudy were making out, with no sense of decorum whatsoever, and I really didn't need to see my little brother doing that. Like, *ever*. Just Short of Chaos was phenomenal, and I worried they might have stolen Insatiable Fire's thunder, until our boys hit the stage and the place went utterly wild. Caleb started the show doing his regular thing but quickly switched to searching the crowd. He spotted me, and his smile brightened as he moved in our direction.

"Holy shit!" a voice came from behind me. "You guys really do know Boner."

"What? Did you think I was lying?" Gabe said indignantly.

"No, no," his new friends assured him. "But maybe exaggerating some."

The one thing the bigger venues had that the smaller ones lacked were the ginormous video screens. On occasion the camera would focus in on Caleb's hands as he played, and it was crazy how fast his fingers flew and still found all the notes. I mean, Phoenix definitely had some pipes, Dakota could play bass, and Levi was a killer drummer, but—at least in my eyes—Caleb was in another league altogether. I'd never realized before how much their sound could be credited to him. Yes, it had a lot to do with how Levi wrote the music and Phoenix sang the lyrics, but his playing set it apart.

"Holy shit," I said under my breath. "I'm sleeping with him." Realizing what I'd said, my gaze flashed to Gabe, but he was oblivious, as usual.

As the evening went on, I could tell Trudy was becoming more and more miffed by Gabe, and I didn't blame her. Ever since Insatiable Fire took the stage, he had been ignoring her and chatting with the two guys who now seemed to—erroneously—hold him in a place of respect. I think the clincher came when Trudy tried to get his attention, and he held a hand up to quiet her while he continued his conversation. Her jaw dropped and she stormed off. She and Gabe called it quits every other week over something or other, and they'd had some real knock down drag outs. Trudy was pretty meek and quiet, except in her relationship with my brother. I had a feeling I would see another side of her tonight. She hadn't returned twenty minutes later, and I tapped on Gabe's shoulder. He tried doing the same thing to quiet me, but I took his outstretched hand and twisted his arm behind his back.

"Ouch! What the hell did you do that for?"

"Trudy has been gone a long time."

He looked around. "She has?"

"Yes, Gabe. You've been completely ignoring her."

He stepped aside and got on his phone. His face morphed into a grimace, with several pain-filled expressions following. "Shit." He peered at me, shouting over the music. "Where did she go in?"

"I don't know. Back...that direction. Somewhere away from the stage."

He rolled his eyes. "Real helpful."

"Well, what do you want me to say? Why don't you text her and ask her where she is?"

"Because." He shut his mouth and his gaze darted about.

"Because she's not talking to you, right?"

"Maybe," he said, tightlipped. "Shit. I need to find her."

"And...?" I prodded.

"And apologize. I get it, sis."

I smiled. He could be a dolt at times, but he knew how to fess up to it and apologize.

Caleb was following what was going on with concern and curiosity, but relaxed when he saw I was not upset.

After their second encore, Matt magically appeared. "I can show you backstage now."

"Oh...umm..." I looked toward the rear of the stadium where we had come in.

"I've already got someone to take your brother and his girlfriend to us. If you could just text him and let him know Max—instead of Matt—will meet them here... Boy. That could be confusing. I should have chosen someone with a different name."

"That's okay. I'm sure he can figure it out." *Fairly sure. He did wonder why the stadium wasn't square...* I texted.

"Tell him Max has bright orange hair. That ought to help. Big guy with bright orange hair and a beard."

I added his directions and put my phone away. "Ready."

"Please?"

"Pretty please?"

Gabe's two friends were giving us puppy dog eyes and putting their hands together as if in prayer.

Matt smiled. "Sorry, guys." He leaned over and quietly added. "You're not sleeping with a band member. Or are you?"

They glanced at each other and hope sprang in their faces. Both opened their mouths to speak at once. "I'm sleeping with Dakota."

Matt tilted his head skeptically. "You both are?"

The shorter guy replied. "It's kind of a...threesome thing. Very kinky," he added, wriggling his brows.

Matt laughed, hesitating. "Okay. Wait here. I'll be back shortly with some passes."

"Yes!"

"Thanks, man. This is awesome!"

They high-fived each other, and Matt chuckled, continuing to lead the way. He opened a door near the stage, and we entered a wide corridor. Dakota's voice bellowed above the general hubbub. He was the first to spot me as we rounded a corner. "Well, look at what the Matt dragged in."

Caleb was behind him, bent over a drinking fountain. He straightened, and I rushed to him like I had in the airport. It was like every cell of mine was urging me into his arms. He swallowed me into his embrace and kissed my upturned lips. All three of his bandmates hollered. "Whoo!" With Dakota adding, "Get it, Boner!"

I ignored them. "You were...amazing. I'm just...so impressed."

Dakota jostled me with his elbow. "You mean turned on, don't you?"

"Well, yes. That too."

They laughed, surprised, I think, by my honesty.

Caleb seemed a little uncomfortable with the praise. I would have thought he'd be used to it by now. "Where are Gabe and Trudy?"

"Well, they—"

"There he is!" someone shouted.

I twisted to see who it was. A guy was approaching us. Caleb, for some reason, shifted, putting himself between me and the stranger.

"I thought I told you not to show your face here again, Chris."

"You did," he said nonchalantly. "Who's this pretty young thing?" He tried to sidestep Caleb, but Caleb shifted to again block him, putting an arm back so he could find me and hold on to me.

"You need to get the hell out of here."

Whoever the guy was, it was clear Caleb didn't like him. I touched him and his muscles were tensed and rock hard.

The guy again swung to the side. "What's your name, honey? You're a hottie."

Caleb rushed the guy, grabbing his jacket and slamming him against the wall opposite us. "I told you to leave!"

Someone grasped my shoulders, and Phoenix stepped over to shield me. I peeked behind me. Levi. He leaned in. "Don't worry. We've got you."

Was I supposed to be worried about this guy? Who was he? I stretched my neck to see around Phoenix.

Dakota was in front of us, on Caleb's heels. "Don't mess your hands up. We've got another show tomorrow," he cautioned. All the action drew the attention of a couple of security guards from further along the hallway, and they were now moving in our direction.

"Okay, okay. Geesh! I just wanted to say hi," the troublemaker said, but his eyes shone menacingly and his jaw was tight.

Caleb slowly unclenched his fists. The guy tugged on the hem of his jacket to straighten it, glaring at Caleb, who turned to the approaching guards. "Get him out of here."

The guy took advantage of Caleb's distraction, sliding so he could leer at me. "Such a waste of a killer body."

In a flash, Caleb took a swing and connected solidly, knocking the guy to the floor. But, not satisfied with that, he jumped on top of him.

Dakota rushed to pull him off, and Phoenix grabbed his other arm. "Come on, man. Let security handle it."

Caleb fought them as they yanked him to his feet and tried to hold him. He strained forward, his face red, a vein pulsing near his temple. "You son-of-a bitch! Don't you even fucking *look* at her." Spittle flew from his mouth. Levi got in front of me, inadvertently pushing me against the cold cinderblock wall.

The security guards were having a hard time getting past Dakota and Phoenix, who were still struggling with Caleb. The guy stood, rubbing his jaw and shifted his gaze to me. "If you ever want to experience what it's like to be with a real man..."

Caleb snarled and dragged both Dakota and Phoenix forward a few feet.

"You got a death wish, man?" Dakota yelled. "Get the hell away from here before I let him loose on you. And after he's finished, it'll be my turn."

The guy had the balls to laugh.

Matt showed up from out of nowhere and clapped onto the stranger's shoulders from behind. "That's enough," he snapped, wheeling the guy around and hauling him toward an exit.

Gabe and Trudy smashed themselves against the wall when Matt hustled by them as he escorted the agitator to the door.

Gabe eyed our group, "What the hell is going on?"

Everyone ignored him.

"Come on, man. Calm down. He's gone," Phoenix told Caleb.

"Just let me go!" I couldn't tell if they released him, or if he tore free from their grasp. "Fuck!" he screamed, the sound echoing in the hallway. Everybody watched him tensely as he paced. "I can't believe— That asshole!" He glanced over and noticed me cowering in Levi's shadow. His expression was filled with remorse, and his voice changed. He raised an arm. "Come here, babe."

Levi moved away, and I hurried to Caleb, encircling his waist and laying my cheek on his chest. His heart was hammering. He smashed me against him, holding my head near to his ribcage. "I'm sorry." He seemed too choked up to say anything else.

"Who was that?" Gabe asked as he skirted Caleb, Trudy glued to his side.

Phoenix pushed his hair from his face, breathing hard. "Did you know him?"

"Yeah. I know him all right," Caleb said stiffly, but he didn't elaborate. It was silent for several seconds. "I'm sorry, guys."

"No, man. We've got your back," Dakota said dismissively. "Your hand okay?"

Caleb held it out and opened and closed his fist. "Yeah. It's fine."

Dakota studied him. "You said...you said you told him not to show here again. He get backstage before?"

Caleb nodded. "Last night. In Boston."

Dakota turned to the two security guards. "Did you get a good look at him?"

They both bobbed their heads.

He stabbed the air in their direction. "That asshole never gets through security again, or somebody's ass is grass, got it?"

"Yeah," one responded, gesturing to the camera mounted behind Dakota. "We'll pull the security tape and make sure everyone watches it. It won't happen again."

"Make sure it doesn't."

I felt sorry for them. But I was pretty sure all of us were filled with too much adrenaline to act polite at the moment.

Gabe leaned in. "Are you okay?"

Touched by his concern, I squeezed his arm. "I'm fine. No one laid a finger on me."

Gabe stared at Caleb. "Could this be the guy who messed with Sophie's scuba tank?"

Caleb blinked. "Well...I wouldn't put it past him, but no. I don't think so. Before last night I hadn't seen or talked to him since high school."

"What's with all the hostility then?" Gabe insisted.

I studied Caleb's face. He shrugged. "I don't know. I honestly don't. He's never liked me for some reason. And I feel the same way about him."

Gabe looked like he was on the verge of asking another question, but Dakota exhaled loudly, drawing everyone's attention. "Who needs a beer?" Not waiting for an answer, he added, "I know I do."

We all gathered in a lounge briefly for a drink. Gabe's awe of Levi, Dakota, and Phoenix was amusing. Trudy clung to his elbow and smiled at them timidly. But after the second beer, Phoenix yawned and stretched. "I hate to be a party-pooper, but I'm beat. I'm going to the hotel to get a good night's sleep."

Murmurs of agreement rose.

"Oh, shit!" Gabe said suddenly. "I never told my driver we were coming backstage after the concert. He probably left."

Caleb waved a hand. "Not a problem. He texted me twenty minutes ago. I had him pull around to the loading dock so you wouldn't have to walk too far."

"Oh." Gabe blinked. "Cool. Thanks."

"I can walk with you if you're ready," Phoenix offered.

Gabe peered at Trudy, who was in the middle of a yawn. "Yeah. That would be great. Are you ready, Soph?"

I glanced at Caleb.

"I'll make sure she gets back."

Gabe looked from him to me, but I was saved from answering by Levi rising.

"I'm going too." He gathered his empties. "I'll see you all tomorrow."

"Eight o'clock," Dakota reminded them.

Phoenix threw him a weary salute, and Levi nodded as he pitched his bottles. They headed out, leaving the three of us alone.

"One more beer?" Dakota asked.

Caleb gazed at me, but I was too lost in my thoughts to respond. "One more. Then we need to shove off."

"Sophie?"

"Hmm?" I focused on Dakota.

"Another seltzer?"

"Oh, no thanks."

He came over to where Caleb and I were snuggled on the couch and handed Caleb one of the beers he had before plopping into his chair, kicking back, and dropping his boots onto the table. "So, Sophie..." He took a long pull on his beer while considering me. "How is your family? The bookstore still going strong? Oh, and as an aside, your brother is a hoot."

The corners of my lips twitched. "That's one way you could categorize him. He's really a sweetheart. But he can say the most asinine things...and follow them with amazingly clever observations. You never know what'll come out of his mouth."

They both laughed.

"And the store is doing good. We bought the building next door a few years ago and expanded into that area while giving the whole place a facelift."

"It's really nice," Caleb interjected.

Dakota sat up, placing his feet on the ground and his forearms on his knees, dangling his beer, half-finished already, loosely. "And what do you think of New York? This bozo showing you around?"

"Yes." I smiled at him. "In fact, he took me to the Rainbow Room."

Dakota seemed amused by that. "Did he, now? I thought that was more your parents' style than yours?"

Caught while taking a swig, Caleb nodded before swallowing and answering verbally. "It is." His brows rose. "We ran into them there, unfortunately."

"Ooh." Dakota grimaced. "Ouch." He twisted to me. "So, what was your take on ol' Mom and Pop Winthrop?"

"Uhh..." I slid a look at Caleb, who shrugged, appearing amused. "It was really only a brief meeting. I didn't have enough time to really form an impression."

"Uh-huh," Dakota said doubtfully. His phone buzzed and he glanced at it. A light came into his eyes. "Ya know, it is getting kind of late." He stood. "I guess I'll get back and turn in myself."

Caleb rose and helped me to my feet. "You ready, Miss Sophie?"

"I am."

Our car was ready at the door and whisked us off. We dropped Dakota at a rear entrance to the Marriott, where I was told they had a secret elevator, which for the most part, made it easy to come and go unnoticed. We were quiet on the trip to Caleb's. He had his arm across my shoulders, but was staring out the window. I watched his face as it went from shadow to light, light to shadow. It seemed like he was a million miles away. When we got to his building, a different man opened my door. Caleb leaned forward and gave the driver at least three hundred-dollar bills, if not more. "Thanks, Al. See you tomorrow."

We shared a few mindless remarks on the way up. Caleb gave me a T-shirt to wear and took a shower. I kept replaying his reaction to the guy he had called Chris over and over in my head. It seemed excessive. There was more to this story. I was sure of it.

CHAPTER FOURTEEN

Caleb

I came out of the bathroom, wearing boxers and a T-shirt; she was sitting cross-legged on the bed in the circle of light from the bedside lamp, staring at the sheets. She was swimming in my T-shirt, which made her appear small and vulnerable. I knew what happened had upset her. It had upset me. But it hurt more to see how it affected her. I regretted losing my shit around her.

I sighed and padded to the bed, sitting on the edge of the mattress. She looked up and gave me a weak smile, waiting for me to talk. I placed my hand on her arm. "I'm really sorry for what happened tonight..."

"You've said that." She put her palm on my cheek. "It's okay, Caleb. I just want to know why you were so agitated."

"Well..." I sputtered. "I didn't like the way he was talking to you."

"I get that." Her gaze raked my face as if reading me, and I suddenly felt naked. "But there's more to it than that, isn't there?"

I really didn't want to go into it, but she deserved an explanation. I rolled onto my back and then scootched to the headboard, stuffing a pillow behind me. She ducked under my arm and I held her. Her nearness comforted me. I collected my thoughts and censored them. She waited quietly for me to speak.

"So, like I think I said, Chris and I went to school together...from about the fourth grade on, when we first moved to New York from New Jersey." I inhaled slowly, unsure of how to characterize Chris's and my relationship. "He...messed with me a lot. I guess you could say bullied me."

"*He* bullied *you*? You're twice his size, three times his size."

I chuckled. "Now, maybe. But I was a beanpole in those days. A stiff wind would have blown me down 5th Avenue. And he usually didn't come at me alone, the pussy," I added under my breath. "I got this," I pointed to the scar above my lip, "courtesy of Chris, his buddies, and a baseball bat." She paled. I had gone too far. I'm glad I didn't show her the other scars.

"Oh, my God."

"I wasn't scared of him tonight. I could pound that little punk to a pulp, if I wanted to." I ran a finger along her arm. "But I was scared he would do something to you. I don't know why. There's no way I would let him past me, and even if I had, Dakota and the guys would have ripped him to shreds." I thought back on it. The fear had been overwhelming. I was afraid he would take the one good thing in my life away somehow. "I shouldn't have lost my cool, though. That didn't make it any better." I studied her. "I didn't mean to scare you. I'm not usually like that. I...I don't know..."

She patted my leg. "I know you're not usually like that. That's what surprised me. But...he provoked you. And...my guess is...your reaction was kind of like PTSD. What happened in the past intensified your response."

I thought about that. "You're probably right." I pinched a fold in the sheets. "But I still shouldn't have morphed into a stark-raving lunatic in front of you."

"Caleb." She rose and straddled me, again touching my face. I cupped her ass. "I'm all right. You're all right. It's over. I'm not upset anymore..." She dropped her gaze. "I'm only sad I have to leave tomorrow, and I won't get to see you for another two weeks."

I slid my hands beneath her underwear, turned on as hell. I needed to do something with all the adrenaline seeing Chris had brought on. "Then I guess we better make the most of tonight."

She scooted backward and yanked at the hem of my shirt. I lifted my arm so she could get one sleeve free, then hastily tore it off and tossed it on the floor. I grabbed the T-shirt she was wearing at the collar and ripped it. I was glad it came apart, or I would have looked ridiculous trying to tear it and failing. She gasped, which aroused me more. I clasped her ribcage and lowered my mouth to her breast, sucking on her nipple aggressively.

"Oh!" She rose on her knees to give me better access and clasped the back of my head. She shrugged out of the torn tee and reached down to find me and somehow—I guess by moving her underwear aside—lowered herself onto me with a groan. She grasped the top of the headboard and used it to absolutely blow my mind. After it was over, she sighed, still clinging to me.

Then she did something that obliterated all else—whispered in my ear "I love you."

That night I lay awake wondering how I could work in a trip to Tiffany's before the band left town.

Sophie

The man looked fantastic in my bed.

"Not that you aren't fabulous, because you are...but don't you think that's a little fancy for the Rum Runner?"

He was sitting watching me get ready, resting against the headboard, fingers laced behind him, wearing nothing but a smile and a sheet.

"I just felt like dressing up." I turned to get a sideways view in the mirror. "I bought this for the gala, then I bought the other one in Philly, remember?"

"Do I ever."

I caught his eye in the mirror, and my cheeks flushed. It was crazy how he could still make me become a pile of goo with merely the tone of his voice, even though we'd been together for nearly three months.

I twisted to attempt to get a peek at the back. "I don't know. Maybe you're right. Maybe it would be idiotic to wear something like this." I reached for the zipper, trying to determine what would be more appropriate.

"No, no, no." He hopped out of bed, buck naked, and came to take my shoulders. "Forget I said anything. They get dressy people in there sometimes. Those executives' wives don't have any other sort of clothes, except for their skimpy swimming suits."

"Hmm." I pouted. "You've been ogling them in their 'skimpy swimming suits?'"

"Now why would I do that when I have the most beautiful girl on the island with me?" His voice was a low growl that sent shivers up my spine, but I tried to downplay it.

"That's better." I kissed him, then returned to perusing my reflection. "Are you sure?"

"I'm sure." He peered over my shoulder at my reflection. The sight of his bare chest behind me was quite a distraction. "And if it would make you feel better, I can wear my gold, fancy dress."

"Oh, would you?" I teased.

He considered the mirror-image of the old-fashioned, digital alarm clock on my windowsill, then twisted to check it again. "Well, I better get something on. Dak said to be there at six."

"I thought you didn't play until seven?"

"We don't..." He searched the floor, then snagged his underwear while I admired his tush. "...but he's anal about some things and being early to a gig is one of them. He says it's bad luck if you're not there at least an hour before."

I glanced at the clock myself. "I guess this'll have to do then." I hunted for my gold purse, spotted it on a bedpost and made a move in that direction, but Caleb stopped me.

"It'll more than do. You look incredible. In fact..." He began to unzip me. "...maybe we should chance a little bad luck."

"Caleb! Hali's going to be there tonight, and I haven't seen her in forever."

"Fine. But later..."

I spun into his arms. "Later, I'm all yours. Now, get dressed." He turned and I slapped his rear.

"Ouch!"

"That didn't hurt."

Hours later I was about to order my second drink. I decided a fancy dress deserved a fancy cocktail and ordered a Last Chance Beach Sunset Mimosa. The combination of the raspberry flavor of the Chambord and the pineapple juice, topped with the champagne, made it both heavenly and slightly lethal, since they went down so easily. I turned from the bar and my stomach dropped.

"Hi, Sophie."

"Steve! What are you...?" I lost the rest of my question in my befuddlement. The last time I laid eyes on him he was riding off in a Last Chance Beach sunset with my cousin. I was surprised by the tears that stung and threatened to spill over my lashes. I'd loved him so much once. Strangely, the betrayal was still fresh. My hands were shaking. I set the glasses back on the wood surface behind me for fear of dropping them.

"I got what I deserved. I came home from an audition earlier than I thought and caught Clarice on the couch with our neighbor being...well...*very* neighborly. You look lovely."

I glanced at my dress then stared at him again, speechless.

He stepped closer and took my arms. I was so shocked I didn't pull away. "Sophie. I'm so sorry for what I did to you. I've regretted it every day since."

I opened my mouth to tell him to drop dead, but my chin was quivering. The tears I'd been trying to keep in check tipped over the edge of my eyelids, tracking down my face.

"Oh, Soph." He gently brushed the tears aside with his thumbs. "I'm so, so sorry."

I was mesmerized by him. I thought I'd never see him again and then *pop*, he shows up. I should be angry, but instead I was shocked and hurt. "I-I need to sit." My voice was weak. I went to slide a stool from under a nearby table and he reached in front of me.

"Here. Let me get that." He'd never done one gentlemanly thing for me in his life. "Is that better?"

I scanned the vicinity. We'd caught the attention of a few people. I turned toward the bar to hide my reaction from them. Of course everybody would be curious about seeing us together again. "What—" my gaze ricocheted from one side of the bar to the other like a Ping-Pong ball. "What are you doing here?" I finally managed to say.

"Well, I came home because of you, of course."

"Because of *me*?" My voice squeaked. I was having trouble controlling it, and I was on the edge of losing it.

"Yes," he returned matter-of-factly.

"You can't think—" Was he out of his ever-loving mind? "You didn't believe...you could simply waltz back into my life?"

He stared at the bar, exhaling with his head bowed and shoulders slumped. It was like someone had deflated him. "No. No. I know I blew it with us." His words were choked. "Biggest mistake I made in my life. Besides trusting Clarice," he said bitterly.

I examined my feelings. I was...relieved. Relieved he wasn't trying to pursue me because...why? Was I afraid I'd give in to him again? I peered at him again, and I couldn't help it. My heart ached for him. But not in the fashion it once had, rather, in pity. He seemed so dejected, and I, of all people, should know what he was going through.

Phoenix's voice trickled into my brain. "...wrap it up. Thank you all for coming tonight..."

They were done.

Caleb will look over here and be ready to kick Steve's ass if he finds out who he is.

I seized my drink and downed it like I was taking pills, throwing it back and wiping my mouth with my hand. "Come on. Let's go." I grabbed him, and we threaded our way to the front door.

Caleb

We were in Last Chance Beach. It had been two months since New York, and Sophie had flown to see me a couple of times, but this was the first time we'd returned to the beach. We were playing at the Rum Runner, the place where we first met. It was a free concert to make amends for bailing on the gala, even though that wasn't our fault. People had paid big money for the tickets to the main event and were no doubt unhappy the gala had been canceled. Levi had offered this concert as a kind of atonement. Hoping people wouldn't pull their funding from Remi's charity.

I'd come to really enjoy playing at these smaller venues where we could break between sets and enjoy time with our friends. Sophie had gotten all dolled up tonight, for some reason, with a fancy new dress that was a shiny gold on the top and layers of sheer white from the waist down. Of course, she could have been wearing the banner outside advertising our gig for all I cared. We'd revisited the argument we had the first night we were there, debating the merits of John Steinbeck and F. Scott Fitzgerald. We hadn't battled about literature in a long time and tonight had a special feel to it. Being back where it all began. Happier than ever. My thoughts went to the blue ring box in my glove compartment and my plan to propose to her.

I looked out, searching the audience for her, my heart singing. My gaze landed on her near the bar. A light fixture directly above them framed the pair. Sophie, peering up at the man in the suit, and he, holding her chin. As I watched, he brushed what had to be tears from her face. I missed a note. I never missed a note. Luckily, Phoenix ended our last set one song early. He rushed to my side.

"What's wrong, man? Do you feel sick?"

Dakota hurried over too. "Is he gonna barf?"

I found my voice. "Who...is...that...guy?" Like the night we met, I was like the Tin Man without his oil can, barely able to speak.

"Who's—" Phoenix followed my line of sight.

"Ho-ly shit!" Dak said in the quietest Dak voice I'd ever heard.

Phoenix's jaw dropped. He turned slightly toward Dak. "Is that—"

Dakota eyes widened. "It can't be."

Levi finally reached us. "What's going—?" Phoenix pointed at Sophie and the stranger, and all three said at once, "Steve Pattison."

"No way!" Levi's jaw went slack. "How could he dare to show his face around here?"

"Wait...Steve? *The* Steve?"

They all looked at each other. I could count on one finger the times I'd seen Dakota Blackstone uncomfortable, and that was the day we went scuba diving, after he and Hali apparently had a little disagreement. And I'd never seen him avoid saying something, but he physically took a step away, shaking his head in mute protest. Their hesitation only served to piss me off more.

"The Steve who left Sophie at the altar?"

Phoenix and Dak swallowed, and Levi watched his shoe make a rainbow arc in the dust on the floor. "Yeah," he finally said, "*that* Steve."

"But don't go jumping to conclusions. Sophie won't have anything to do with—" He turned to search for her and I spotted them. Sophie was holding his hand, and they were leaving. "—him," Phoenix finished weakly.

Dak finally found his voice. "Don't get mad."

"I'm not mad." And to my amazement, I wasn't. Because I was dead inside. I proceeded to put my guitar in its case. They all stood around, gawking at each other. "Aren't you going to take care of your instruments?" I asked, barely able to keep the edge out of my voice.

"Yeah," Dak answered, grabbing the other twos' shoulders and retreating. "Yeah. We're packing up."

They huddled together, no doubt discussing how to handle me, while I continued to unplug my amp and loop its cord into ovals.

"Umm...Boner," Levi said tentatively.

"Yes."

"We have people who do that now."

I froze. We hadn't put together or broken down our setup for years, but I was on such autopilot, I had reverted to our days in the beginning. "I was merely trying to save them a little time, but if you don't want me to help them, I can stop," I lied.

"Oh, no. By all means, coil away."

They eyed me.

I made another loop then quit abruptly and dropped the whole thing at my feet. "You've taken all the fun out of it." I snagged my guitar case and slung it onto my shoulder, but as I went to leave the stage, the three of them shifted like a single unit to block my path.

Dak crossed his arms. "Where do you think you're going?"

"To the bathroom."

"With your guitar?" Phoenix questioned.

I took a breath. "To the bathroom, then home to bed. Okay?"

They looked at each other and, one by one, moved aside. I marched past them and started to storm down the hall to the john. But feeling them watching me, I deliberately slowed my pace. When I reached the bathroom, I threw a glance over my shoulder. They were huddled again. I ducked into an adjacent corridor. Halfway to the end, I went to pass some kid and he said, "Caleb Winthrop! Ussie?"

"Huh?"

He got his phone and opened the camera. Putting his arm around my shoulders, he held the phone up to take a selfie with me.

I ducked my shoulder and continued my journey to the front door. "Just leave me alone, would ya, kid?"

"Whoa. Snotty, much?" he called after me.

I squeezed my eyes shut for a second but kept walking. Not good for PR, but I didn't give a damn. I made my way past a crowd of people who were having their IDs checked and barged through the door into the fresh night air, only to find Sophie on my left, resting against the building with her arms crossed, talking to Steve. I turned to my right and kept moving.

"Caleb?" she called after me. "Are we leaving now?"

"I'm leaving now."

"You're leaving now?" She sounded confused. "Wait. Caleb? Wait!"

I increased my speed, but she caught me and placed herself in my path, bringing me up short. "Where are you going?"

I stepped off the sidewalk and over a yellow parking block into the lot running adjacent to the street and walked at an angle. "Back to my hotel."

She chased after me. "Back to your hotel? Without me?"

"That's right," I said through gritted teeth.

"Caleb! Stop!"

I halted, seething inside, and turned to her.

She caught her breath. "What's wrong?"

"What's wrong?" I lifted my gaze. Leaning against the building now with one dress shoe on the brick wall, he was still waiting.

Of course he is.

"Nothing's wrong. Why don't you go with *Steve*," I said mockingly, "and enjoy the rest of your evening together." I began to wheel around and continue to the car, but she grabbed my arm and I lost it, the fury taking control. "Is this all a game to you? You led me on to imagine this is something it's not, to—I don't know—make him mad, get revenge, maybe, and—" I was so angry I couldn't think straight or finish my argument. "Fuck this! I'm out."

I took off again but she didn't follow. "You're just going to leave me?" She sounded pissed.

Good.

I reached my car and threw my guitar in. Noise from the Rum Runner drew my attention. My posse. But they held up to talk to Steve.

Fucking traitors.

She was moving toward me now. I scrambled into the front seat and started the car. She knocked on the window. I lowered it, grinding my teeth, not looking at her. "Yes?"

"You're just leaving me. How am I supposed to get home?"

"I'm sure Steve will take you." Repeating his name irritated me all the further. "Or, ya know what?" I got my wallet and withdrew a hundred-dollar bill. "Here. Call yourself an Uber."

She was teary-eyed but crossed her arms, stubbornly refusing to take the money.

"Suit yourself." I dropped the money, put the gearshift into reverse, and barreled out of there, gunning the engine. I checked my rearview mirror. She was still standing there, but her head was bowed and her hands were covering her face. As mad as I was, the guilt still cut into my core, but I shut it down, going numb for the rest of the ride.

Once at The Sands, I opened the glove box and retrieved the little velvet cube holding the engagement ring.

What an idiot I was. Again.

An idiot to believe she was in love with me as much as I was in love with her. I put the box in my jacket pocket and mechanically exited the car. Leaving my expensive guitar, I strode toward the hotel. It didn't matter if the guitar got stolen. Nothing mattered. Tears mounted, but I fought them back. I swung through the revolving door.

"Good evening, Caleb," someone called. Remi was at the desk.

"Hi," I bit off. I took the elevator to the suite I was sharing with Phoenix this time, although I hadn't planned on staying there.

Plans change.

Once inside, I stopped to catch my breath. I wanted to smash everything in the room.

Why not? I'm a rock star, after all. We're known for trashing hotel rooms. Not Insatiable Fire, but what the hell? I might as well.

But I was too tired for breaking things, as much as I desired to. Out of the corner of my eye I spied the wet bar. I poured myself a scotch and sat on the balcony. Forty minutes later, I watched my crew pull into the parking lot. They didn't look up as they tore across the asphalt, no doubt eager to confront me.

Great. Could this night get any worse?

CHAPTER FIFTEEN

Sophie

His car left and I broke down.

I reined it in as Savannah and Hali drew near me, but their sympathetic expressions sent me over the edge again.

"He just...he just threw some money at me and left." I cried and they wrapped their arms around me and tried to comfort me.

Phoenix, Dakota, and Levi reached us.

"What happened?" Levi asked as he tried to catch his breath.

Savannah raised her head. "He threw money at her and left."

"Come on," Dakota growled at the other two. They took off for somewhere. Probably to get their car and go to the hotel. Steve was gone.

Savannah drove me home. Hali sat in the back seat, with her arm around my shoulder. I was numb. When we got there, Savannah turned. "Are you sure you don't want one of us to stay with you?"

"No, I'm fine," I said tiredly. "I'll call you in the morning." I plodded up my steps, unlocked my door, and waved at Hali, who had switched from the rear to climb in next to Savvy. Once inside, it hit me like a train on fire. Caleb was gone.

As I passed in front of the mirror, I caught my reflection, the tear-stained face of a girl in a party dress. It reminded me of my "wedding day." The white tulle at the bottom mocked me. Suddenly I hated that dress. I dropped my purse and yanked on the zipper. It got stuck, and I nearly ripped the dress in my rush to get it off. I was wearing new lingerie that I'd hoped Caleb would be removing. I clawed at my bra clasp and stripped until I was naked. I didn't have any curtains on the windows, but it didn't matter. No one was in the office buildings on the opposite side of the street anyway. I crossed my arms over my naked body.

The stick-figure drawing of Caleb he'd taped to the wall was staring at me. I tore it from its place, crumpling it before tossing it aside. Hot tears streamed down my cheeks, and I released a frustrated scream. The image of him handing me money out his car window floated back to me. I took a tube of paint from my easel and chucked it across the room. It hit the window, but was too little to do any damage. The expenditure of energy was satisfying, though. I threw another, and another, until the paint tray was empty of tubes, then added brushes and pencils to the list of missiles thrown. When nothing handy was left to throw, I screamed and toppled my easel. I thought about going into the kitchen and breaking dishes, but my fury was spent, leaving me tired. I threw myself on my bed and cried myself to sleep.

Caleb

Dakota stormed in the door. "Where are you, asshole?"

Levi made an attempt to calm him. "It's late and we're in a hotel. We need to keep our voices low."

"I don't give a shit. Does it look like I give a shit?" Dakota responded.

I slid the door open and entered, leaving my empty glass on the ground near my chair.

"Oh, there you are." Dakota charged across the room, and I put my fists up to defend myself, but Phoenix got in front of him.

"This isn't helping," he said steadily.

Dakota stared at him darkly, seething and dragging air through his teeth. He switched his gaze back to me but didn't come after me. Physically, that is.

"You threw money at her like she was some kind of whore?" he raged.

"What are you talking about? I gave her money for an Uber, and she didn't take it, so I dropped it."

"Same difference. Do you know what it's like to leave a girl who you lo—care for, drowning in a puddle of tears?"

I didn't answer, just walked over and threw myself into a chair, although his words hit my gut like tiny missiles.

"You didn't even ask her," he continued, getting louder, "*didn't even ask her* why she was talking to Steve."

"I didn't need to," I shouted, sitting forward agitatedly. "I caught them on the verge of kissing."

This brought him up short, but Phoenix picked up the cause. "Kissing and on the verge of kissing are two completely different things."

I threw a hand in the air in disgust.

"She was only talking to Steve because he was upset."

I slid my gaze in his direction again, suddenly interested to hear what he was saying.

Phoenix sighed and came to sit on the couch near me. "He learned the girl he ran away with before their wedding cheated on him. Sophie's a very sympathetic person. She felt sorry for him, but he told us she made it clear she was not willing to renew their relationship."

I stared at him mutely with my jaw hanging open for a second, then covered my face with my hands and lay back in the chair. "What have I done?"

"You've made a real ass of yourself, that's what you've done," Dak responded.

"You know what?" I said tiredly, exhaling and rubbing my temples briefly. "You can talk to me when you care for someone as deeply as I care about Sophie." I jerkily reached into my pocket and pulled out the ring box, setting it on the table like I was throwing down the gauntlet. "When you are ready to propose to her, and you see her with an ex-boyfriend in a very intimate position."

They all gaped at me.

"Fuck." I hadn't intended to tell them that. Hadn't intended to tell anyone until I'd asked Sophie and she'd said yes. "I don't need this bullshit." The tears almost blinding me, I went into my bedroom and slammed the door behind me. I sat on the edge of the bed, hanging my head in mourning over the perfect relationship I'd just trashed.

Twenty minutes later, I heard Dak and Levi say their goodbyes. I left my room, and Phoenix was still on the couch. "Where are you going?"

"To Sophie's."

"Caleb."

I turned around. He tossed me the ring box. I caught it and stared at it for a second, then shoved it into my pocket and left.

I sat in my car for a while, parked outside her apartment, looking at the ring. I opened the glove box and threw it in there before climbing her stairs and knocking on her door.

"Who is it?" she said groggily.

"It's Jack the Ripper." I was still angry, but now that rage was directed inwardly. "Who the hell do you think it is at 3:30 in the morning?" Despite what the guys had told me, I still had a flash of apprehension, imagining Steve opening the door in only his underwear.

The deadbolt slid back and she opened the door. "What are you doing here?"

Seeing her, her hair all tousled, squinting at me with tired eyes, awoke something tender in me. "Can I come in?"

She pried her lids open a bit wider. "Are you intending to yell at me some more?"

I repositioned a strand of her hair that had fallen into her face. "Not if I can help it."

She sighed. "Sure. Come in. Whatever." She trudged to her bed.

She was naked, the moonlight highlighting her curves where it kissed them, and I had to ignore the stab of lust that hit me. I came into the room and closed the door behind me softly.

She ripped the sheet off her bed and wrapped it around herself then sat on the edge of her bed, staring into her lap.

I switched to the opposite bed but had to step over several paint tubes. Her place was a wreck. "What happened here?"

She rolled a shoulder. "I got mad."

"Did you ever think of becoming a rock star?" I joked. Then I sobered. Instead of sitting, as I had intended, I moved to the window and watched the street below, trying to find the right words to say to make her understand. I turned to her. "Sophie..." That was all I could manage before becoming choked up. She raised her head and eyed me. I blinked, and had to look to the side to keep the tears from falling. I couldn't peer into her beautiful, stricken face, knowing I'd done that to her. I swallowed. "When I saw him touch your cheek..." I couldn't go on.

"But you understand I'd never do that to you. Could never do that to you. I told you I'd never hurt you."

Her words seemed to free me. I rushed to her, falling to my knees in front of her. "I know, Sophie, I know. But the sight of him... And then I found out who he was..." It sounded lame, even to me. I dropped my gaze. "I'm sorry, Sophie. I'm so, so sorry." I lifted my chin and a tear slipped by my guard and slid down. "I realize I was an idiot. Can you ever forgive me? I only did it because I love you so much."

"That's not love, Caleb. The way you treated me was not love."

How could I deny what she was saying? I lowered my butt to my heels, my hands to my thighs. "You're right. Of course you're right." I stared at the floor, my mind like gears covered in peanut butter, as I tried to sort through it all. "It was selfish. I was being selfish. Thinking purely of myself and my own feelings." That reaction might have been appropriate with Heidi, because I didn't love her and she didn't love me. But even then... I was beginning to see myself in a new light, and I didn't like what I was seeing. "I...hurt you. And what's worse, I meant to do it. I was so angry I meant to hurt you. That's unforgivable." I put the heels of my palms on my temples, and it was deadly quiet for several seconds. "I should go."

She grabbed my arms. "No, wait."

"No. I should go, Sophie," I wailed. "I'm no good for you. You deserve better."

"Don't I get to decide that?"

I peered at her, confused. If I was broken, then she was broken too. What Steve had done to her, what *I* had done to her, she presumed she deserved this. I lost the tenuous grip I had on my emotions and sobbed.

"I just left you there to fend for yourself. What kind of guy does that to the woman he loves?"

"You were upset."

"No!" I shouted. "Don't do that. Don't excuse me, Sophie. You should hold me accountable."

"Caleb," she said softly. "You made a mistake. We all make them. What's important is you learn from it."

"But that's the thing. I'm not sure if I can. Here I've sat in judgement over my parents because they are self-absorbed, and I do the very same things."

"But, unlike your parents, from what you've said, you have the desire to change and grow. I believe you can do that."

Can I? I know I want to, but...

"I want to, honey. I really do. But...I don't know if I can."

"The only way to know is to try."

A ray of hope shot through me. "I don't ever want to act like the jackass I was tonight."

"Okay."

"I don't ever want to hurt you."

She hesitated. "But you will. And I'll hurt you. It's what we humans are best at, it seems. But we are capable of so much more too. And you can see it everywhere if you search hard enough." She grew quiet, and I thought about what she'd said. "Like Dakota, Phoenix, and Levi. They were so...kind to me." Her voice became choked.

I lowered my head. "After I was a jerk."

"Caleb, look at me."

I obliged her.

"They've all had their turns at playing the jerk too. None of us are above being human and selfish at times, but owning up to it and trying to change—that's what makes the difference."

She shifted her gaze to something over my shoulder. "It's late."

"I should leave."

"No. You should stay." She stood and unwound the sheet covering her, lifting and snapping it before releasing it to float onto the bed. Her naked body in the moonlight seemed like a marble statue, created by a master. She slid under the sheet and lay on her side. "Come here."

I was scared. This frightened me more than anything Chris had ever done to me.

She patted the mattress next to her. "Come on."

I stood and took off my shoes and socks. She watched me. I joined her in the bed. I moved slowly and carefully, afraid to do anything to mar this second chance I had gotten.

"Put your head here," she murmured, indicating her chest. Reeling in my desire for her, I laid my cheek against her soft skin and closed my eyes. She raked her fingers through my hair soothingly. I'd never had anyone do that to me before and it was blissful. We fell asleep like that.

After five days in Last Chance Beach, Insatiable Fire took to the road again. As in the past, Sophie flew to see me on several weekends. Missing her terribly, I decided to surprise her and fly into Summerville and spend a day with her on Last Chance Beach, then fly back. It was a last minute decision, and not well-thought out, so I arrived at her place only to find her gone. I tried to remember from our phone conversations what she had coming up. I hurried down the stairs and into the bookshop, running into Mr. Lockhart first. While I hadn't won him over entirely, our relationship was much better.

"Caleb!" He set a box of books on the floor and shook my hand. "Sophie didn't mention you were in town."

"That's because she doesn't know. I came in to surprise her. Is she working?"

"No. She worked earlier. Did you try her place?"

I frowned, hating the idea of missing one moment with her. "Yeah. She wasn't there."

Mr. Lockhart lifted his chin, gesturing to someone behind me. "Perhaps Gabe will know."

A stack of books was walking toward us, apparently carried by Gabe. "Hey, Caleb! Gabe will know what?"

"Where your sister is."

"Yeah. She went home. To your home, I mean."

I brightened. Mr. Lockhart was picking up his box again. "Sir, would you mind if I went there to surprise her?"

"Of course not. I'm sure she'd like that." He gave me a smile which about knocked me over and left.

As we watched him make his exit, I said out of the side of my mouth. "I think my charm is working. I'm making progress with him."

"Oh, yes," Gabe responded. "You've progressed from being despised to merely being hated. Congratulations."

I jabbed him in the ribs with my elbow.

He laughed. "Are you here long?"

"Just until tomorrow. My flight leaves at 12:30."

"Where are you flying back to?"

"Atlanta."

He gaped. "Atlanta? You could have driven."

"Yes, I could have. But that would have taken at least a half-hour more, and that's a half-hour I wouldn't have spent with your sister. Speaking of which, I'm done with you." I grabbed his shoulder with one hand and extended my other arm. "Next time I'm in town we'll go for a beer." We shook hands.

"Sounds good. Take care, bro."

I hopped in my rental and drove straight to the Lockharts' house, excited to at last see Sophie. An unfamiliar car was parked in the drive, but I thought nothing of it. But as I was passing the front window, light in my step, I saw them. Sophie in Steve's embrace. My shock was so great, it didn't compute at first. But after I was able to work through the reality of what I was seeing, I was crushed. I turned to hightail it out of there, the betrayal turning my stomach to ashes.

"Caleb! What are you doing here?" Her gleeful voice stopped me in my tracks. I closed my eyes, pushing down the hot tears pressing on my lids. "What a surprise."

I wheeled around and held my hands up to fend her off, as she was running to me. "Sophie." She halted. Glancing in the window, I caught him watching us, a smirk of victory on his perfect fucking face. My lips curled into a snarl in response. "I can't believe this. I can't believe you— How long has this been going on? The whole time?"

Her brow furrowed. "What are you talking about?" She peeked at the window too. Steve withdrew. "Oh. Steve? He just came by to say hi."

The heat began to rise on the heels of the dead, cold shock. "Oh, I bet he did! Does saying 'hi' always involve mauling you? I mean, Sophie—" I tried to get a grip. "I thought I meant something to you. But I can see I was wrong. So very, very wrong." I couldn't stand looking at her, so beautiful, yet false. I spun, intent on getting as far from the scene of the crime as I could, as quickly as possible.

"Caleb, wait. You're misreading things again. Steve and I are only friends."

"Sophie! Wake up! He wants you back."

"No, he doesn't. And even if he did, I love you."

I stopped, swallowing bile. How I wanted that to be true. I slowly pivoted. Steve was in the window again. No doubt tallying his score against me. Clenching my jaw, I shifted my focus to her. "I'm not into sharing. It's either him or me."

"What?" Her gaze grew wide. "You would make me choose?"

I squeezed my eyes shut. "There shouldn't even be a need to choose. I'm such an idiot." The rage tore from my throat. "*Such* an idiot! *Again*! Fuck this. I'm done." I could hardly see through my tears, but I willed them not to fall as I walked away from her. There would be no other woman after this. I was finished with relationships.

"Caleb?" Her voice broke. "How could you believe I— Why are you doing this to me again?"

To you?

An excruciating headache sliced through my temples, and it was hard to make her out above the rush of blood to my cranium. I fumbled briefly getting the car door open, but managed to get in and drive off. A block from her house I was forced to pull over. I laid my forehead on the steering wheel.

Why is this happening to me?

Then I heard it clearly. The me. I was thinking only of myself again. I drew in a deep breath and sat up.

I didn't even listen to her. Didn't take a moment to stop and consider maybe I'd misread things.

I made a huge U-turn without regard for safety. Luckily, no other cars were on the street.

Sophie wouldn't do that to me. There must be an explanation for what I saw.

I couldn't return to her fast enough. I had to apologize. I swung into her driveway and threw it into park. Jumping out, I didn't even bother with shutting the door. All I needed and wanted was to be with her and apologize for, once again, acting like a jerk.

I need to take it all back. I need to undo the damage I've done. Tell her how—

In the window, I spied them embracing again. But this time it didn't even bother me. Despite what Steve thought, he wasn't going to come between Sophie and me. Then her mom came rushing in, and Sophie moved from his embrace to hers, and I caught the look on her face. She was utterly devastated. The raw pain I witnessed knifed through me.

I did that. I hurt her again. Why can't I quit doing that? Why can't I control my emotions for once and not jump to conclusions?

I spun and plodded to my car.

Why am I always fucking hurting her?

I got in and closed the door. Gripping the steering wheel so tightly it hurt, I realized I was broken beyond repair. Having no experience with being loved, other than my time with her, I didn't know how to do it, couldn't do it properly. I was suddenly so tired. So fucking tired. Sick of myself, the person

I couldn't escape from, who was my constant companion, and would never stop hurting her.

I love her.

Then do what's right and get as far from her as you can, as quickly as possible. Let her live the life she deserves.

I left town vowing to never return, and I shut down. Not only buried the thought of Sophie and me being together, but withdrawing into myself and locking away my emotions. I didn't want to hurt anyone again. Didn't want to hurt me again. It was over.

CHAPTER SIXTEEN

Sophie

Weeks had passed since Caleb's surprise visit home. I'd gone through everything until my brain hurt. I considered what it must have appeared like to him. I recalled how he wouldn't listen to me or believe in us. At first, I refused to call him. Then I realized it was hurting me as much as it was hurting him, but by then he had blocked me.

I tried to return to life as usual. Made an attempt to again put the pieces of my life back together. My life without him. I ate like I was supposed to, went to work like I was supposed to, acted like I'd never met Caleb Winthrop.

I was helping a customer find a book, and Steve walked in. I held up a finger. "I'll be with you in a minute." I continued giving the lady several suggestions of age-appropriate books for her granddaughter, then found Steve perusing books on our sale table.

"Hey. Are you searching for something in particular?"

"You."

I looked at him quizzically.

"I came to see if you wanted to grab lunch."

"Oh. I still have an hour before my lunch break. Can you wait that long?"

He grinned. "Sure. No problem. I had some errands to run anyway. I thought we'd check out that new place."

I thought he was talking about the new Italian place that had opened a block over. "Great. I haven't been there yet."

"It's a plan, then. I'll be back in an hour and we can walk, if you want..."

"That sounds perfect. Thanks, Steve."

Ever since he'd returned, Steve had been given the cold shoulder by pretty much everyone on the island. Small communities don't forget transgressions. And, although part of me thought he deserved it, the other part of me was pained to see him ostracized and alone.

Maybe having lunch together will cheer him up.

Steve left, and I continued to robotically perform my job, acting like my mind wasn't on Caleb, although it was. When noon rolled around, Steve was waiting outside the door, his hands stuck in his jacket pockets.

"Have you been here for a while?"

He grasped my forearms and gave me a kiss on the cheek, which seemed kind of strange, but I wrote it off as him being in a particularly good mood. "Only a few minutes. Shall we?" He stuck out his elbow, and I hesitated a moment, but put my arm through it briefly and used the excuse of turning to look at something in a shop window as an opportunity to detach myself.

We got to the corner, and instead of continuing on, he opened a door to the building there, holding it for me.

"Oh. I thought we were going to the Italian place?"

"No. I wanted to try this place." It was Up On The Rooftop, where Caleb and I had gone on our first date.

"Oh. Okay. But I've been here before."

"Well, I haven't. Come on. I'm starving." He put his hand on my back and nudged me forward, causing me to almost stumble on the threshold.

"You need to pick up your feet when you walk, Sophie. You're always dragging your feet."

His tone rattled me. It had a startling familiarity. He was sounding like the old Steve, not the one who had returned a humbler, kinder man. I brushed it off as he seemed very pleasant after that, until he thought we'd been waiting for our server too long, although the place was packed.

"Shit. I guess I'll have to go get the drinks myself," he said irritably. He pushed his chair away from the table and stood.

As he was turning around, I laughed. "Don't you want to know what I want to drink?"

"No. I've got it," he said as he left.

"Okay then." I laced my fingers on the table with a sigh.

He came back with a bottle of champagne and two glasses.

"Whoa! Are we celebrating something?"

He smiled. "Just an opportunity to have lunch with a pretty lady."

The hair on my arms rose, but I fought the unease, unsure of the reason I had to be uneasy.

He's merely trying to be charming or something. I mean, he'd have to be insane to think I'd have any interest in starting up a relationship with him again.

I cleared my throat, which seemed to have gone dry. "Oh, well, thank you."

He poured himself some champagne and had a drink. Then went to pour mine as what seemed like an afterthought. I put my hand over the flute.

"No thank you. Remember, I still have to work."

He brushed my hand aside and filled my glass. "Oh, don't be a stick in the mud, Sophie. Surely a glass or two of champagne isn't that big of a deal."

I narrowed my eyes at him.

You can pour me a glass, but you can't make me drink it. I considered leaving then and there, but I was starving.

When the poor waiter did arrive, Steve made some very loud statements about this being the worst service he'd ever had. The waiter, who must have been barely twenty-one, apologized profusely, but Steve wasn't done chastising him.

I reached for my flute. *Maybe I do need champagne.*

Steve gestured to me. "Obviously it's not important to you my date here only has an hour for lunch."

"Steve, it's fine," I said quietly. "I'll text them and let them know I'm running late."

I slid my gaze around the room. Everyone was staring at us. Some openly, some trying to act like they weren't.

A heavyset man with a twitchy mustache bustled up. "I've got this, Tim." The kid couldn't get out of there fast enough. "Is there a problem here, sir?"

Great. The manager.

It gave Steve the opportunity to begin his whole diatribe again. I thought about stepping in, but I knew he'd be livid if I did, and I dreaded having his verbal abuse turned on me.

Is that an excuse to let this continue?

I reached across the table and put my hand on Steve's. "Could we maybe just order?" *And stop acting like a jerk.*

He blinked several times. "Of course. I'm sorry." He turned to the manager, and his smile flat-lined. "I'll have the Reuben and the lady will have the chicken quesadilla."

The manager took his menu. "I'll get that order in right away."

"Make sure you do."

"Excuse me," I said to the manager. "I'd like to order for myself." I gave Steve a pointed look, then quickly perused the menu as I *had* planned on ordering a chicken quesadilla. "I'll have the hummus plate. Thank you."

The manager exhaled and his face brightened. "Of course. I'll put a rush on that." He exited as quickly as possible. I again scanned the room over the rim of my flute as I took another drink. Some of the guests still frowned at us, but most had returned their focus to their meals or conversations.

I leaned in. "That was extremely embarrassing, Steve."

"Embarrassing?" He checked the room too, and released a breath loudly. "I apologize. But we'd been here ten minutes and—"

"Please don't start again." *I wonder if I could get that hummus to-go…*

"You're right. Perhaps I'm a bit cranky today."

Perhaps?

We sat silently for several moments, absorbed by our own thoughts.

Something he'd said stuck out at me. "You called me your date."

He'd been staring off, but returned his gaze to me. "What?"

"You called me your date. You told the waiter your 'date' had to get back to work."

"We're having lunch together," he said as if talking to a school child. "Therefore, you are my lunch date."

"Okay. I want to make sure we're on the same page. I hope you realize I'm not now, nor ever will I be, interested in dating you."

"Well," he huffed. "Thanks for sugarcoating it." He looked to the side and pouted. I refused to take the bait. Several seconds passed in silence. "You know, you needn't be so blunt. I don't need for you to highlight the reasons that I don't measure up against a rock star."

"That's not what this is about."

He took a long drink of his champagne, examining me, then rocked forward. "Isn't it, though?"

"Listen—" I started, angry, but also suddenly tearful because of his referring to Caleb.

"I'm sorry. I'm sorry," he said, squeezing my arm. "I guess I'm a little out of sorts. Let's dance."

His abrupt change of subjects was like someone shifting mid-gear causing my thoughts to stall. "What?"

He placed his napkin on the table, stood, and to my horror, offered me his hand.

"Steven," I said in a low voice, glancing around again, "I'm not going to dance with you."

"Why not?"

"Because..." I blustered, "one, it's lunchtime and no one's dancing, two—"

"You didn't let that stop you at the Rainbow Room."

A chill washed over me. "H-how did you know about that?"

His thin smile unnerved me all the more. "Trudy is a great source of information. Especially with a few mojitos in her and a well-placed compliment or two."

Trudy and I had talked on the way home when there was an open seat next to me. I should have known better than to confide in her. Still, I couldn't believe what I was hearing. "You've been spying on me?"

He tilted his head. "Hmm. I don't like the word spying. Let's call it intelligence gathering."

I threw my napkin on the table. At this point I was no longer concerned if people were listening to our conversation or not. "I don't care what you call it, it's still spying."

"Let me guess your second objection." He sneered. "You don't want to dance with me because you did that here on your first date with Mr. Rock-and-Roll."

How does he know that? Did I tell Trudy that? Or Gabe? I don't think anyone knows that besides me and Caleb. Had he somehow gotten the information from Caleb?

My mind raced.

I have to escape from here. But if I storm out, he'll follow.

"I'm going to use the restroom. I'll return in a minute and we'll discuss this."

He didn't sit, and I could feel him watching me all the way to the restroom. I threw the door open. Luckily no one was behind it.

"Oh, shit. Oh, shit. Oh, shit!" I grabbed the edges of the sink and tried to calm myself, but, looking down, I realized my hands were shaking.

Maybe someone is after me and maybe that someone is my psycho ex-fiancé.

Because, I'd decided, he definitely is psycho now. No one in their right mind would think they could dump me on my wedding day for my cousin, and then show up a couple months later and win me back. Should I call Declan Moran, the police chief, or was I overreacting?

A toilet flushed.

Shit. Someone is in here.

A tall, pretty blonde in a tight red dress and platform heels exited from one of the stalls. I recognized her as one of the people following Steve's tirade with the waiter. Seeing me, she slowed her steps, eyeing me warily. I didn't have the energy to fake doing my hair or washing my hands, so I simply stared into the sink next to her. The water ran. She got soap. It ran again. She stole glances at me the whole time, eventually not looking away as she waved at the dispenser and tore a paper towel from it.

"You okay?"

"Yes. I'm sorry. I'm just trying to find a way to leave here without that guy at my table realizing."

A slow smile spread across her face. "Do you have your cell phone?"

I nodded, not sure where she was going with this.

"I'll text you in a minute. When I do, get the hell out of Dodge. I'll make sure that asshole boyfriend of yours has no idea you're leaving. What's your number?"

I rattled it off.

"Got it. I'll get a drink at the bar, and I'll text you after I'm done."

With that, she left. She seemed excited to be helping me.

I took some deep breaths while I waited, then the phone rang.

"Hello?"

"Get moving. I have this." I cracked the door open and a commotion reached me. Steve was yelling, "Shit. Why don't you watch where you're walking?"

I chanced the briefest look back. The girl skirted Steve. "Sorry about that." Steve had something red splashed all over him and was assessing the damage to his shirt. I burst through the same door I'd used when I'd fled

from Caleb. But this time I didn't risk taking the elevator and took the staircase to the street level instead.

"Sophie!"

Panic made my feet fly faster, but I turned an ankle taking a corner.

"Sophie! Wait! Where do you think you're going?"

He was gaining on me.

"Dammit, Sophie. Stop." He grabbed my elbow and spun me around one
step from the bottom. He scowled at me for a moment, then smashed his lips
on mine, backing me against the wall. I fought him, but he held me tight until I was able to work my arms between us and shove him. He leaned on the
banister opposite me, panting.

"Don't you ever come near me again!" I screamed, almost hysterical. I
hobbled along the sidewalk in the direction of the bookstore.

From behind me, he groaned. "Sophie."

I moved as quickly as I could, grimacing with each stride. As I grasped
the store's door handle, he shouted, "Sophie, please. Wait!"

My dad left the register and came to me. "Sophie. What's wrong?"

"Daddy." I leaned on him and gulped in air. "Steve might come in here..."

"Yeah?" His gaze raked my face, then lifted as Steve came running into
view through the shop's front windows. He pulled me nearer, staring aggressively at my ex.

Steve stood, gasping for air for a moment, then turned and disappeared.

By the time the shop closed at ten, I had calmed considerably. Dad had
me call and talk to Declan Moran, who added the information I gave him
to the case file and reassured me I could call him any time, day or night, if I
needed help. The floor swept, the lights turned off, we exited, DJ, Dad, Gabe
and I, and one of our newer employees, Polly Smithson. It was determined
Polly was parked in the same direction as Gabe, so they walked across the
street together. I gave my dad a kiss on the cheek. "Good night, Dad. Thanks
for everything."

"Are you sure you're all right now?"

"Yes. I'm fine. See," I held my arms out, "my hands have stopped shaking
and everything."

He looked down the street. "Okay. See you tomorrow."

"Nope. It's my day off, remember?"

"Oh, yeah. Thursday, then. Good night."

I walked toward my place. Scanning the shadows, I was startled to see a figure near the corner of the building.

"Gabe?"

"Nope." He moved into the light and I almost screamed. Someone grabbed my shoulders.

"Steven. You're not welcome here."

I started breathing again, though still shallowly.

"I only came to apologize, Alan."

"It's *Mr.* Lockhart to you," he said icily. "And I don't appreciate you lurking here in the dark, waiting to get my daughter by herself." He gestured to the storefront. "And I'm pretty certain Caleb wouldn't be too happy about it either."

It was odd to hear him say Caleb's name.

I looked at Steve's face. It was hard. "Well, Caleb ain't around, is he?"

"Not at the moment," my dad countered, "but he will be. And even if he isn't, I'm here." My dad straightened to his full five-foot-eight. "And I ain't going anywhere." He copied Steve's tone.

Headlights swept us, and Steve put up his hand to block them from shining into his eyes. The car slowly pulled to the curb. "Everything all right, Mr. Lockhart?"

It was Sam Ruiz. My dad studied Steve. "No, Officer Ruiz. Steven, here, was just leaving." Under his breath, he added, "If I see you near this place again, I'll get a restraining order. You got that, Steve?"

Steve stared at him, then crossed in front of us, moving down the street and whistling with his hands stuck in his pockets. Sam's door opened and she got out. A foot on her running board, her arms on the top of her car, she focused on Steve's back. A car stopped behind her and Sam signaled for him to pass in the turn lane. "I'll be patrolling the block tonight, Mr. Lockhart. Chief's orders. Sophie, you have my number, right?" She'd given it to me in the hospital.

"Yes." My voice came out shaky. I cleared my throat. "Yes," I said stronger. "I have it."

"Good. I'm going to circle and make sure Mr. Pattison there is truly leaving. You all have a good night." She returned to her vehicle and pulled a uey then drove away.

My dad took my shoulders and looked me in the eye. "You go straight up to your room and you lock the door. Both locks."

I cocked my head. "Daddy, don't worry. I'll be fine."

He nodded. "I'll watch you go in."

I climbed the stairs to my apartment, unlocked the door, and twisted to wave at him. He had taken a step off the curb and was combing both ends of the street with his gaze. Just like Gabe had the night after Caleb left for the first time. It warmed me.

Despite my rather crazy day, I fell right asleep. I woke in the middle of the night thinking I heard something and listened intently. My phone was buzzing. I didn't recognize the number and hesitated, but something told me to answer.

"H-hello?"

"Sophie, hi. It's Phoenix Blackstone." Like I knew dozens of Phoenixes.

I bolted upright. "What's wrong?"

"Wrong? Oh, nothing's wrong. Exactly..."

"Phoenix, it's..." I held my phone out to check the time, "after midnight, something must be wrong."

"Shit! Is it really? I'm sorry, Soph. I'll call you in the morning."

"Don't you dare hang up," I said quickly. "Are you there?"

"Yeah."

"Good." I snapped on the lamp by my bed and swung my legs over the side of the mattress. "Now what's going on?"

"It's...Caleb."

"I kind of figured that. What's wrong with him? Did he hurt himself? Is he sick?"

"No, no. Nothing like that. It's just...he's not reading."

Was I hearing him right? He called me in the middle of the night because Caleb wasn't reading? "What?"

"He's not reading. And you know how weird that is, Sophie."

"Well, yeah, but...I'm not sure how I can help with that..." *Or why you think it's important enough to call me about it?*

"Ever since what happened between you—"

Had he told them I cheated on him with Steve, which I definitely didn't do...

"—whatever that was—"

I heaved a sigh of relief.

"—he's been acting strange."

A rustling muffled Phoenix, who appeared to be talking to someone. "I am telling her. Shut up!"

There was a slapping noise and a corresponding yelp.

Phoenix continued. "He's had the same book in front of him for weeks."

Again, he spoke to someone else, his voice tight. "If I'm doing such a shitty job, then why don't you handle it?"

"Fine."

Dakota.

"Hi, Sophie. This is Dak."

Yep.

"What Levi here is trying to tell you—"

"*I'm* Levi."

Oh, Lord. They're all three there.

"You mean Phoenix. You know, your *brother*." They sounded like they were crowded into a phone booth, and they no longer seemed to be trying to hide their arguing.

"Anyway, what was failing to be communicated—"

There was a *thud* and then, "if you don't stop it, I'm going to beat the shit out of you."

Then Dakota began talking as if nothing had happened. "He's not eating. I mean, he's eating, but not like Boner usually does. On the bus he sits and stares at the window. When we're at a hotel, he spends every waking minute at the gym. Probably trying to burn off some of that testosterone he isn't using." *Muffled laughter.* "I mean, he's getting seriously jacked." *A murmur of agreement from the other two stooges.* "And speaking of testosterone, he won't have anything to do with the sweet young things who end up backstage, and there have been some lookers lately. In fact," he spoke slowly, as if just coming to this realization, "none of the whor—ouch! Why'd you do that?" An indistinguishable mumble followed. "Fine. But don't kick the shin. That shit hurts." He returned to talking to me. "None of the *women*," he said for some-body's benefit, probably Phoenix, "backstage have been able to score at all. Levi's taken. But what about you, little brother?"

"What about you?" Phoenix rebutted.

A few seconds of silent standoff proceeded Levi's voice saying, "One problem at a time. Let's focus on Boner."

Dakota started again. "So, Boner...on stage...it's not like he's missing any chords but...it's like his playing has no heart in it."

"No life in it," Phoenix said in the background.

"Yeah, that," Levi concurred.

"Yeah, no life in it. There's something wrong with him," he concluded, "and we need you to come here and fix him."

I waited for a reaction from the peanut gallery, but they must have been nodding in agreement or something.

"Dakota..." I let out a breath. "I'd love to help you guys but...he's not even answering my phone calls."

"She says he's not answering her phone calls," he relayed. "What about texts?"

"No. I think he's blocked me." I sighed. "Why don't you put me on speak-er phone so we can all talk together?"

"Okay, just a sec... Can you hear me?"

"Yes. I can hear you, Dakota. Hi, Levi. Hello again, Phoenix."

"Hi," they said morosely.

"Okay," Dakota started again. "So...I recognize Caleb acted like an ass when Steve showed up. Believe me, we dragged him over the coals for doing that. But...here's the thing, Soph, we guys really suck at this whole relation-ship thing." I caught a low murmur of agreement from the rest. "We don't know what to say, we don't know how to act... And with Boner, there's—this really seems to go against the bro code, but so is calling you. I guess we're des-perate." He inhaled. "There's a reason he does the things he does. Not that I'm excusing him, because I'm not, but...he was cheated on."

I blinked. "He was?"

"In the worst way. Heidi totally played him and slept with several of his friends. Not us," he added quickly. "It was before he met us."

"Oh." I put a hand on my forehead. *That would have killed him. No wonder he didn't believe me.* "Oh, geez. That sucks. That really sucks."

A murmur rose from the other end of the line as they all agreed.

"That makes so much sense, though."

"See?" Dakota said. "So, you'll come, right?"

It was like they thought I could wave a magic wand and make everything better.

I wish I had that power.

"But like I said, guys, he doesn't want to see me. He won't even talk to me. How am I supposed to fix *that*?"

"Sophie?" It was Levi. "He loves you. I know what love looks like, and he loves you. If he's banishing himself from you, it's because he came to the conclusion it was for your good somehow."

"He won't talk to us, either," said Phoenix. "We've tried."

Dakota added his two cents. "But we think if you were here, you could talk some sense into him."

I stared out the window at nothing. Silence fell on the other end of the phone for the first time. I sighed. "Okay. I'll give it a try."

"Oh, thank God," Phoenix said weakly.

"Hot damn!" was Dakota's shout. And I couldn't hear Levi's response over them.

"I'll have to make some arrangements, but I'll be there tomorrow. You're in Nashville, right?"

"Hmm...you're keeping tabs on us?" Dakota teased.

"Yes, Nashville," Phoenix said. "We'll be there by two."

"Okay. Text me the address you want me to show up at and I'll be there."

CHAPTER SEVENTEEN

Sophie

Hidden by a curtain, I watched them get off the bus, utilizing a crack between drapery panels to spy. Caleb stepped out and my heart zinged. He was definitely more buff, but he seemed gaunt and...thinner, somehow. His expression was flat. Dakota stretched exaggeratedly, and his gaze searched the lot. Phoenix and Levi, too, seemed to be scanning the vicinity, perhaps looking for me. Caleb walked in my direction and through the double doors to my left.

"Caleb?"

To say he was surprised was an understatement. Floored would be a better description. "Sophie?" He lowered his bag to the carpet. "What are you doing here?"

"I came to talk."

His mouth hung open for a second. "To me?"

I walked toward him and his body stiffened. Not a good sign. "Yes, silly."

"How did...?" he slowly rotated his head. They all jumped when they were spotted between the double doors and scurried around, stepping on each other in their hurry to get out. Caleb's jaw was tight. "They called you."

"They were concerned about you." I advanced another foot, and this time he retreated an equal distance.

"This was a mistake. You shouldn't be here."

I clasped my hands, needing something to do with them because I wanted desperately to touch him. "Why?"

"Why?" he parroted. He again looked outside. It appeared like Dakota was watching us and relaying what he saw to Levi and Phoenix, who had their backs to us acting like they were giving us privacy. Caleb peered down at the ugly red carpeting spattered with gold lassos at our feet. "You just shouldn't." He sounded so forlorn. It hurt my heart. He lifted his gaze and glanced at the parking lot again. "They shouldn't have called you."

"Caleb...can we simply...talk?" I took a peek at the front desk where two employees seemed to be following our conversation with interest. I lowered my voice. "Somewhere else. You and me, alone."

He stood there.

"Come on, Caleb. It can't hurt to talk, can it?"

"I don't see why? It won't change anything."

"Please."

"Okay," he huffed finally. "Stay here, I'll get a key."

I tried to hide my elation over my miniature victory. I looked at the parking lot. Dakota held his arms out, palms facing me, and mouthed something. I gave them a thumbs up, but my smile disappeared when I turned my head and noticed Caleb staring at me, leaning on the counter with his legs slanted like he had at the scuba shop. But this time he was frowning.

The clerk swept his arm to the right, and Caleb had to pay attention. "Take these elevators to the fourth floor and your suite will be the last two doors on your left. You can use either to enter."

"Thanks," he said gruffly. He eyed me. "Well, come on."

I cleared my throat and walked in front of him. He thought I didn't see it, but he flipped his bandmates the bird. People were already filing off the elevator. But one wet little girl wearing fins and holding a snorkel remained on board. We got in with her. Blonde, with freckles and a pair of braids, she was adorable. "Going swimming?" Caleb asked her sarcastically.

She didn't say anything. Just stood there swinging her hips from side to side. She studied me and whispered loudly, "I'm not supposed to talk to strangers."

Caleb snorted.

We arrived at the floor marked "P" and Caleb held the door for her, but she didn't move.

"Well, come on. This is your floor, isn't it?" She nodded then peered at me.

"Go on," I urged. "It's okay." She left but never turned her back on Caleb, pressing against the opposite edge of the door as she passed him.

The door closed. His arms crossed in front of him at the wrists, he tilted his head to stare at the numbers, but his lips twitched. Finally, he commented without turning. "You're a stranger, too, you know?"

I sputtered, trying to contain my laughter. The first floor dinged, but we didn't stop there.

"You look good," I ventured.

He raised an eyebrow but nodded. "Thank you." The second floor dinged. "You look..." he exhaled, "great."

Heat flooded my cheeks. We were silent for the rest of the way up, but when we got to the fourth floor, he held the door for me. I hesitated, my lips quirking. He smiled but nudged me with his bag. "Get out." Mimicking the little girl, I slid past him leaving as much space as possible between us. He chuckled as he led me, his shoulders more relaxed. I determined things were off to a good start. We located the room at the end of the hall, and he ran the card through the first door's lock. He opened the door to the bedroom, but shut it quickly. "Wrong door." Moving to the next, he unlocked it and stood aside for me to enter, his face more serious. I entered and glanced around. "Nice," I commented, with lack of anything better to stay. I stood nervously, shifting my weight from foot to foot.

"You can sit if you want."

"Oh. Thanks." I took a seat on the couch, straightening the skirt of my sundress.

He stood in back of one of the chairs, gripping the top. "So? What did you want to say?"

What did I want to say? "I miss you."

He jumped like I'd thrown a bucket of cold water on him, then paced in front of the window silently. The sunlight came from behind him and blinded me. Then he crossed between me and the window, and I received a second of relief, before being blinded again. He stopped, and put his hand on his forehead briefly, then ran it down his face, ending at the chin, and covering his mouth. He sucked in air and released it noisily, then sat in the chair and leaned forward, his fingers intertwined between his thighs. "I've missed you too, Sophie. Terribly. But it doesn't change the fact that you're better off without me."

I couldn't help it. He was near enough I caught the cedar, sandalwood, and leather scent of his skin. I ran my shoe along his calf, what I could reach of it, where his socks were exposed. "I think I'm very good *with* you."

He looked at my foot. "I'm trying to be serious."

I withdrew it and tried to loosen the knot at my neck where the halter top dress was tied, my leg now bouncing nervously. I was so not good at this sort of thing.

He closed his eyes for a moment. "I'm sorry. I'm not good at this. I've hurt you again, even though that wasn't my intention, which goes to show, I'm right. You shouldn't be with me."

"You were correct about Steve," I blurted. His gaze widened. I had his attention. "He was trying to get back together with me."

He hopped to his feet and stood behind his chair again, gripping the top. He started to say something, rethought it, and shut his mouth. He came to have a seat again, and, to my vast surprise, took my hands. "Sophie, I don't belong with you, but I don't believe Steve does either. You deserve better than both of us."

"I do deserve better than Steve. When he made his move and I turned him down...let's just say he wasn't very happy with me."

"He didn't try to hurt you, did he?"

I realized, too late, this probably wasn't the best direction for this conversation to go on. "No, he—"

He jumped to his feet again. "You hesitated." He took up his pacing again on the opposite side of the room. "I swear to God, I will fucking rip him to pieces if he put a finger on you."

"Caleb."

He eyed me. I patted the chair. "Please come sit."

He thought for a moment, then crossed the room with precision, stood in front of the chair, and sat, carefully folding his hands and leaving them in his lap. "I'm sorry. I didn't mean to upset you."

I touched his knee and he stiffened. "I'm not upset."

"Do you want to tell me what happened...with Steve?"

Not exactly. "He tried to scare me, but my dad and Samantha Ruiz ran him off."

"Samantha Ruiz?" He seemed puzzled fleetingly, then drew in a breath. "The cop? You had to call the cops?" His muscles were tensed, ready to propel him to his feet again.

"As a precaution. It really wasn't a big deal. I—"

"I'm coming back with you."

That caught me off guard. "Huh?"

"I'm coming back. I'll stay away from you. I only want to...camp...on your doorstep...a little. You won't even know I'm there."

"Caleb. This isn't what I came here to discuss."

"Huh?" His gaze darted around rapidly. I could tell he was creating a mental checklist. *I'll need ammo, a sleeping bag...maybe multiple weapons...*

"Caleb," I said louder, startling him from his thoughts. He looked up. "The guys told me about Heidi." I hadn't meant to say it, but it tumbled out.

His eyes narrowed. "I don't know what that has to do with this. It didn't affect me."

"Caleb, it would affect anyone. It affected me when Steve did it to me."

"But I don't see you going ballistic any time a girl comes near me."

I offered a wry half smile. "That doesn't mean I don't want to."

He blinked. It was like the information did not compute. "Really?"

"Hell, yeah. I'm as jealous as the next girl, but I trust you." I wrapped my hands over his. "I trust this. I trust us."

He exhaled. "Yeah. How do you do that? I just...go nuts."

"Yes, I know. We're two different people, Caleb. You can have those feelings. Feelings are never wrong. It's how you choose to act on them that makes the difference."

He sank back in his chair, lacing his fingers behind his head, and watching me for a moment. Then he swooped down into his former position, leaning forward with his hands clasped. "Are you sure I can't do physical damage to Steve? Because I can be very stealthy."

"Caleb!"

One side of his mouth lifted, and I wanted to kiss it. "Okay, okay. I won't do Steve bodily harm." He said it like it was a sentence he had been told to write a thousand times. "But, if he ever hurts you, or even threatens you, I'm not gonna sit still, Sophie."

"Well...if you ever consider me in danger—"

His eyes glowed and I held a hand up.

"*Seriously* believe I'm in danger...then you can act in whatever manner you deem is appropriate."

He studied me. "I don't know, Sophie. I don't want to ever cause you pain again."

"Caleb, you think if you're with me, you *may* do something to hurt me. But what I *know* hurts me is being without you. I love you. And I want to be with you."

A noise came from the bedroom, along with squabbling voices. "You freaking crushed my foot."

"Shh!"

Caleb smirked, and he put a finger to his lips. He crossed the room noiselessly and yanked open the dividing door. All three of them were crowded on the opposite side of the door and almost fell into the room.

"Oh, hi," Dakota said sheepishly. "Imagine finding you here." He looked from Caleb to me. "Have you guys kissed and made up yet?"

I moved to Caleb's side. "Not fully..."

Caleb smiled and took my face between his two hands. "Sophie Lockhart, I love you." He didn't turn. "Did you hear that, gentlemen?"

"I don't know about any gentlemen, but I heard it," Dakota quipped.

"Good." He shut the door on them and kissed me.

CHAPTER EIGHTEEN

Caleb

I swore to Sophie that I wouldn't destroy Steve, but that promise didn't prevent me from siccing the cops on him.

Chief Declan Moran listened to me patiently and asked a few questions. Then he rose, strolled around his desk and leaned against it, crossing his arms. "We will definitely check it out, Mr. Winthrop, but my gut feel is that Steve Pattison—being the spineless weasel that he is—wouldn't have the intestinal fortitude to do something to Sophie." He paused. "He also impresses me as someone who's too lazy to do much of anything that would require a modicum of thought or effort, like sabotaging someone via scuba tank."

"But as I said, he basically threatened her and her father. They—"

He held out a hand. "I am aware of the incident as one of my officers was there. I'm not dismissing your concerns. I'm trying to tell you to widen your net and keep on guard. My cop senses tell me this isn't about Sophie as much as it's about Insatiable Fire."

I blinked. "What? Why do you say that?"

He unfolded his arms and grasped his desk on either side of him. "For one, no one could know who was going to take that tank, but there would be a good chance of one of the band member's taking it, since you made up fifty percent of the group. That would be a win for the perpetrator in this scenario. Two...Last Chance Beach is a very sleepy community, Mr. Winthrop. We don't have much crime. And Remi Boyd's attack, the vandalism with the water sprinklers at The Sands, and a booby-trapped scuba tank is way beyond our normal business—unless they were performed by the same person." He stood and walked around his desk again. "I don't have any concrete evidence supporting this theory, though...it's just a feeling. Bottom line is, we don't know who committed these crimes, but we know they're still out there. I'm advising you to be vigilant, ready for an attack from any angle until we learn more."

I got to my feet and shook his hand. "Oh, you can bet I'll be on the lookout for anyone intent on harming Sophie. That's for damn sure. I appreciate you listening to me today."

"Of course. And, again, I want to reassure you, I will check into Steve. Until we know for sure he's not a threat, he *is* a threat in our books."

"I appreciate it."

He walked me to the door, making small chat, but when we shook again before I left, he held on for a moment and looked me in the eyes. "We're going to get whoever this is, Caleb. Don't you worry."

I knew his words were meant to encourage me, but I was more concerned than ever. If someone was targeting Sophie because of her connection to the band...if something happened to her, we would be partially to blame.

That's just not going to happen.

Weeks had passed in which I considered getting as far away from Sophie as possible, to keep her out of danger. But that meant leaving her alone with a maniac on the loose. I decided in the end it was better to stick close to her side so I could protect her.

At the moment though, I was more nervous than a sheep at the shearer's as I led her across the sand, and it had nothing to do with bad guys. We were on Last Chance Beach, months after we first met, back for the delayed gala, which was now linked to the annual Fall Festival.

"Can I open my eyes yet?"

"Nope." I turned my head to inspect everything. Moonlight, check. A soft breeze, check. The smell of the ocean, check. A huge heart made with votive candles, check. Savvy had insisted it be a heart. A soft quilt, check. A mysterious giftwrapped package, check. The obligatory champagne on ice and two flutes, check. A heart full of love, check, check, and double check. I took a deep breath. "You can open them."

Her face glowed. "Why, you little romantic devil! You've done it again."

Over the past month I'd taken her on various highly romantic, proposal-worthy dates to throw her off. Kept her guessing and made her less suspicious about tonight, the big night. She pushed onto her tippy toes and kissed me. With any luck that kind of kiss would be mine forever.

"Did I surprise you this time?"

Her fingers still latched behind my neck, she observed the scene again. "Did you ever. It's lovely." She looked at me, rubbing noses. "I'm one lucky girl."

I kissed her. "No. I'm the lucky one."

She cast her gaze across the area again. "Is that a present I see there?"

I smiled. I loved how much she was into surprises and gifts. "It is."

"Is it for me?" she asked, batting her eyelashes.

I led her into the circle. "You little squirrel. You know it is."

She laughed.

"But not until I'm ready."

She scrunched up her nose in the most adorable way. "Darn."

"I won't make you wait long. Would sitting here be okay?" I indicated the blanket.

"Absolutely."

We took a seat. She was facing the ocean; I was at her back, with my legs around her, like we had done the first time we came to the beach together. She crawled two fingers over the quilt in the direction of the gift, and I slapped her hand. "Not yet."

"Oh." She pouted. "Party pooper."

She settled into my arms, and I lowered my head until we were cheek-to-cheek and squeezed her. "I just want to sit here and enjoy this."

"Mmm," she murmured contentedly.

The waves crashed and bubbled, singing their age-old song. The breeze gently lifted our hair. The moon made the ocean shimmer like a thousand diamonds. We sat and absorbed it all.

I kissed her temple. "I could do this forever, you know? Sit here with you, listening to the ocean."

She sighed. "Me too. It's so peaceful. No customers. No Gabe."

We chuckled. "Well, I suppose I've made you wait long enough."

She clapped. "Oh, goody!"

"Okay. There are special instructions with this gift," I said as I handed it to her.

"Of course there are." There had been several other gifts with instructions on our recent romantic dates. She'd been in training for tonight.

"Okay. You may unwrap your gift and only unwrap it."

"This is so exciting. You give such good gifts."

"Thank you. I think you'll enjoy this one in particular."

"Hmm." She shook it. "It's another car, isn't it?"

One of her gifts had been the convertible sitting behind us. Being a rock star had its perks.

"Nope." It was pretty clearly a book.

"Oh, shucks."

"Just open it. I don't understand why you have to be so slow."

She liked to peel each piece of tape back carefully and make it a whole event. "Come now," she replied sternly. "You unwrap the way you want to, and I'll unwrap the way I want to. Did you, by any chance, get this at Beach Reads?"

"Nope." Although I had been by the bookstore to ask her dad, and Gabe, for their blessings.

She gasped, putting her hand on her chest. "You went to a competitor?"

"Maybe. If you'd just open it, you'd see."

"Okay." She quickened her pace a modicum. Pretty soon she had a hard-copy of *The Great Gatsby* lying in her lap. She'd told me it was her favorite book the night after we met. She let out a squeal, but waited for further instruction. I had taught her well over the course of the last several weeks.

"You may open *only* the cover."

She obediently flipped to a blank page.

"Okay. One more."

"What?"

"Turn one more page." Another blank page. "Turn to the title page," I said impatiently. Spanning the area under the author's name was his autograph. Pretty neat writing for a guy too.

She sat up quickly, crossing her legs. "Oh, my God! Is this for real?" She whirled around. "Is this really his signature?"

"Yep."

"Oh, my God!" she shouted again. "You—" She put a hand on her chest, barely able to speak. "You got me an autographed copy of *The Great Gatsby*. I'm going to cry." I'm not sure why she had to announce that. It happened every time I gave her a present. "Oh, Caleb. I don't know what to say. This is...this is...incredible. I can't— I'm speechless. Fitzgerald himself could not find words to describe how happy and grateful I am for this gift." She ran trembling fingers underneath the signature. "F. Scott Fitzgerald," she said reverently.

I was beginning to think the proposal might be sort of a letdown after this. "There's more."

She gasped. "What? No."

"Turn the page," I said tenderly.

Tremulously, she lifted the page. "This is— Caleb...this is a first edition."

I chuckled. "I know. And it's been certified and appraised and all that. It's legit." And it came with a mighty hefty price tag too. Three times what I paid for her maxed out Beemer. Collectors weren't hip on selling pieces of their collections. I went through fourteen people before I found a lady who I pleaded with, trying to capitalize on any sense of romanticism she might have. She listened to what I needed it for and eventually was moved to sell it to me.

"You shouldn't have done this. I mean...I thought the car was over the top. How did you find this?"

"It wasn't easy."

"I'm sure it wasn't." She ran her hand along the back and gave me one of her wicked smiles. "There are...strings or something on here. What are they for?"

I tapped her nose. "Don't mess with that. You'll have to wait and see."

"Ooh. I love it when you're mysterious."

I grinned. "Flip to page twenty-four."

She stared at me for a moment, then down at the book in her lap. She riffled carefully until she found it. I had planned to highlight the line, but Savannah said Sophie would slice my balls off if I did anything to mar this sacred book. Only she said it more daintily. I think she said Sophie would castrate me. Paige agreed, saying, "Oh, yeah. She'd cut you in a heartbeat." Thus motivated, I finally came up with the idea to insert a page of paper to cover all of the other lines so nothing but the one I wanted was showing in a window I made.

She read. "'I was alone again in the unquiet darkness.'" She gazed at me quizzically.

"That day I was stupid and selfish enough to tell you to make a choice between me and Steve, I returned to apologize about two seconds after I left. But I got a glimpse of your expression through the window and saw how much I'd hurt you. I knew I had to go. But, after having been with you, I couldn't revert to my old life and be happy. You made me feel less alone, and without you, I was empty."

"Oh, baby." She put a hand on the side of my face and kissed me.

"Now, page one twenty-seven, please."

She skimmed through the pages eagerly. "'Once in a while I go off on a spree and make a fool of myself, but I always come back, and in my heart I love her all the time.' Again, she looked to me.

I shrugged. "He says it better than I can. Even though I left, I never, not for one millisecond, stopped loving you." I cleared my throat, and my voice was a little shaky all the same. "Okay, turn to the end, but don't remove what you see. It's for me."

She flipped as instructed and understood what the elastic ties were for. They trapped a tiny manila envelope with my name on it to the back cover, because, again, Savannah was worried tape might blemish the treasured volume.

"*You* get a present this time?"

I slipped it from the bands. "That is yet to be determined." I stood and helped her get to her feet. "Up you go."

I opened the flap on the envelope, squeezed the sides, and blew some air in there to open it wider. I peered inside, prolonging things to heighten her anticipation and my enjoyment. I flicked the bottom to loosen it, turned it to release the contents into my palm—high enough she couldn't see it—and made a fist to hide it.

I slowly knelt before her and was surprised by how caught off guard she was. I would have thought my purpose over these past months was pretty obviously leading to this moment.

"Sophie, none of the books I ever read prepared me for the lightning bolt that struck me the night I met you. From page one, you had my heart, honey, and I want to continue our story together, to spend each breath with you until the ink runs out on the page." I glanced down. "I know I don't come close to deserving you," I lifted my head and looked her in the eye, "but I will try with *every cell of my being* to become a better man and perhaps a little worthier of taking your hand," as I said it, I brought her knuckles to my lips, "and holding it forever. If you'd just do me the unmerited honor of accepting this ring—" I opened my fingers, "—and agreeing to be my bride, my love forever, then I will try my damnedest to make your life one lived happily-ever-after."

She was covering her mouth, holding in the sobs shaking her, her tears glowing in the moonlight.

"Sophia McKenzie Lockhart, will you marry me?"

She nodded rapidly.

I put my forehead on her knee. "Oh, thank God." I struggled to my feet, threw my arms around her, and squeezed the shit out of her, raising her off the ground. "I love you," I murmured in her ear.

"I love you too," she sobbed.

We stayed like that for quite some time, savoring the moment. The moment we committed to sharing the rest of our lives together. We'd had our bumps along the way, misunderstandings, misbehavior (on my part), and worries, especially after the scuba accident. But we'd worked through them, not as smoothly as we could have, but we'd learned and grown from our experiences. I never realized I was missing Sophie in my life, but now that I do, I don't ever want to be without her again.

I set her on her feet and was filled with such a surge of elation that I lifted our hands into the air and shouted to the waves, "She said yes!"

And I'm going to see to it we live that happily-ever-after.

NOTE FROM THE AUTHOR

Thank you for reading LEAD ME ON, part of the LAST CHANCE BEACH ROMANCES. I hope you enjoyed it. Now that you've read the book, won't you please consider writing a review? Reviews are one of the best ways readers discover great new books. They don't need to be fancy or long, just a sentence or two honestly describing your opinion of/experience with the book. I would sincerely appreciate it.

Want more from M.J. Schiller?
Page forward for an excerpt from ~
ROCK WITH THE RHYTHM
A Last Chance Beach Romance

Phoenix

Women gulping down drinks in fish bowls could work to a guy's advantage, as it might put his woman in the mood. Or, it could work to his disadvantage, if she has too much and ends up laying on the tile at the foot of the porcelain deity all night long. I liked to watch couples from the high platform of the stage while I sang and try to determine which scenario would play out for them.

But tonight I was focused on a couple in particular. A couple of girls. One was screaming "Insatiable Desires", —the song that catapulted us into the limelight—over and over again at the top of her lungs. The other was Savanah Drew.

"Insatiable Desires" was actually on our setlist in a few songs, but the girl was annoying me. I'll take requests. In fact, I love requests. I had even taken one earlier from this same girl. But this wasn't a request, it was a demand, and I was starting to feel like an organ grinder's monkey.

I turned to my boys. "So, we're going to play her song, because we don't want to be total pricks and it was on the setlist...but it's going to be at the end of the night."

They nodded and grinned, agreeing with me that not giving in was the best course of action. But I had my doubts. Mostly because the party in question was still screaming as Savanah shushed her.

I wasn't really paying attention to the loud mouth though. I was eyeing Savanah. Even though we'd been in the same class at school, she was a complete mystery to me. I was intrigued because she seemed different than the people she ran around with in high school.

Does she still see them?

I knew nothing about her life now. We'd come back to Last Chance Beach a couple dozen times since we'd first left to try to make it to the big time eight years ago. But whenever I returned, I was pretty tied up with family. And even had I not been, I would have never asked Savanah out. The island had its own little caste system when I was growing up, and Savanah and I had been from different stratas. Her Dad was the CEO of a Fortune 500 company. Mine was a supervisor down on the docks. Hers wore $500 an ounce aftershave. Mine smelled of fish. Growing up, my family wouldn't have even been able to afford the golf cart that took the Drews from one end of their property to the other. She was the princess in the castle. I wasn't fit to tend her gate.

But now I was returning a very wealthy man.

I wonder if a pile of platinum records evens the scales some...

I knew to some people it wouldn't matter what my net worth was; I would still always be the son of a dockworker and therefore unworthy. The questioned remained, was Savanah one of those people?

I had seen her the previous night when we played at The Rum Runner and had encouraged our lead guitarist, Caleb, to ask out her friend Sophie. At least Caleb had made an attempt at conversation with Sophie, while I, the hypocrite, had chickened out on approaching Savanah. Luckily my boys were none the wiser, because they had no idea that I'd had a crush on her since the dawn of time.

But here she was again tonight. At the Shellfish, of all places. The place had to be the biggest dive on the island. I never would have expected her to show up here.

There she goes again, surprising me. A girl who comes to The Shellfish can't be a snob, can she?

I started to think I might have a chance after all.

But maybe she just came because of Sophie.

It was clear that Sophie had a thing for Caleb, and vice versa. Did Savanah just come as backup for Sophie? When I saw Caleb dancing with Sophie, I knew I had to take the chance. Caleb was socially awkward to the extreme, and he was stepping way outside of his comfort zone. Mostly because I pushed him. I, on the other hand, usually had no problem in social situations. It was just when I was around Savanah that I lost any ounce of suaveness I possessed.

Savanah was dancing now with the loud mouth, while Caleb danced with Sophie. Normally, Savanah seemed a bit uptight. But her wild friend seemed to be rubbing off on her. It was that or the fishbowl they were sharing. She was laughing and shaking her ass along with the rest of them, which was highly unusual. I tried not to stare, but the way she was moving was making that increasingly difficult. The stiff-postured, conservative girl had left the building and had been replaced with a sexy-as-hell vixen with some seriously sweet moves.

It's time to man up, Phoenix.

And that was my intention as I worked my way through the crowd to her on our next break. The closer I got, the harder my heart beat against my ribcage, and the hands that played rhythm guitar for one of the hottest bands in the country became sweaty.

What the fuck? Are you still in high school? She's a woman. You're a man. Just ask her out, you dumbass.

I almost bailed at the last minute, had, in fact, passed her, but I back-tracked as if giving her a second look.

Play it cool.

"Savanah? Savanah Drew?"

She blinked. "Yes, Phoenix. You'd think you would have recognized me. We only went to school together for all of our lives."

Shit. Now she either thinks I'm an idiot, or she's insulted I can't remember her. Smooth move.

"Yeah. Of course. I just didn't recognize you at first. Did you change your hair?"

I inwardly rolled my eyes. Her hair was the way she always wore it. Long and mahogany-colored. Although she had it up tonight.

She frowned. "No. It's the way I've always had it."

"Yeah. It must be the lighting or something," I said hurriedly. "How are you?"

She was still looking at me curiously. "Good. And yourself?"

"Oh, good. Good. Great, in fact. The band is doing really well."

"Yes. I'm aware of that."

I'd wanted to impress her, but it came off as bragging. She put a hand on my arm, bringing me out of my inward musing.

"Listen, Phoenix. I want to apologize. Paige is being..." She looked over at her friend, who was messing with some guy's hair. He seemed annoyed. "...well, obnoxious." She returned her chocolate brown eyes to mine. "I've tried to quiet her, but she's just...a little wound up tonight. The fish bowl probably wasn't the best idea..."

"Oh," I rolled a shoulder, "it's not bothering me."

She raised her eyebrows. "Really? Because you seemed aggravated. And I don't blame you," she quickly added. "It can't be fun having fans shout requests at you all night long."

I tried for an easy smile. "Oh, I don't mind. It's part of the gig."

"Maybe. But Paige has taken it a bit far." She sighed, again searching out her friend.

Interesting...

I wanted to keep her talking. "What's she like, your Paige?"

"Well, she can be kind of...quirky." Her roaming gaze stopped.

"What do you mean by that?"

She nodded toward the stage and I looked. Her friend was in one of the two cages made for dancers on either side of the raised platform. Paige grasped the bars and threw her head around in a circle, swinging her hair.

"But...there's no music."

Savanah crossed her arms. "Yeah. I know."

As we watched, Paige licked one of the poles.

Savanah grimaced. "Ooh. That's so unsanitary." She continued to watch, like a guard dog. "She can be a handful," she said, as if to herself.

For a moment, it was like she'd let the mask she always wore slide, and I could see how tough it was being the one who was responsible all the time.

"Well..." I said carefully, "if you don't mind me asking...why are you friends with her then?"

Her gaze snapped to me, her jaw tightened, and I thought I'd screwed things up. Then she exhaled. "Paige has been through a lot. She moved here from Missouri after a bad breakup with—excuse my French—an asshole of a boyfriend. It doesn't excuse her behavior toward you, but...I don't know..." She trailed off. Her gaze on her friend was sympathetic now, and maybe a bit worried.

I tried to lighten the mood. "Well, no harm done. Just to show there are no hard feelings, why don't you let me buy you two a drink?"

"Oh, I appreciate that, Phoenix, but I think we've had enough." She edged toward the stage. "I better go get her before she breaks her other leg." I'd heard she turned her ankle at the show the night before and had been surprised to see her here with a boot on. Savanah stopped moving, looking me in the eye. "It was really good seeing you again, Phoenix."

The soft and sincere way she said it zinged straight to my heart. "Yes. Same..." She was already halfway to the stage. "...here." I groaned. My God, time and distance had done nothing to nullify the effect she had on me. I watched her coax her friend out of the cage and help her down the stairs, then I lost them as they headed toward the restrooms.

So...our first conversation wasn't the best...

But I vowed to do better on the next. I knew I had nothing to fear now. Savanah Drew was a sympathetic creature. If she was going to reject me, she would let me down easy.

But I didn't get the chance. Savanah and Paige disappeared shortly after that. Later, when Caleb told us he was walking Sophie to her car, my resolve became even stronger. If Caleb was taking a chance, surely I could do the same. I would woo Savanah Drew or I would go down in flames. I had to at least give it a try.

TO FIND OUT WHAT HAPPENS NEXT, PURCHASE ROCK TO THE RHYTHM!

ALSO FROM M.J. SCHILLER

ROMANTIC REALMS COLLECTION:
TAKEN BY STORM
AN UNCOMMON LOVE
LEAP INTO THE KNIGHT
LADY OF THE KNIGHT
A KNIGHT TO REMEMBER

ROCKING ROMANCE COLLECTION:
TRAPPED UNDER ICE
ABANDON ALL HOPE
BETWEEN ROCK AND A HARD PLACE
ROCK ME, GENTLY
MIDNIGHT MELODY

LOVE AND CHAOS SERIES:
ROCKED BY GRACE
ROCKED BY LOVE
ROCK IT TO THE MOON
ROCK OF SALVATION (Coming soon!)

REAL ROMANCE COLLECTION:
UPON A MIDNIGHT CLEAR
THE HEART TEACHES BEST
DAMAGE DONE
BLACKOUT
HOMETOWN HEARTACHE
TAKE A CHANCE ON ME

DEVILISH DESIRES SERIES:
TO HELL IN A COACH BAG
DAMNED IF I DO
THE DEVIL YOU KNOW
SATAN, LINE ONE
PITCHFORK IN THE ROAD
SIN WORTH THE PENANCE
HELL HATH NO FURY
TEN MINUTES IN THE SIN BIN
DEVIL'S IN THE DETAILS
DEVIL'S ADVOCATE
HADE'S NIGHT

INSATIABLE FIRE SERIES:
BEATING IN TIME
LEAD ME ON
ROCK WITH THE RHYTHM
BASSIST'S INSTINCTS

ABOUT THE AUTHOR

Bestselling author M.J. Schiller is a retired lunch lady/romance-romantic suspense writer. She enjoys writing novels whose characters include rock stars, desert princes, teachers, futuristic Knights, construction workers, cops, and a wide variety of others. In her mind everybody has a romance. She is the mother of a twenty-seven-year-old and three twenty-five-year-olds. That's right, triplets! So having recently taught four children to drive, she likes to escape from life on occasion by pretending to be a rock star at karaoke. However...you won't be seeing her name on any record labels soon.

www.ingramcontent.com/pod-product-compliance
Lightning Source LLC
Chambersburg PA
CBHW070928250626
47159CB00009B/3170